Vrykolakas

The Evolution of the Vampire

Book 3

Shawn Boyd

Printed in the United States of America

Prologue

Moving into the 5th century, our heroes are spread thin. Not only are China and India fighting the infestation, but Vietnam, Korea, and Japan have seen the manifestation of this evil as well. Vampires and were-creatures have gone north into Mongolia and are spreading further and further west as Ju-Long, the first of his kind, travels toward Rome with Lalita, his succubus mate.

Ling and Naina, with their incredible speed, defend the lands of India and take care of Marcos, Naina's adoptive father, whose health is beginning to fail. They celebrate their love for each other, worry for her father, and are frustrated by the increase of demons despite their best efforts. The Raksasha live in small covens, fighting not only our heroes, but also each other over territory.

Biao and Jie stop to see their Sherpa friends on their way back to China. Jie faces a tough decision that could change his life for good. Biao worries for his brothers back home. Te, the healer, is still missing despite Zhan's best efforts to track him down. Cai, and the young apprentice Gan, continue to chase the were-animals that plague their homeland. With them is a new secret weapon, Yang Bo. In the meantime, the number of xiang shi are on the rise again in the north as remnants of Ju-Long's presence there are left unchecked.

Japan faces a new enemy as Quon and Yun-Qi, two of Ju-Long's original warriors, make their home there. They go unnoticed, operating secretly for a while, until they unwittingly create more of their own. They are hunted by a band of soldiers led by a man almost as psychotic as their former master.

Balavan, Jia-Li, and their small band head northwest and end up in Mongolia. There they meet a ruthless leader who captures them, then employs their services. The group travels west with his army as he lays waste to his enemies and heads toward

Constantinople. There, a showdown between Ju-Long and Balavan, the monk he turned into a Raksasha, looms over the rights to Jia-Li.

Ju-Long and Lalita finally reach her homeland and find new threats to their existence. Xiong and Amal meet up with a man who might be friend or foe as they pursue the xiang-shi and his succubus. Not even the Roman Empire, already threatened by outside forces, is prepared to deal with this new evil. It has many names in the land of the Empire. Vrykolakas . . . Vampiro . . . Vampire . . .

Jie lay back breathless. He had only been with one other woman, and that seemed like forever ago. He lost her to the xiang shi when they took his home city of Fanzhou, along with the rest of his family. They had been back in the village of their Sherpa friends for a week, and were going to be headed through the mountains and back to the monastery the day after tomorrow. He was torn between loyalty to his friend, and the mission they were on, and what was feeling more and more like love every minute. After this, his decision was even harder. She was so beautiful, the sex was incredible, and she had told him that she loved him.

He said it back.

She rested her head on his shoulder and coiled herself along his tall frame. Nyimi sighed in satisfaction as she cuddled against him. The feel of her smooth skin, the softness of her breasts, and the flowery scent of her hair threatened to arouse him again. It was hard to believe that a woman so beautiful desired him.

He had fantasized about her during their first stay here, and for weeks thereafter. It was funny, even then he figured he never had a shot with her. She was into his friend, Ling, a handsome, humorous, charismatic man that all the ladies seemed to fawn over. Not to mention, Sangye, a Sherpa friend, had a thing for her that almost led to a fight between Ling and him. Ling was back in India with his soulmate Naina. Sangye was wed to Maya and they were expecting their first child any day now.

No, Nyimi wasn't a great cook, but that was okay, Jie was. She wasn't the hardest of workers, but she did her share. She would make beautiful daughters and handsome sons though. *Children.* Jie hadn't thought about having children of his own since

Fanzhou. Everything from then until the past few days was about survival and the mission. If there was only some way he could get Nyimi to come back to China with him.

It would never happen like that.

She was too delicate a flower to cross the Himalayas, despite her Sherpa ancestry. Her dream was to live in Nepal, away from the village and its hardships.

Jie wondered how Biao would take it if he had to resume the journey home by himself. Guilt swept over him. Who would watch his friend's back? Who would cook for him? Who would be there to talk to him on the long road back to the monastery? His heart was pained at these thoughts.

Nyimi nuzzled against his chest and began to snore ever so gently. *What are you going to do, Jie? What are you going to do?*

Biao was glad to see the sun come up. He, Topgye, and Dorje had been on the night watch. Since the Yeti attack last time Biao had passed this way, the village had not had any major problems. It was hard to believe that was almost a year ago. There was news from some of the villages north of them, that on occasion a blood drinking demon would steal one from their numbers during the night.

That is why, despite the absence of a threat in the area, this Sherpa village remained vigilant, especially after sundown. Biao enjoyed being back in the company of old friends. It had been many moons since Jie and he left the comfort of Marco's place and his brother Ling. It would be many more moons before Biao saw home again.

Jie was just stepping out of Nyimi's hut as Biao passed. It took him by surprise, but he tried not to let it show. "Morning, my friend. Did you rest well?"

"Yes. Everything go alright last night?"

"Quiet. Just how we like it."

"Good." Nyimi stepped out behind Jie, yawning. Biao knew the pair had become fond of each other, but this was the first time they had spent the night together. He wondered if he was about to lose a friend the way he had lost Ling.

"Hey, Biao."

"Hello, Nyimi."

"I'm hungry," she said, going up on tip toe to kiss Jie on the cheek, "what's for breakfast?"

Biao let out a little laugh. "I'm going to go to bed. You two enjoy the day. It looks like it is going to be a beautiful one."

"You want me to w-wake you for lunch?"

"Nah, Jie. Maybe dinner."

"Sleep well."

Biao walked toward his hut, or Dorje and Lahmu's actually, whom he was staying with. First Ling and Naina, then seeing Sangye with Maya, and now Jie with Nyimi draped all over him, it seemed love was in the air for everyone—except him. He had to admit he was a little jealous, but his time would come. Now was not that time.

Biao missed Xiong and Amal as well. He went into the hut and to a small partitioned off section where he slept. Biao kicked off his boots, undid his belt, and laid it aside along with his crossbow and quiver of bolts. He laid down, wondering if Xiong and Amal had killed Ju-Long yet. Or had they in fact met their end? There was no way to know. He might never know. They were too far away, and Zhan, even with his telepathy, could not reach them at this point. Biao offered up a prayer for them, as well as one for his brothers back home, then drifted off to sleep.

After breakfast, Nyimi went back to bed. Jie was busy helping Sangye and several others finish a new hut, the one Sangye and Maya would raise their family in. It was easy to see the happiness on Sangye's face, and the pride he took in building their new home. Nyimi already had a hut, left for her by her deceased parents. They only had her, and fell ill when she was very young. Her mother died first, her father succumbing to the same illness a month later. She was raised by the entire village, everyone taking care of the beautiful little orphan girl.

As Jie worked he pictured adding on to her place to make room for the many children they would have. The thought brought a smile to his face and joy to his heart. For a long time now he felt as if he had nothing to live for, so death had no hold over him. Now it was different. Nyimi brought love back into his life, gave meaning to his existence. He had a reason to live, a future that involved more than fighting demons and being lonely. He was a mere mortal. Jie knew he would not live as long as the brothers he fought beside. If he wanted to settle down and start a family, the time was now. *How am I going to explain it to Biao?*

They had made good progress on Sangye's home during the day, but evening was upon them. Time for dinner and then rest. Jie was sore, but it was a good sore that came from working hard and accomplishing something. Maybe after they ate he could convince Nyimi to give him a rub down.

Rita, Topgye and Sangye's mother, Lahmu (Dorje's wife), and Maya had prepared the food. Biao joined them for dinner and began discussing the long trip home they would embark on tomorrow. Fortunately, Nyimi was sitting away from them. She and Jie stole glances at each other and smiled, but Jie was happy she could not hear the present conversation. He was seventy-five percent sure he was staying, but he couldn't find the words to tell Biao. His friend was excited to be heading for home once again.

"I figure we head out at first light. It will be a long, hard journey through the mountains, but we'll make it. You keep us fed, and I'll keep us alive, partner." Jie just nodded as Biao spoke. Others would be pulling watch tonight, and Rita and Lahmu would be up early to feed them breakfast and provide them with rations to start their trek. Jie could feel his heart strings pulling in two different directions.

"I'll probably stay up awhile, I slept a little longer than I planned on. It will give me a chance to say my goodbyes."

"I'll p-probably hit the bed early."

"Try not to let Nyimi keep you up too late," Biao laughed.

"Sh-shut up."

Jie went to the creek and washed up. Biao had superior strength, he could take care of himself. His friend also had supernatural speed. Biao would definitely make better time if he didn't have to wait for Jie to catch up.

He got to Nyimi's hut to find her waiting for him. "I wasn't sure you were coming here tonight. I hoped, but I wasn't certain."

"Why wouldn't I?" Jie replied. *She knew I was coming. Why else would she be naked under that thin blanket?*

"I wasn't sure if seeing me one last time would make it too hard for you to leave."

"My mind is not made up yet."

"What can I do to convince you to stay?" She pulled the blanket off her, exposing her gorgeous body. Long dark hair, beautiful breasts, and a set of legs that took your breath away. He knew those legs led up to an amazing ass, all of it on a five-foot seven frame, tall for a woman of this village.

"I'd say you're off to a g-good start," Jie smiled. "I could just st-stand here admiring that body all n-n-night long."

"Why just look at it when you can love it, touch it, squeeze it?" Jie undid his belt and laid it aside. Nyimi sat up a little, propping her head up with her elbow. She watched as he undressed. Jie was six-foot five and she had insisted that he had larger muscles than she had ever seen before. His shirt came off first, exposing what she labeled his huge arms and massive chest. He could already feel her soft body pressed against his rock hard one.

Jie turned around and dropped his pants. Nyimi took in the sight and he watched with keen interest as a shudder ran through her body.

Jie turned to her. "I am g-going to m-make l-love to you until neither one of us can m-m-move."

"Put your money where your mouth is, big boy."

"I'm gonna put my m-mouth here, there, and ev-everywhere." Jie laid down beside her, running his rough hand along her smooth skin, starting at the shoulder—then cupping her right breast. He leaned in and kissed her neck as his hand moved over her abdomen. He traced over the curve of her hip as his lips brushed hers.

They made love until they were both spent. She was breathless, but smiling. He smiled and let out a little laugh as he found his own air again. "That was fantastic. You are amazing."

"I love you, Jie."

"I love you, too." Jie rolled off to the right. They both lay there sweaty and exhausted, until Nyimi half rolled onto him and planted a kiss on his lips. *How could I ever leave her?*

Biao had been lying down for about an hour, unable to fall asleep. He really had slept too long during the day, and was anxious for the morn to come. That's when he heard the yelling. The night watch was calling for help.

Biao sprang to his feet. He hadn't bothered to take his boots off yet, so he grabbed his sword from its scabbard and raced outside. The cries for help came from the west part of the village. He was on the east. He heard several men shouting 'demon' in their native tongue. He was sure a xiang shi had found its way here and was trying for an easy meal. It would not find one tonight.

He recognized two of the voices, Pema and Norbu. They had helped escort him and his brothers into Nepal as they raced across India to find Ju-Long. As he approached he saw a third man leaning over the body of a fourth.

"What happened?"

"A blood drinker grabbed Pasang when he was away from us relieving himself. When it seemed to be taking too long, we went to check on him. His brother, Tensing, spotted him first," Pema said, pointing at the man kneeling next to Pasang, "a demon had him, sucking the blood from the vein in his neck. The devil dropped Pasang right there, and looked as if he was going to charge us. That is when we lit him up. All three of our bolts hit him, two in the abdomen and one in the right thigh. None of the shots were fatal—and by the time we reloaded the beast had disappeared."

"Which way?" Biao asked.

"West, into the trees and toward the high ground," Norbu answered.

"What did he look like?"

"Like one of us. Either a Sherpa or some other native nomad."

"Either of you recognize him?"

"No," they answered in unison.

"Take care of him and stay sharp. I'll be back." Biao took off into the woods hoping he could catch the injured blood sucker and finish him.

Kalden ripped the first arrow from his abdomen, stifling a scream as he did. This was the first time he had run into trouble since the time deep in the mountains when that meh-the-like man demon nearly killed him. He was very careful to slip in and out of places with his prey unnoticed, and he never hit the same village twice in a row. He had run a circuit north of here, making rounds in numerous places. The people up there were starting to catch on to his little game, so he headed south. Word must have traveled, because this was the first time he ran into more than one sentry on duty.

He strained and ripped the second one out. That brought a roar from his throat. He leaned back against the tree, resting before he pulled the third one, lodged deep in his upper thigh, free. After that he would fly away from here as fast as he could and find another less resistant meal. But first the last arrow had to come out. The pain made it way too hard to focus before that.

Biao could hear the creature. It wasn't far, and he was on the right path. He wished he had brought a wooden weapon. He would have to decapitate the demon if he wanted to defeat it by sword. He slowed down for a moment and looked around. There was a fallen branch that looked sturdy enough to forge a short spear from. The tip didn't need to be completely sharp, just enough to puncture the skin—he would use brute force to drive it the rest of the way through.

Kalden tugged the third arrow out of his leg with a yelp. As he lay there trying to recover and refocus, he thought he heard someone approaching on his left. He sniffed the air several times. The light breeze that was blowing toward him carried the scent of a human with it. *Foolish,* he thought. *I guess I will feast and then fly.* Kalden got to his feet, and slid behind the tree while he waited for his prey to come to him.

Biao came upon a small area that was partially clear. He spotted three bloody arrows a few feet from a large tree. His enemy had been here, and hopefully hadn't got far. He tightened his grip on the sword in his right hand and the makeshift spear he held in his left.

The human had slowed its pace and was moving cautiously across the open area. Surely the man would be armed and alert. He would have to move on his victim quickly. Kalden prepared himself to spring into action. He listened to hear if there was actually more than one set of footsteps coming his way. His suspicion that the man was armed was confirmed as he spotted the tip of a sword come into his line of sight.

Something slammed hard into his side and Biao fell over. The demon was on top of him. He had dropped his sword and caught the beast by the throat as it tried to sink fangs into him. The blood sucker had his arm with the spear pinned down. Its free hand was tearing at the hand he had on its neck, the nails digging into his skin like mini daggers.

Biao thrust his hips upwards and rolled left, putting himself in a mounted position on top of the xiang shi. He still had it by the throat, and it still had a grip on both his hands. He was now pressing down instead of up, making the choke much more effective. He wasn't sure what crushing the demon's neck would do, but he was gonna find out.

The creature released its grip on the arm he was choking it with and delivered two fast, hard blows straight to his nose. Blood poured from it and the demon opened its mouth to receive it. Claws raked down his face, then across his forehead. More blood spilled from the fresh wounds. It ran into his eyes affecting his vision. A series of rights rocked the left side of his jaw. He felt another tooth break loose. That made four including the three he lost in a fight with a human servant on the southwest coast of India.

Dazed and half blind, the demon rolled Biao off and then jumped on his back. This scene was becoming all too familiar. Then the beast let out a scream, followed by another, even more agonizing one. The xiang shi fell off him, still yelling in pain. Biao heard the sound of something sinking deep in flesh and bone. The screaming died immediately.

"Biao, are you okay?"

"Jie? Where did you come from?"

"I awoke to the cries for h-help from Pema and Norbu. By the time I got to th-them, you had already headed after the d-d-demon. I followed right a-away."

"Well, you seem to be developing a habit of saving my ass when we are in this place. First the demon Yeti, and now the xiang shi."

'Your f-f-face is a bl-bloody mess."

"Yep, and if this keeps up, I'll be gumming my food soon," Biao said as he spit a tooth out on the ground, "thanks, Jie." He spit a hunk of blood and mucous out. *This is way too familiar.* "I don't know what I'd do without you."

Biao had to delay resuming his journey home for a week to heal. Thoughts of his own mortality swam through his head again and again. This was the third time he was near death. It was the third time a normal human had saved him. He thought about Jie and Nyimi. He dreaded the thought of traveling alone, yet he wanted his friend to have a chance to have the life a person should. Biao thought he might never experience that life himself.

Jie struggled with guilt. Yes, Biao was capable, but the recent fight with the xiang shi proved that everyone needed someone to watch their back. In the meantime, he was lost in love with Nyimi, and he knew he couldn't leave her. But if something happened and Biao didn't make it home, Jie would never forgive himself.

The week had been bittersweet. Pasang had to be staked to make sure he didn't return as a xiang shi. Afterward, he was burned in a funeral pyre, his brother sobbing and inconsolable the entire time. Then late last night, Maya gave birth to a handsome baby boy. They named him Dawa, and Jie got a chance to hold him for a moment. It made him long for a child of his own. He had yet to tell Biao that he wouldn't be going back with him. He would have to face him in the morning and profess his decision to stay and marry Nyimi.

Jie knew Biao would be up at the crack of dawn, ready to leave. He got up, leaving Nyimi sleeping, got dressed and went outside. It was a short walk to Dorje's hut. He fully expected Biao to be waiting for him. No one was outside. He knocked on the hut wall next to the entryway. He could hear Lahmu yell from inside "Come in."

"Good morning, Lahmu. Biao still s-sleeping?"

"He went out with Dorje and Topgye two hours ago."

"He say when he'd be b-back?"

"He left a message for me to give to you. He wanted to let you know that he truly valued your friendship, and was grateful for all you did for him. He wants you to take care of yourself, Nyimi, and your future children. He said if you had a son, Biao was a good, strong name—feel free to use it."

"He is g-gone?"

"Yes. He left so it would be easier on you and your decision to stay. Dorje and Topgye are escorting him part of the way. They will be gone for a couple of weeks."

"Damn. I am g-g-gonna miss him." A tear welled up in his eye. He wiped it away before it could fall.

India, 401 AD

Meena struggled on her own at first, but her determination to exact revenge kept her going. It had been several months since she ran out on Ju-Long. He had wanted her to make love to his twin female Chinese human servants and succubus girlfriend. She was not ready for that. When her father, Prince Amit, locked her away for falling in love with a peasant boy from the Sudra caste, she was forced to do terrible things. The two women who took care of her were mean and preferred each other's company over that of a man. Not that any man in his right mind wanted to have sex with those two hideous women.

They were careful to make sure she remained a virgin, but they forced her to perform oral sex on them. They were strong— far stronger than she. And they were dirty. They smelled horrible, and sometimes made her lick their vaginas and assholes clean after they urinated or defecated. When she refused, they would beat her rib cage until it was black and blue.

Meena had thought about killing herself more than once back then. She also fantasized about killing them. When she escaped, she soon discovered that her father had executed her love shortly after he locked her away. If she could get to him, daddy would die as well. But tonight, those two hags were going to meet their end for sure.

Ju-Long had given her the power to do it. He had taken her virginity, then turned her into a Raksasha. She would still be with him if he hadn't tried to make her be with the women. She actually went back to the Caves of Ajunta a few weeks after she ran, ready to beg for Ju-Long's mercy and forgiveness. She wept when she discovered the monks had taken the caves back and the Master was nowhere to be found.

She had been so lonely, and now had no idea where her maker was and if he was even still alive. It was that night she resolved to make it on her own, and exact her revenge. All that was standing in her way was a couple of guards at the rear of her father's palace. She would make quick work of them, then enter and go to the dungeon where she had been held, and the pair of hags she sought resided.

Ling, Naina, and Marcos were thoroughly enjoying the extravagant dinner Prince Amit had invited them to. He had hired Naina, and her brother Amal, to find his daughter. They had turned up empty handed, and the Prince was losing hope of finding her again. Her escape and disappearance had strained relations with the Vaktakas, who ruled much of the south. His daughter was to be wed to one of theirs, and when she took off and their entourage went home empty, things began to get ugly along their mutual border.

Naina and Ling continued the search, since her brother Amal and his brother Xiong traveled west in pursuit of Ju-Long. They didn't find a trace of her either. Whether she was alive, dead, or turned they had no clue. The only thing they were certain of was she was no longer with Ju-Long.

Meena came to the bottom of the steps. A single torch was lit, barely illuminating a fraction of the dark, damp, musty smelling chamber. She knew one of the women was close. She could smell the rotten crotch old bitch.

The woman stepped out of the shadows. "Garina, we have a guest."

"Who is it, Chaaya?"

"I don't know, sister. Step into the light so I can see you better, darling."

Meena paced forward until she was fully in the light of the torch. "Oh, my! It is Meena! Oh how we have missed you, you naughty girl!" Chaaya cackled.

"Oh, goodie! Nobody licks ass like our little whore princess!" Garina added as she came to stand beside her sister. "Foolish little girl, I am going to make you go down on me until your tongue is raw and bleeding."

In a blur of movement Meena shot forward, plunging her fist through Garina's chest, ripping her heart out and showing it to the woman before she died. Chaaya let out a guttural scream that echoed throughout the dungeon. Meena shoved the heart into Chaaya's open mouth. "Chew on that, bitch!"

Meena grabbed her ears. "Remember when you used to grab my ears and force me to lick that disgusting gash you have between your legs? Never again!" Meena twisted her head violently, feeling Chaaya's body go limp as she heard the snap, crackle and pop of bones.

"There, that is done." Meena started to ascend the staircase. *Daddy, I'm home.*

The music was loud, and a half dozen girls were dancing around the hall entertaining the Prince and his guests. There was a time Ling would have been mesmerized by scantily clad women dancing around him. Not now. At the moment he was staring into the eyes of the only one he ever wanted.

He turned to the sound of something crashing. A guard had been tossed across the room and landed on a table next to him. Over by the doorway, three guards with swords drawn, were stepping between the Prince, who was out of his seat, and a woman with blood all over her hands and arms.

"Meena!" Naina yelled. She was already on the move.

The prince was moving as far away as he could while his men tried to hold off his daughter. Meena had already killed two of the guards when the third drove his sword all the way through her abdomen. She grabbed the man's hand while the blade was still in her and snapped his wrist, then delivered a punch that sent him flying into the oncoming Naina. Meena recognized her from their youth when her father had brought her and her brother Amal to the palace for dinners—just like the one tonight.

She remembered that Naina had supernatural speed and could fight. Her brother Amal had the ability to move objects with his mind. Meena hadn't seen him, but knew it was time to exit. She wanted her father dead, but not at the cost of her own existence.

Ling watched as the woman pulled the sword from her stomach and tossed it aside. The Prince's daughter had been turned into a demon. He stopped to help Naina to her feet, and when the two looked up Meena was gone.

The pair ran out of the room and down the halls, twisting and turning as they sped toward the back of the palace. Naina assumed that was the direction Meena was headed. The front of the palace had tons of guards inside and out. The rear was probably how she entered and was the far easier path to make an escape.

They passed two guards who were down, and heard the yells and footfalls of many others as the whole palace was alerted. The pair came to the rear exit to find the doors wide open and a couple more dead guards. As they ran out they could see Meena, taking off skyward with an unconscious man in her arms. "I really hate the ones that can fly! Pisses me off!" Ling shouted shaking his fist in the air.

China, 402 AD

"Our brother returns. Let us go and greet him."

"Te is back?" Wei asked.

"No. It is Biao," Zhan replied. "Unfortunately I still cannot locate our other brother. He is either dead, or so far out of reach I cannot contact him."

"I pray it is the latter, eldest one." The pair walked out of the monastery and into the bright, beautiful sun just starting to set in the western sky. They could see a horse and rider approaching from that direction.

Biao could make out a tall thin figure that had to be Zhan, and a huge monstrosity standing next to him, which was unmistakably Wei. He had been on the road for over two years. The site of home almost brought a tear to his eye. He urged his horse from a trot into a gallop, wanting to cover the final distance as quickly as possible. He could dismount and actually outrun the steed he was on, but he was tired. Excited, but tired.

The boys prepared a meal and were serving it to the three brothers and Huang-Fu, a villager and close friend that had joined them. Biao could hardly believe how much the young apprentices had grown since he last saw them. Some were no longer apprentices, but actual monks.

This was the first solid meal Biao had had in a while. With Jie staying behind, food had been scarce, and never this tasty. He wondered how his friend was doing. It had been a long road home without him.

"He is fine," Zhan said.

"Who?"

"Jie, isn't that who you are worried about?"

"Reading my mind."

"Hard for me not too. You are thinking hard enough about it that you are actually projecting."

"Oh."

"He and Nyimi are expecting their first child any day now."

"Can you let him know I made it home safe?"

"I already have."

"What about Ling and Naina?"

"Both fine."

"Xiong and Amal?"

"Out of my reach. Have been for a year." Zhan frowned.

"Te?"

"Can't locate him either."

"Cai?"

"He is out with Gan and Yang Bo, tracking down the cats, and keeping an eye out for xiang shi."

"And how are those boys?" Biao took another bite. The food was delicious.

"Gan seems to have a part of all our powers and then some. He is strong like you, Xiong, and Wei. He is fast like Ling, can speak with animals like Cai, and has a touch of my gift and Te's gift of healing. There seems to be a new discovery all the time. He can also fly like Ju-Long. Apparently the bite of the xiang shi and the blood from each of us we gave to save him, have given him more power than we could have imagined."

"Wow. And Yang Bo?"

"As I relayed to you some time ago on your journey back, he has become a man-panther. Other than eating raw meat, he is safe to be around. We had to keep him locked up for a while, but once he started to gain control he became an invaluable asset."

"So, I'm home, what would you have from me?"

"At the moment, nothing. You need to rest and get your strength back. You have lost quite a bit of weight."

"I'll give you two weeks, then I am going to make sure you are up to date on your hand to hand combat training," Wei said. "With Xiong long gone, and Gan and Yang Bo not around, I have to go easy all the time. Now you're here I can be a little rougher."

"In other words, in two weeks I am going to take an ass whoopin'?"

"Yeah." Wei smiled.

"Welcome home. Get your strength back so I can pound on you. Gee, thanks."

"It's my pleasure." The four men laughed.

***

Two months passed. Biao was just getting used to sleeping in a bed again, and not jumping up at every little noise. He regained the weight he lost and took several lessons (aka beatings) from Wei. It was good to be back home. He just wondered how long it would last.

There was a growing number of xiang shi spreading in the north again. Kuang-shi (blood suckers who were part Yeti, part human, and all demon), who were unwittingly created by Ju-Long, plagued the west, and the south and east were being hit by a growing number and variety of man-animals. It was only a matter of time before he was out on another mission. Hopefully the next one didn't involve mountains.

Biao was out feeding and tending to the horses when Wei walked up. "Not today, big brother. I'm still sore from the last hurtin' you put on me." Wei, who was in charge of weapons and combat training at the monastery, was around five-hundred pounds and nearly eight feet tall. He was the strongest of all the brothers, and second oldest. While he didn't possess the great speed Xiong and Biao were gifted along with strength, both of his youngest brothers combined were no match for him. His skin was almost impenetrable, having stood up to the fangs and nails of the xiang shi, and the claws of a were-panther. Pain? Something he rarely felt.

"As much as I would love to whoop up on ya, that's not what I am here for. Cai and the boys are back and we have business to discuss."

"Our resources are spread thin, and they are about to be thinner," Zhan said as he handed his empty bowl to one of the apprentices. He decided to let everyone eat before getting down to business.

"How so, eldest one?" Cai asked.

"As you know, Xiong and our ally Amal track Ju-Long. Ling and Naina protect India, and Te is still missing." Zhan took a drink of water and cleared his throat. "We are going to have to divide ourselves further to accomplish anything. I will be remaining here to watch over the monastery and village. Gan and Wei will be heading north to cut into the expanding number of xiang-shi, then west to check out these kuang-shi."

"That could take years. Wei cannot travel at great speeds," Cai interjected, "why not send Biao?"

"Shut-up, Cai. He's finally letting me out of the house. Leave it be." Wei had always been the one to have to stay behind. He was ready to travel.

"Wei is the only one here that can give blood to Gan every two or three days without repercussions. Besides, Biao will be busy elsewhere, as will you," Zhan continued. "You will be taking Huang-Fu and twenty men along with twenty of the older apprentices out to chase down the man-animals. You will be taking Chin with you."

"Is he ready?" Cai asked.

"He has control of his beast." Zhan answered.

"Control of his beast? What the hell happened to him while I was gone?" Biao was puzzled.

"We were out on a mission nine months ago. We tracked down one of the tigers that became infected during the great battle with the xiang shi. We were able to destroy the beast, but it killed two men and injured Chin," Cai answered, reliving the ugly scene in his mind

"So he is a man-tiger now?"

"That is correct, Biao," Zhan replied. "Your mission remains the same, Cai, as far as the infected cats are concerned. With the man-animals, Yang Bo and Chin have shown us that they aren't all evil like the xiang-shi. If they were good in their human life, they may be good in this form."

"So, what do we do then?" Huang-Fu asked. He had been on the first hunt with Cai when they captured a man-panther and brought him back. They learned how to kill them using a silver weapon, but Yang Bo was turned. He was scratched by their prisoner while it was in animal form.

"Destroy if necessary. If they have good in them, let them live. If you can, recruit them. Yang Bo has proven he can be an asset, despite his condition. Right now, we need all the help we can get."

"Why am I not going with them as well?" Yang Bo interrupted.

"Because I need someone who can keep pace to go with Biao."

"And what prey tell am I doing?"

"Yours is the most important mission of all, Biao. I have seen Te. I don't know where he is, but he is alive, though a prisoner. You two are going to find him. You have to find him."

"And where will we begin our search?"

"The last place he was seen. It is a town in a Chinese territory known as Vietnam. The place itself is called Me Linh," Zhan explained, "from there I have no clue, but it's the best we got."

"When do we leave?" Biao asked.

"Cai and his group will start out in a week or so, after Cai has caught his breath. Wei and Gan, you leave in the morning. Biao, you and Yang Bo will leave as soon as possible."

Eastern Himalayas, 405 AD

Norjumbu saw the fire in the distance. Whoever it was, they were just outside of his territory. He made his way close to the border between his domain and that of a mated couple like him. He had come to terms with what he was a long time ago. He was nearly seven feet tall, much taller than the five-feet five he had been as a human. He could still see some of his old self when he looked into a pool of water at his reflection. He was also like the demon meh-teh that had made him this way. His jaw was huge, with large fangs jutting out of his mouth. His chest was broad, hands (or actually claws) oversized, and his feet were enormous. Norjumbu was covered in a thin layer of white hair that had a slight green hue to it. It wasn't as thick as the meh-teh's fur, but it was more hair than any human had.

The two men by the fire wore no heavy clothes or protection against the cold—and though Norjumbu was impervious to it, he knew it was freezing. He also knew that whoever they were, they were not just mere humans. He could tell the smaller one was still over six feet tall. The second one was enormous, Norjumbu's size or bigger. He could easily cross into the neighboring territory and snatch the smaller man, escaping before anyone noticed, but something told him to forgo that thought. He lived off both blood and flesh, and he had fed last night. The lower half of the human he snatched was waiting for him back in his lair.

Something about this pair was dangerous. Something told him to avoid all contact with them. Something told him to run and hide.

Wei and Gan talked about their time north of the great wall. The pair had tracked down and staked or beheaded over fifty xiang shi. Many of the demons who figured out what they were doing fled to faraway places. They spent an additional year making sure the northern part of China was free of the beasts. They also ran into a pack of man-mastiffs, like the were-panther Wei had had to kill back at the monastery several years back. Two escaped and they were unable to track them down. The other five they killed—three males and two females. They hadn't expected to run into man-animals in that area, but they had packed a couple of silver weapons, including some silver tipped arrows, just in case. Thank Buddha they had.

Then they had headed west. Thus far they hadn't found a single kuang-shi, but like their Yeti relatives they were elusive creatures who knew these mountains better than Gan and Wei ever would. They would travel south along the eastern mountains and see what they came across, then head back to the monastery, somewhere they had not been in over three years.

"How are you feeling, Gan?"

"Okay."

"You haven't had blood in three days. You need me to open a vein?"

"It probably wouldn't hurt. The hunger isn't serious yet, but the craving has made itself known." It was no easy feat to break through Wei's tough skin. Gan couldn't penetrate it with his fangs, so it was up to Wei to open up a spot for his friend to drink from. He had to take a dagger in one hand, and drive it as hard as he could through the opposite forearm near the wrist. He bent more than one blade over the past three years. Thankfully he always found a replacement.

The wound would not stay open long, and by the time Gan needed blood again it would be completely healed. Wei felt little pain for the most part, but this smarted every time. Tonight was no exception.

Aden and his mate, Jaya had seen the fire and knew humans had stumbled into their territory. They had cautiously crept closer to the men, hesitant to move on the pair because of the size of the one, and the fact that they wore no heavy clothes in this freezing cold place. Something about the pair was unnatural. They could be those human looking blood drinkers. Aden and Jaya had dealt with a few of them before. They were formidable opponents, but could not match the strength of the kuang-shi, as the locals referred to him, his mate, and others like them.

The duo were using hand signals to communicate. They could speak, but it was a mixture of their native Tibetan language and grunts, groans and growls. It made perfect sense to them, but no one else understood it. They remained quiet while they decided whether they would attack or not. Then the smell of blood came and it decided for them.

Gan was drinking from his left wrist when Wei saw them coming. They were large, fast, and moved with a grace that betrayed their size. One was female. Though they were covered in hair, the breasts were unmistakably that of a woman. "We got company, Gan!"

The two were on their feet as the kuang shi slammed into them. The female hit Gan and they went flying backwards. Wei centered his balance and caught the male, but the force still knocked him to the ground. They rolled several times, Wei's training allowing him to wind up on top.

Wei rained blow after blow down on the demon. The beast was not ready for the strength he was now faced. Wei was able to connect with its face multiple times. An especially hard right broke one of the beast's fangs off. That is when Aden caught Wei's wrists in his huge claws, and the power struggle was on.

Gan was able to escape the female's grasp after they slammed into the ground. He took to the air to assess the situation and draw both his swords. The female leapt for him but he was just out of reach. She couldn't fly. Some of the stories talked about a flying kuang-shi. She obviously wasn't one of them. She was strong. She was fast. But could she fight? Gan was about to find out.

Wei and his opponent took turns rolling each other. The beast was stronger than anything he had ever faced. It wasn't a trained fighter though, relying too much on its brute strength to conquer its enemy.

Wei was back on top, but the demon still had both of his wrists. "Let's see how thick that skull is!" The beast's face was already a bloody mess from Wei's initial punches. Now it was time to see if he could add to the damage. The first head butt rattled him as well. The beast was definitely hard headed. The second one he landed closer to the bridge of its nose. Blood was running into the creature's eyes, affecting its vision.

As he drew back for a third head butt, the demon Yeti released his left wrist and went to block Wei's attack with its right. It was what the big man was hoping for. Wei yanked his right hand free, trapped the beast's right arm with his—isolating it, and went with a move he had practiced a thousand times but never used in an actual fight.

Wei applied pressure to the creature's forearm. It was fighting against him, but he had it locked up tight. Aden took his left fist and began pummeling the back of Wei's head. When the big fella finally snapped its right forearm, the beast bellowed in agony. Wei sat up and grabbed a stake from his belt. Aden caught his right wrist and stopped Wei's downward swing in mid motion. While it was occupied trying to fend off one attack, Wei drew a second stake in his left hand and drove it into the demon's chest. It didn't sink in far enough. Aden released the one hand and clutched the other as Wei tried to drive the stake in further.

That left Wei's right hand free and he plunged the stake it held hard enough to reach its mark. The beast convulsed for a moment, then went still.

The female was bleeding from multiple wounds, including defensive ones on her forearms. She was quick and deceptively agile. Gan missed with both swords more times than he had hit her. Still she came at him. He tried several times to get to a spear so he could finish her. Each time she either tackled him before he reached them, or delivered a blow that sent him flying sideways.

Jaya heard her mate scream out in pain, and that was the distraction Gan needed. He dropped the sword in his left hand and swung the other one with both. They were close to the same height, and Gan leveled his sword toward her neckline. It went halfway through before it became lodged. Blood spewed from the side of its neck. Gan tried to yank it free, but she wrapped her huge paws over his and the hilt of the sword.

The look in her eyes was sad and desperate at the same time. Gan almost felt sorry for the beast. It was as if she was trying to beg for mercy, but all that came out were gurgling noises. Then her eyes got wide as her body went limp. When she fell Wei was standing there. He had driven a spear through her back and into her heart.

"You're bleeding," Gan said.

"I think it is the demon's blood."

"No, it's yours. I can smell it."

Wei looked around for some clean snow. There was plenty of the blood colored variety around him. He moved over until he found some pristine powder and gathered some of it. As he began using it to wash his arms off he noticed little scrapes and cuts. Apparently the kuang-shi had the strength and talons sharp enough to penetrate his skin. That was worth noting.

From a higher vantage point Unk looked on. He watched his parents get murdered. He was only six, halfway to maturity for his kind, and already five-feet tall and over two hundred pounds. His father was tough, as was his mother, but they had been taken out by two very human looking creatures. Granted, one of them was huge, but they both were more than they appeared. He knew he couldn't do anything about it now, lest he too be killed, but he did burn the images of the men into his head. Someday he would find them and rip them apart for what they had done.

Norjumbu watched the entire thing. His instincts that told him to avoid the pair had been correct. They had just taken out his neighbors and appeared no worse for wear. He looked across the higher ground and spotted Unk. Unk's mother, Jaya, had crossed into his territory almost seven years ago. They had fought, mated, and fought again. He had kicked her out of his domain and she had taken up residence in the territory adjacent to his. Not long after that, Aden had come along and the two became a family. Several months later, Unk was born.

He secretly watched the child as he grew. As the boy got older, Norjumbu was certain it was his. He never challenged, knowing that he could not defeat Jaya and Aden together. Now, his heart poured out to the boy. If he could convince Unk to come with him, he would take them both to a safe hiding place until these men left the area.

Japan, 412 AD

For over a decade Quon and Yun-Qi quietly resided outside the city of Kymamoto on the furthest southwest island of Japan. They made a dozen human servants, six males and six females, to guard them by day. Both xiang shi, or as they were called in these lands, Banpaia or Tenma, enjoyed the company of men, but Quon also had a taste for women.

They were very discreet when they fed, always traveling away from their home. They also discovered that over time the hunger lessened. Quon and Yun-Qi were always stronger after feeding, but they could actually skip a day now without serious consequences. The pair would fly somewhere, snatch a victim, feed, and then drop them in the salty sea to be devoured by sharks and other fish. They had several lairs they could hold up in scattered about the islands should they be delayed and have dawn catch them before they could return home.

The couple first stayed in a cavern not far from the shoreline. The pair wished for more than just a life lived in caves and dirty, dark, damp places. They made two servants to begin with, a large male named Eito, and a beautiful woman called Masumi. Quon and Yun-Qi took their time in finding a good place to call home. They used their ability to fly, which they gained while fighting and feeding on a Chinese dragon during their time with Ju-Long, to scout out some unoccupied land not too far away from civilization.

When they came across this area they knew instantly it was where they would settle. The next five human servants they made were males. Not just any men, but men who were skilled craftsman and builders. It was a long process, over two years in the making, but when it was finished they had a beautiful Shato fit for royalty, with a secret underground crypt where the pair slept the day away. They financed themselves the good old fashioned way for the first several years. Theft. Once they accumulated enough wealth they got into the shipping business, which was run by Eito. Eito and Masumi were their front. They were the wealthy couple who owned the beautiful home and ran their very successful shipping and trade company. Of course it didn't hurt when the real owners, for lack of a better term, ate the competition.

Other than to feed or take care of necessary business that Eito could not handle, Quon and Yun-Qi rarely left the land they owned near Kymamoto. While there were many Chinese immigrants in Japan, they were not particularly popular here, and the less attention they drew the better. They frolicked with each other and their servants. They still had not unlocked the mystery of the *kiss* which would allow them to make more of their own, but they really didn't care. If they wanted more companionship, they would simply make another servant.

Their family was growing. Three of the female servants had given birth, two had sons and the third a girl, all sired by the male servants. Yun-Qi loved children, and their presence added to the xiang shis' front. Another male servant, Yasahiro, acted as Eito's brother-in-law and right hand businessman. Tamako played the role of his wife. The other servants were simply that—servants.

The couple kicked around an idea for quite a while and decided to finally implement it. Back when they were with Ju-Long, they would capture humans and hold them prisoner. This practice would supply them with fresh blood for a while without having to go on the hunt every night. Quon discovered that they could survive and be at full strength with only a third of the blood an average human held. So they formulated a plan.

Separate from the main house, a second structure was built. The above ground part was a storehouse for food, tools, and other supplies. An underground chamber beneath it was a prison for their human 'livestock'. It would hold twenty comfortably. If they each fed on one human a night (two total), and went down the line, each victim would have ten days or better to recover before they were called upon again for blood. They would be fed and given plenty of water. Other than being imprisoned, they would not be mistreated. When their bodies could no longer recover, they would be killed and replaced. Both agreed it was a brilliant plan.

All went well for a full cycle of the moon. Then, while Quon and Yun-Qi were away on business (killing a rival who had attacked and sunk one of their ships) all hell broke loose.

***

Rei woke up thirsty. *Or am I hungry?* For the past week or so she awakened to find this feeling in the pit of her stomach. This time it was stronger than ever. The last thing she remembered was the demon sinking its teeth into her again. Like the other two times he was gentle, and thanked her for her sacrifice. Each time he finished she felt weak. He drank her blood as if it were wine. She would be tired for the next few days, waking only to eat, drink, and relieve herself in one of the pots they provided for her and the other prisoners.

Then, as she started to feel strong again, the demon would feed on her once more. This time, as she rose from her slumber something was quite different. The urge she felt was almost maddening. She looked over at the man lying on her right. She could hear the whoosh of blood as it flowed through his veins. The pulse that beat on the side of his neck was calling her. She licked her lips and her tongue rolled over one fang and then another.

Typically there was a male or female guard by the stairs, getting them what they needed, making sure their chamber pots were emptied, and preventing any of them from making an escape attempt. She looked around the room which was dimly lit by four torches, and saw no sign of a sentry on duty. Rei glanced back at the man's throat. She wasn't sickened by the thought, but rather

33

quite aroused by it. She slid over closer to him, then claimed her prize.

***

"What do you mean you don't know what happened? You had one main order, Eito! Keep the prisoners safe. That included keeping them!"

"I am sorry, Master Quon. We have failed you. I have failed you." Eito fell to his knees and laid his forehead on the ground.

"Yasahiro, explain this to me one more time."

"The night before last, a male and a female prisoner managed to escape. It appeared they had fed on two of the others—in the same manner you and Master Yun-Qi feed."

"Go on."

"They broke their bonds that chained them to the wall and took off."

"Where was the guard?"

"I went back to the main house," Taro, one of the other male servants, spoke up.

"Why?"

"I was hungry, Master Quon. I had forgotten to bring anything with me, and Ishi was not going to be coming with the prisoner's food for several more hours. They were all asleep. I thought it would be okay. It is I who have failed you." Taro went to his knees, lowering his face. "I beg your forgiveness."

"It is my fault he was not back in time," Ishi said, going to her knees, "I was awake when Taro came in, and I'm afraid I might have distracted him."

"How?"

"I am ovulating, and I was hoping to become pregnant."

"All three of you, on your feet," Quon yelled, "and you made an effort to find the escapees?"

"Yes, Master." They replied in unison.

"Jun went with me. He and I scoured the area, even traveling into Kymamoto. We searched through the night and into the afternoon with no luck."

"And last night?"

"We had two guards on the prisoners after that at all times. Jun and Kichi were on duty. We found them when Taro and I went to bring the prisoner's food and relieve them." Ishi had tears in her eyes. "Jun's heart had been ripped out and Kichi's throat was gone. She told me three nights ago that she believed she was pregnant with her second child. It was a horrible site." Ishi buried her face in her hands and began to sob even harder.

"Two more of the prisoner's had broken free, and fled. The rest had gotten the key off Jun's dead body and freed themselves." Taro added.

"Yasahiro and I personally went after them. We tracked some of them to Kymamoto. It was mid-morning and we heard rumors around the town that a dozen crazed individuals had come to town crying that Tenmas had captured them and kept them prisoner. Four of their companions had also become Tenmas. The demons had drank blood from all of them.

That got the visitors locked up in another prison. There they told of the huge Shato where the blood sucker's lived, and the outbuilding that had the dungeon they had been held in. A group was being formed to head out the next morning and investigate the crazy accusations. That's when we headed back."

"So they will be here sometime after dawn?"

"I am afraid so, Master," Eito answered. "That is why we have already prepared for evacuation."

"So, your mistakes have cost us our home, and two of our people. I should kill you all for your poor judgement and lack of vigilance!"

"Easy now, Quon," Yun-Qi finally chimed in, "it is not all their fault, and we have made an important discovery."

"And what would that be?"

"If the prisoners who escaped the first night, and the ones who killed Jun and Kichi, fed like us, then we have discovered how to create our own. The *kiss* is feeding off them without killing them or destroying their bodies. Apparently it is a three part process, because the first two who escaped were the only ones we had fed on for a third time."

"What about the other two? We only fed from them twice."

"True, but the newborns, I'll refer to the first two as, fed off them. Apparently it doesn't matter who does it—the third bite is a charm."

"Huh. So how does that let them off the hook?"

"They were outmatched. They had no clue what was going to happen."

"So we give them a pass?"

"I love our home, but I long for a new adventure. Let us take one of our ships and head to a new place."

"And start all over?"

"Yes, my love. It's not like we don't have eternity."

"Masters, first let me thank you for your mercy," Eito spoke up, "then let me explain the plan I have already set in motion."

"Go on,"

"I have sent the other two men, Naoko and Akio, along with four of the women, Dai, Fuyu, Tamako, and Masumi toward our shipyards near Hakata. They carry most of our wealth, along with the three children. I have kept a cart and two horses back to pull you in your crates when the sunrises, and enough mounts for the rest of us. We will head there as soon as you are ready."

"I've got a better idea," Quon spoke up, "how about you all head out and meet us there. We have a safe place to stay near the shipyard. We will fly there and await your arrival. I'd much rather do that then be an open target traveling cross country by day."

"As you wish, Master."

***

Rei, and the man she escaped with, Hiroshi, successfully survived their first two days, or rather nights, in their new forms. Much of that was thanks to Hiroshi paying attention to conversations that were held by their captors. They both knew naturally that they needed blood to survive. The hunger made that a given. But through the things he overheard, the demons who made them could not be out during the time of the sun, lest they die. The ones who guarded them, their human servants, were created by the demons to protect them by day. That meant the demons, or Tenmas as Hiroshi referred to them, must be vulnerable by day.

While they had no clue how to create their own human servant's, they did know to find a hidden resting place out of the sun during the day. By night they were stronger and faster than they ever dreamed possible. Hiroshi had also heard the Tenmas talk about flying. He attempted to launch himself through the air, only to come crashing down. Rei followed, soaring into the night sky, much to the dismay of Hiroshi. While jealous that she could fly and he could not, there were two things they had in common, a lust for blood—and each other.

Hiroshi was thirty-one, an inch shy of six feet tall, and was built like his job had been in his former life—a farmer. He was lean but muscled, and well weathered. His hair, which he preferred to keep short, had tinges of grey scattered in its natural jet black color. Rei was quite the opposite. She was barely five feet tall, had long jet black hair, soft skin, and while not overweight, had large breasts and a plump behind. That was not common for the women of her village. She was only nineteen, had no children, but was set to be married next month.

She liked the man she was to wed, but did not love him. It was arranged, as many marriages were, by their parents. She would have been the loyal wife and made herself a life with him. While scared at first, she was totally happy with this existence and her present company.

Their plan was to stay on the move for a while. Feed, travel to a new spot, find a safe lair, have wild, crazy, unbridled sex and do it all over again the next night. That was what they were about to do right now.

***

Gou received his orders from the clan leader, and had forty-five mounted warriors with him for this mission. At only twenty he was younger than most of the men he led, but he had proven himself in battle and was a natural born leader. He was also known for his foul temper and fits of rage, as well as his lack of mercy for his enemies. At six foot two and two-hundred thirty-five pounds of muscle, he was an imposing figure. He typically kept his waist length black hair in a tight braid, which was the case right now.

A long, ugly scar ran down the right side of his face starting above his eye and ending at the bottom of his jaw. He received it when three men jumped him. Apparently, he raped one of their wives. She was just one of many, and he never found out who she was or which one of the men was her husband. He killed all three of them, but one cut his face before he died. He had many scars over his body, from knives, daggers, an arrow, and where he was burned by a torch one of his enemies used as a weapon after Gou disarmed him.

The scar on his face was even scarier than it was ugly. Gou wore it like a badge of honor. It only reinforced the reputation he earned as a ruthless badass who was not to be crossed. You either had great respect for him, or you feared him. For Gou the two were one in the same.

They arrived at the Shato around mid-morning to find it empty. The place was huge and the occupants left behind all the furnishings and most of the decorations. They fled in a hurry. They found the outbuilding, and the underlying dungeon, just as the crazy people that came running into town had said. There were two dead bodies, one male and one female, that had been brutally killed. Even in death the woman was attractive. *I would have showed you a real good time, sweetheart.*

Some of Gou's men picked up a trail heading west. There were hoof prints and the tracks of horse drawn carts. He heard in the past that the owner of this place ran a shipping business. Hakata was a possible destination. That was the direction Gou led his warriors.

***

Eito and his group caught up with the others by late afternoon. If all went well they would make the shipyard shortly after nightfall. He hoped if they had pursuers their lead was sufficient to make their escape without any confrontation. The Masters would be awake when they got there. Hopefully they were already having a vessel readied for their departure. Masumi was his wife, not just for the front they put on, but for real. There had been no ceremony, or anything official, but he was hers and she was his.

Sure, they both belonged to the Masters, and shared themselves with the other servants, but there was true love between them, as well as a son. Daiki was the oldest of the three children the group had. He was only eight and already almost five feet tall. He was a miniature version of his father. Eito himself was six foot seven, and taller than every man he had ever encountered—three inches taller than his father. He wondered if his son would someday be the first person he ever looked up to.

Of course the masters would have to be protected, but right in line after them was Masumi and Daiki. He would sacrifice the others, and himself, to see that they lived on. If the enemy caught up with them before they could set sail, they all would have to fight. Except Masumi. He would have her flee with the children at the first sign of danger. No one would argue over who went with the children, as long as someone did.

Haru was the next oldest child. He was five and average size for his age. His parents, Jun and Kichi, were dead. Bashira was only two, and her mother, Fuyu, was a strong fighter and would definitely be in the battle. Her father, which could be any of the men—because Fuyu had slept with them all around the time of conception, was unknown. She was the spitting image of her mother, her features giving no clue as to which man had sired her. Akio had taken on the role of her dad, but there was only a one in six chance (one in seven if Quon could still reproduce in his form) he actually was. The only non-contestant was Yun-Qi, who had never slept with any of the women.

***

Quon and Yun-Qi rose just before sunset. Once it totally disappeared they emerged from their hiding place and went to work. Yun-Qi spoke with two of his captains. One ship was unloaded and ready, but wasn't due to go out again for three days. The second had just docked and was being unloaded. Their four other vessels were out to sea. Yun-Qi informed them that they would be taking the one that was ready, to load it with provisions and gather the crew. They would be transporting ten other adults and three children as well, so he ordered them to ready quarters for their guests.

"I have checked on the others. I can sense they are safe, but are worried. They are still a ways off." Quon informed his partner. "I am going to fly back and see if they are being pursued, and approximately how much time we have if they are."

"Good," Yun-Qi replied, "I will supervise and hurry along the preparations here." When he was with Ju-Long and the other warriors in his small army he could never reveal what he truly was. With Quon he could be exactly who he wanted to be, though he still had to be careful. He wasn't sure which trait the rest of the world would see as more evil—his love for men, or his thirst for blood. Yun-Qi leaned in and kissed Quon on the cheek while reaching down and cupping his mate's manhood. "Be careful lover. I want to have sex with you on the high seas later," he whispered.

***

Hiroshi and Rei snagged a couple of drunken sailors as they were relieving themselves behind a building. They drug them into a half empty storage shed, fed on them, then hid their bodies behind a stack of crates. "Where to now?" Rei asked, standing on her tip toes to lick a line of blood that was running down Hiroshi's neck. It brought a soft moan from him.

"Let's do it a little different tonight."

"How so?"

"We've taken enough coin off our victims the last few nights, we can rent a room. There is an inn I saw up the street."

"And stay there all night?"

"No, Rei. Just to make love in a bed, in a room—instead of some cavern, or storage shed."

"We've had fun in those places, but I'm game. Think anyone will realize what we are?"

"You look just as human as any. We'll just have to watch smiling too big."

"Our fangs do shrink back a little after we feed."

"And in places like this, as long as you have the money, people don't ask a lot of questions."

The room was small and needed some cleaning, but the bedding was soft, and the candles they lit gave it a romantic touch. Rei was beautiful, but in the candlelight she became gorgeous. Hiroshi sat in the one chair the room held, next to a small table. She was standing in front of him, pulling her dress over her head.

Rei straddled him and they kissed passionately, her mouth hungry for his. He kissed her cheek, then ran his tongue lightly over her neck, before nibbling on her ear. "I want you, Rei."

"Any way you want it, Hiroshi, that's the way you need it. Any way you want it," Rei whispered.

***

His people were being pursued. They still had a sizable lead, but a large band of men, trained soldiers on horseback, were closing the gap. They would make it to the ship, but there would not be much time to set sail before the enemy was upon them. Quon swooped low until he was flying parallel to Eito's horse. "They are coming. We won't have much time."

Eito jumped in his saddle a bit until he realized it was Master Quon. "Sorry, you startled me, Master."

"I'm going to try to slow them a bit, but we are going to have to find a way as to not lead them right to our docks."

"Yes, master."

He continued to fly alongside Eito. The entire group now realized Quon was there. "I am thinking that as you go through town you ditch the horses and carts and head to the ship on foot. There is a stable behind an inn. You can leave them there. I will see to it one of our captains retrieve them tomorrow. While our pursuers scavenge the city looking for us, we can set sail and be safely away."

"Yes, Master."

"In the meantime, pick up the pace. Oh, and give me you crossbow and arrows."

***

Gou drove his men harder. He was going to spill blood tonight, he could feel it. Whatever these things were, he would find them and he would kill them.

Quon aimed for the man leading the charge. Hopefully taking him out would send the others in disarray. It was harder to hit a moving target, and he had never fired from the air. He tracked the man and pulled the trigger, hoping his arrow would find its mark.

Gou felt the bolt slam into his shoulder. He yelled out, but kept upright. He pulled on his steed's reins and brought it to a stop, then reached over and ripped the arrow out with a groan. His men slowed, looking all around for an enemy to engage. One of his warriors let out a scream. He saw him fall, an arrow in his abdomen. Another bolt struck home, taking a soldier through the chest. Gou's head was on a swivel, looking for the source of the attack.

Quon had hit the leader, but it was not fatal. The group had come to a stop and he had taken out three of the others. It was easy work now that they weren't moving as much. They scrambled looking for him, but had no clue where he was as he flew around picking them off.

A total of seven of his men were down. Gou's rage was building. "Show yourself cowards! Fight like men!" He saw a bolt sink into the face of another of his warriors. Somebody was shooting from high ground, though there was no high ground. He scanned the sky and saw what could not be possible. "The demon is in the air! Dismount and aim your bows to the northwest skies!"

Quon fired one more shot, then reached back for another arrow. His quiver was empty. His last arrow, directed at the screaming leader, missed its target but hit his horse. Then Quon saw missiles headed his way. "Shit!"

Gou's mount had taken off when the arrow buried itself in its hind quarter. The demon had shot higher into the sky evading their fire, then took off west at incredible speeds. Gou ran to another horse and climbed on. "Mount up! We ride!"

***

Hiroshi collapsed on top of her, both exhausted and satisfied. "You are so beautiful. If I have to spend eternity in the dark, there is no one I'd rather do it with."

"Do you really think we will live forever?"

"I don't know, Rei. I know that I feel like I am sixteen again. I just want to make the most of every moment, of everyday, and I want to make the most of it with you." Hiroshi rolled over onto his back. Rei curled up against him, lying her head on his shoulder.

"I am hungry," she said, kissing his chest.

"Yes, I believe we have used up our earlier meal."

"Shall I fetch us a snack?"

"That would be wonderful." He brushed his hand through her hair. "Or I can go. Or we could go together."

"I would like to go another round. Here. In this room. It was a wonderful idea you had. Are you feeling up to it?"

"Feed me and I will be."

Gou was pissed. The cowards he thought were his men had mounted up alright, then turned and headed the other way. He had looked back as he spurred his horse west to find not a single one of them rode with him. He would deal with them later. Right now he was going to make whatever it was that put the arrow in his arm pay.

He had tracked the horse and carts to a stable. The keeper had told him they might have checked into the inn across the way. Gou wasn't sure how many of them there were, but they would all die by his blade before sunrise. He had checked with the man running the inn and no large group had checked in. He ordered a drink, slammed it, and ordered another. His shoulder had quit bleeding, but it was a little sore.

As he finished the second one and pondered a third, a beautiful young lady came down the steps. The woman was looking around, as if she was searching for company. Gou tapped his cup on the bar and the man refilled his glass. He tossed a coin on the counter, double what the drinks cost, and walked over toward the stairs.

"You looking for me?"

Rei smiled at him. "You looking for a good time?"

"I am the good time, lady."

"Oh. Well than I guess I am looking for you." She winked. "I have a room. Follow me."

Hiroshi was at the far end of the hallway, slumped over like a passed out drunk. He heard Rei lead their meal into the room. He was to wait a few minutes, then slip into the room and they would feed.

Rei had just stepped into the room, and heard the man behind her close the door, then the clunk of his belt and weapons hit the floor. She took her dress off, still facing away from him. He pushed her down face first on the bed and she felt his length press against her ass. "Easy there, lover boy. What's the rush?" He pushed her face into the bedding hard.

"Shut up, bitch. I like it rough." He leaned down and bit into her shoulder.

"A biter. Oh, I like that." Gou turned her over and slapped her face.

"Didn't I tell you to shut up?" She spread her legs and he climbed in between them. "That's better."

Rei wrapped her legs around him and clamped down tight. At the same time she grabbed his head and pulled it in, sinking fangs into his neck. He was strong, fighting against her and bringing himself up on all fours. She tightened her grip as he used his right fist to punch at her ribs. Then Hiroshi was there, draping himself over the man and biting into the opposite side of his neck.

Gou cursed them, never screaming or begging for his life. He felt himself grow weak, stopping his assault on Rei's rib cage. His body collapsed on top of her as everything went dark.

***

The last of the passengers and cargo was loaded onto the ship. The servants were busy helping the captain make way as half the crew was pretty drunk. They had no idea they would be setting sail tonight so they had been drinking hard believing they had two plus days before setting out again. Two of them had not reported for duty. The captain himself had given up his personal quarters to Quon and Yun-Qi, who stayed on deck until the vessel had made it into the open sea.

They headed into their room once everyone else felt safe. "We still have a few hours until dawn. Shall we?" Yun-Qi asked

"I have given the captain his orders. We will be traveling along the coast of Korea. He is to find a suitable place to make berth before sundown this evening."

"Oh, I was hoping for someplace more exotic."

"It is just a stopping point on our journey, my love. We must eat. I do not wish to feed on our crew." Quon smiled. "We can make our final destination wherever your little heart desires."

"I love you."

"And I you, Yun-Qi."

"Come over here and let momma take care of her handsome man."

***

They placed the man's body under some blankets and got dressed. They had about an hour or so before dawn. He had made for a fine meal, and they had made love longer than either of them had anticipated. There was no regret. The couple left the room and headed down stairs. There was an old woman who had replaced the man at the bar.

"Our friend is sleeping," Rei said, laying some coin on the counter, "he traveled most of the night to get here. He is exhausted. We will be back this evening," she lied. "Will this be enough to hold the room until then so he can rest?"

"Number?" the old woman said gruffly.

"Excuse me?"

"Room number. What is room number?"

"Oh, of course. Room *Ni.*"

"This place busy during day. Drunk sailors very loud all time. He may no get good rest."

"He'll be fine. He is dead tired. Just don't bother him." Rei smiled at the woman.

"We need to go," Hiroshi said, tugging at Rei's elbow.

"You have a pleasant day." The old woman scowled at Rei after she said it.

"You want my day pleasant? You stay and deal with idiots, let me be with him." She winked at Hiroshi. "I show you better time. She too young to know my tricks." Hiroshi smiled and winked back as Rei drug him toward the door.

***

Gou awoke to complete darkness. He threw back the blankets and realized he was still in the same room the woman led him to.

47

He wasn't sure if the demons thought they had killed him, but they failed. He would be ready for them next time—and there would be a next time. He would make that bitch bleed from every hole she had.

Speaking of blood, he always enjoyed spilling it, but right now drinking it was the only thing on his mind.

Me Linh, Vietnam, 400 AD

The three panthers that waited for their fourth, Lim, to arrive found some unwelcome visitors had come to call. They attacked Cai, who was the first to stumble upon them, along with three of the warriors from the village next to the monastery back home, and two of the apprentices. Gan located their general position, but it was inside a building with many rooms. They split into three groups to search for the man-panthers. Even in human form they had proven to be deadly, snapping the necks of two of the men almost instantly. Cai and the others had silver daggers drawn, but they seemed useless against the speed and strength of the man-panthers.

One of the apprentices managed to stab the lone female among the trio in her side as she tore the throat out of the third warrior. He was subsequently thrown into the wall by one of the men with her. The other apprentice lay on the floor as the second man transformed into a panther. Cai tried to get to him as the female screamed, pulled the dagger from her side, and slashed it across Cai's abdomen, opening a large cut in his stomach going from one side to the other. Cai fell, holding his insides in place. Blood gushed out as he writhed in pain.

Gan entered the room, a silver dipped sword in each hand. He ran the sword in his right hand through the woman's back, impaling her through the heart. He twisted it inside her making sure the heart was destroyed. One of the men took a swing at him and Gan lopped off his arm with the sword he held in his left hand. The creature roared in agony and backed away.

The one in panther form had bitten and clawed his way through the unconscious apprentice's chest cavity. When it heard the screams of its companions and saw Gan it sprinted out the door. Gan withdrew his weapon from the woman, then finished the now one armed beast, decapitating it with a smooth scissor strike using both swords. He took a quick survey of the room, then dropped his weapons and went to Cai. The smell of blood was calling to the part of him that was xiang shi. Gan fought those thoughts, and the thought of sinking fangs into Master Cai, finishing what the woman had started. The struggle was real.

Disung, in his panther form, saw a group of men coming at him from the right as he entered the hallway. He turned around and saw no one in the opposite direction. He tore off down the long corridor.

Te was behind a group of four men and four of the boys. He heard them yell and ready themselves. Something or someone was coming at them. He was not built for speed, nor was that his gift. He stepped up his pace, but was still a ways behind them.

Disung reached the end and turned right, the only direction he could, into another long hallway. There were more men coming at him, but there were more the other way, including the dangerous one that had taken out his kin.

Te watched as the huge black cat began ripping into the group in front of him. He saw three of them go down so quickly he barely had time to react. One of the warriors and two of the apprentices had stabbed the beast, but it continued to fight, maybe even harder.

Huyen had been following the group at a distance through her building. While her place had many rooms, there were only three guests staying here. She had come to check on them when she saw this group searching for someone, or something, in her halls. She had taken the three panthers in, using them from time to time to do her bidding. They weren't like other animal demons she had owned in the past—these three were hesitant to serve her at first. They were not inherently evil.

She took care of that initial resistance with a show of power and a little mind control spell she had used a thousand times while on this plane. The tall man in the rear stopped, raised his hands in front of him, and sent some form of energy out. It didn't feel like magic, especially *Ngai* magic, but it was powerful. *What are you?*

Disung was wounded, but winning. He could feel the intense burning inside his body coming from several different places where daggers had been thrust into him. The pain was most intense in the two wounds that daggers were still stuck in. He had killed five already, and wounded the others. He readied himself to make a break for it. There was no telling when reinforcements and the dangerous one would show up.

Then it hit him. He felt like his heart was being shredded. All of his internal organs seemed to have a knife slashing at them. Disung collapsed on the floor, unable to breathe. Something began to scramble his brain, and that was the last thing he felt.

Te hated that side of his gift. He was born to heal, not to injure or kill. Just like he could take away illness, mend broken bones, and bring calm in a troubled situation, he could also reach inside another and rip them to shreds internally. Today he wished he could have reacted quicker.

Huyen was in the form of an old man, the persona she used as a property owner in this city. *Impressive* she thought, watching the tall man's handiwork. *I might have to keep you.* She moved up behind him and laid a hard blow to the back of Te's head with the cane her old man form carried for effect.

She looked up and saw at least a dozen men coming down the hall toward her and the tall one who laid on the floor at her feet. She raised her left hand "Dem lai vong." The bodies hit the floor.

Gan stopped the bleeding and did as much as he could for Cai. He needed to get him to Te quickly. Whatever commotion was going on in the hall, it was silent now. They must have subdued the last of the man-panthers. Gan picked Cai up gently and moved out into the corridor.

He reached the end of the hall and rounded the corner. The bodies of his comrades were littering the floor. He set Cai down and began checking for a heartbeat on each one. There wasn't a single wound, not one drop of blood on the men or the apprentices, but they were all dead. He went to the group that was a little further up. There was blood everywhere. In the midst of his people was a naked human body, covered in blood and bodily fluids.

Te. I did not see Te. Gan began backtracking, double checking every face. He found no sign of Master Te. Gan yelled for his mentor, his booming voice echoing through the halls.

After spending a half hour scouring the building and surrounding area, Gan ended his search. Cai was passed out, but still alive. That was when Gan made the decision to fly Cai back to the monastery as fast as he could. He wasn't sure if they would be able to save Master Cai without Master Te, but it seemed like the best option at the moment. He would fly non-stop at the fastest speed he could achieve. But first, he was going to need to feed.

Phuc was more than half drunk as he staggered down the street, flask of rice wine in his hand. It was a beautiful, bright, sunny afternoon and he would have been out playing with his kids on a day like today had they still been alive. The two had fallen ill and passed over a year ago. His wife had died three months later from the same illness, and he had pretty much been drunk every day since.

He staggered over to an old building that hadn't seen any real use in years. He leaned on the outside wall and knocked on the partially open door. "Herro? Anybodily home?" Phuc hiccupped. Then a hand shot out and grabbed him, yanking him into the building in an instant.

Gan bit into the drunk man's neck. His plan was to take just enough to put him at full strength and curb the hunger until he got back home. The taste of the blood, fresh and warm, was erotic. Feeling the man's heartbeat in his mouth as he drank life in was overwhelming. He sucked harder and faster, unable to break away from the embrace of the blood and the powerful energy it poured into him. Whatever control he thought he might have was gone.

Phuc could feel himself grow weak. He felt no pain, no sorrow for himself. What he felt was relief. Finally, there would be an end to his torment. "Thank you," he whispered as he felt the last threads of life slipping away.

***

Gan flew as fast as he could and was back at the monastery by the following morning. Lin-Yao, Huang-Fu's wife, cleaned and dressed Cai's wound, the bandaging cloths wrapped around his torso helped hold his insides in place as the cut itself was still wide open and they had no idea how to close it.

Lin-Yao, a very beautiful and intelligent woman who was as tough as they come, overheard the conversation that Gan, Zhan and Wei were having. All the others were dead, and Te could not be found. She was saddened by all this, but inside was thankful and rejoiced in the fact that her husband, Huang-Fu, had not gone on this particular hunt.

"How is our patient?" Zhan asked.

"He seems stable right now. There is a lot of pain, and he is fevered, though I did not see signs of infection when I cleaned the wound. He has made it this long with such a serious injury, so that is a good sign. Only time will tell for sure." Lin-Yao cleared her throat. "He has passed out again from the pain. I am going to go gather some roots and herbs to make into a tea. The ones I am thinking of should ease his pain and help him heal."

"Thank you, Lin-Yao. You and your husband have been invaluable to us from the day you arrived."

"You look troubled, my son, and it is not just about Cai, Te, and the others. You are blocking hard, and I do not wish to forcibly pry, but there is nothing you can't talk to me about, Gan."

"I am hungry, Master Zhan."

"For food?"

"Blood."

"I will open a vein and fill a cup. What else troubles you?"

"I don't want it from a cup, chalice, bowl or flask."

"What is it you want then? The blood of the enemy who did this to our people."

"Yes. But no. I want blood straight from the source. Any source."

"Come and drink from my wrist then. Maybe you will find it better fresh."

"I know it is better. I have tried it like that."

"On Te?" Zhan looked puzzled. Gan refused to make eye contact with him.

"No."

"Cai?"

"No. On a normal human before I flew back here. I was low on energy and needed to feed before I brought us back. One donor was missing, one donor was dying, and everyone else was dead."

"So you found a local?"

"Yes. I only meant to take a little, enough to sate the thirst." Gan shook his head in shame. "I couldn't stop. I drained the life from him. I felt his heartbeat fading and didn't care. At that moment I was one of the monsters."

"And how do you feel now?"

"Like one of the monsters." Gan looked up and Zhan could see the burning need in his eyes.

***

Huyen had gained two new pets to replace the two she lost, and one was on the mend thanks to the tall one named Te, the same man who had nearly destroyed her kitty cat Disung. Te had been a tough case. She had to use an incredibly hard and powerful spell to force him to do as she bid. Then she found out he had not just the ability to ravage an enemy's body on the inside, but also the ability to heal.

She found Disung barely clinging to life when she returned just before dawn the following day. That's when Te, finally under her control after an exhausting night, offered to heal the man-panther. He had removed the two silver daggers from Disung's body, then laid hands on the man and began to mend the damage he had done. Disung was conscious and could speak, but a long ways from full recovery. Repairing his own handiwork was exhausting. Te would have to rebuild his own strength before going at it again.

Then she met Phuc, a blood sucking demon who had a more human appearance than any other blood drinker she had ever encountered. He tried to make Te his meal, but she stopped him. His mind was easy to control, especially after she supplied him with what he needed most. Not her blood, that was way too special for a low level parasite like him. She made him wait, then fetched him a young lady off which she allowed him to feed.

He feasted on the girl greedily, draining her life the way his had been drained the day before. Sated and satisfied he was more than happy to do her bidding.

***

The next day the four had to flee. The girl Phuc drained the day before attacked a man in broad daylight in the presence of a crowd. Many of them screamed *ma ca rong* as she drank in the blood hurriedly, much of it spilling down her chin. The man she fed on was actually one of her uncles. Soldiers came with weapons and she fought her way out, getting sliced up by several of their blades as she ran. The men gave chase, but they could not match her speed. She lost them halfway through town. The entire city was on alert within the hour. They weren't just searching for the girl, but for whatever had made her into this abomination. She hadn't been in this state when her father and mother last saw her yesterday morning.

They headed south by horse and wagon. Disung was still healing and Te was too slow of foot to keep up with her and Phuc's speed. It was going to be a long journey.

***

Cai was slowly on the mend, Te was still missing, and Gan's blood thirst had gotten the best of him. He pounced on Zhan, biting into his neck feverishly. Zhan cried out to Wei through his telepathy then pried into Gan's mind imploring him to fight it. The aura of his apprentice had all but disappeared as the xiang shi took over.

By the time Wei got there and pulled Gan off, Zhan was starting to pass out from the blood loss. The young apprentice fought to get out of Wei's hold, but even his superior strength was not enough. Zhan stared up at the two of them, Gan's feet dangling above the floor, and saw something that frightened him even after everything he had been through in the last several years. Gan's face was demon like, blood dripping from the corners of his mouth. It was soon after that Zhan found a flask and drank for the first time in a long time.

Gan was now sequestered in a strong hold, though he was remorseful and ashamed of what he had done, especially for attacking Master Zhan, he agreed that he should be locked away from others until he could learn to control the demon inside him once again. No one was allowed around him except Wei. He would learn to drink straight from the source through Zhan's behemoth brother. Wei was the only one who could force him to stop if he couldn't stop himself. Today was the first time he had blood fed since Zhan. Wei had to knock him out to get him to stop. This was going to be a long process.

Uncharted Land, 420 AD

Huyen enjoyed their travels, and picked up a couple more pets along the way. She had no idea where they were now, but it was new, different, and as intriguing a place as she had ever been to. They spent twelve years exploring the Chenia, Funan and the Maylay Kingdoms. In a place named Tarumanagara they met two more blood drinkers named Quon and Yun-Qi. The couple owned a shipping company that ran from there to Vietnam, China, Korea, Japan, and all points in between. The pair and their entourage had been living comfortably there for five years.

They were different from Phuc. They could not comprehend how he, a xiang shi as they referred to themselves, could walk in the daylight. The two had to be persuaded, by threat of force, to allow Huyen and her happy band of travelers to join them. Of course, as the two would soon find out, they had joined her crew, because while Huyen allowed them to run their business, she ran everything else.

They spent several years based in Tarumanagara, but traveled to many different places as the xiang shi couple tended to and expanded their enterprise. Then, while setting up business in a new place called Papuans, they were told of a land that was basically untapped. It was south, and had a huge coastline, much larger than Papuans.

The man telling the story had been there once, on a ship run by a captain that was now deceased. They had met heavy resistance from the natives and had to turn back. Half the crew and the captain were killed before they could escape. The place had unusual animals, sounded bountiful in parts, and had a mystery to it that intrigued Huyen.

Quon and Yun-Qi made note of it. Six months later they returned to Tarumanagara, pondering a trip south. Business and circumstances made them hold off on the journey to this unknown land, but finally they set sail back to Papuans, then south to this unchartered place.

Their ship had anchored just off the north coast of this strange land, and the first creature they met was an enormous *ca sau*. It was larger than any of them had ever seen. From its long, tooth filled snout to the tip of its massive tail, it was at least seven meters long and weighed thousands of pounds. It drug a crew member off one of the rowboats and took him under. He never came back up.

The shore was lined with them, their armor-like exterior soaking up the sun. As the four rowboats hit the beach—the fight for survival was on. By the time it was over three *ca sau* were dead as well as two more crew members and one of the human servants, Akio. Everyone else made it far enough inland that the humongous beasts lost interest and quit chasing them. The captain, his first mate, and Eito and Masumi were still on the boat. Eito and Masumi were keeping watch on Quon and Yun-Qi until nightfall.

A week later they had met the natives who were unfriendly as described, but were soon worshipping Huyen like a goddess. Funny how the death of a few can bring about compliance from many. No one understood a damn thing they were saying, except Huyen. She interpreted for the others, who used the Aborigine natives to help them gather materials and construct a decent place to call home while they were here. When construction was complete, Quon sent the captain and the surviving crew members back to Tarumanagara, along with Eito and Masumi's son, Daiki.

Daiki was sixteen and an inch shorter than his father, but still growing. He could easily reach seven foot by the time he was done. He had been raised in the shipping business, and was already taking over for his dad most of the time. Also headed back would be Fuyu and her daughter Bashira. Fuyu was a strong woman who also knew the business well. Not to mention that she and Bashira had just lost their pseudo husband/father, Akio. They needed to get away from this place and the horrible site of Akio being ripped apart by two crocodiles engaged in a tug of war over his body. The plan was for them to return in a year and see how things were progressing.

Quon and Yun-Qi took to flying around at night, exploring this amazing place. They encountered some of the wildlife, including a hopping animal that carried its young in a pouch. The natives called it a *kangaroo*, which basically translated into *I don't know*, according to Huyen. At first Quon thought she didn't know what it meant, but when she said "I don't know" she was giving him the definition.

There were other animals that carried their young in pouches, like the now named *Tasmanian devil*, and the *Tasmanian wolf*. There was also a strange looking animal that spent most of its time in trees—eucalyptus trees to be exact. The natives had given them the name *koala.*

One thing there seemed to be plenty of were snakes—and dingoes, a dog that could be either feral, or tamed and living with humans. Quon and Yun-Qi had encountered a nasty pack of them one night, led by a crazed man who could also take the form of a mopoke, a dismal night bird with a very harsh cry. That had been one hell of an encounter.

Thoorkook was perched high in a tree when he spotted the two men approaching, walking hand in hand. Soon he would let out his distinct call, summoning his dogs to him. They had not had a good meal in a couple of days.

The siblings who thought they had killed him thousands of years ago had only made him more powerful. The brothers, both named Byana, had taken revenge on him for sending his dingoes to kill their sons. First the brothers changed themselves into giant kangaroos and tracked down his dogs. Once they had finished them, they turned to Thoorkook. In a duel, the brother fighting him stabbed Thoorkook in the throat. Assuming he was dead, they turned him into the bird he was now, the damage to his throat giving him a raspy voice and strange call when in his mopoke form.

It took three centuries to figure out how to change back into his human self. By then, the brothers were long gone. Thoorkook collected more dogs, sharing some of his power with them. They were more vicious and nasty than the ones he had before. He had also brought two Tasmanian wolves and a Tasmanian devil into his fold, aligning them with the dingoes. He tracked down all the brothers' ancestors he could find and let his animals feast on their flesh and blood.

Thoorkook watched as the two men came to stand under his tree. They kissed passionately and began to unclothe each other. It had been a long, long time since he had seen two men together. He enjoyed watching, but also loved to join in. In the past he had slept with both men and women he was attracted too. After, he would feed them to his animals. It had been decades since he had sex with a human. Maybe he would hold off calling his pets for a while.

One of the men was on all fours, the other behind him, when Thoorkook approached in his human form. They were both attractive and muscular, though the one who was giving was larger than the man who was receiving. They had jet black straight hair, and their pale skin was unlike any human he had seen before. They were so lost in the throes of passion they didn't notice Thoorkook until he was right upon them.

Quon saw the large Aborigine male and was on his feet, fangs bared, in an instant. His partner looked up, the man's large, flaccid member a foot from his face.

At six feet tall, the native man was the same height as Quon, though leaner. The man threw his hands up in an 'I mean no harm' gesture. He spoke some words Quon could not understand in a very harsh voice that did not match his expressions. Then Quon noticed the scar on the man's throat. "What do you want? Get away from him! I will finish ripping your throat out!"

The man shrugged innocently. Obviously he didn't understand Quon either. Yun-Qi stayed where he was, mesmerized by the size of the man's phallus.

Thoorkook used his hands to express his desire to be with them. Quon was on high alert and wasn't putting it together. "I think I know what he wants, lover," Yun –Qi said as he reached a hand toward the man's member.

Thoorkook shook his head yes and stepped closer, allowing the smaller, pale man to grab his length. Quon was ready to launch himself on the dark male when Yun-Qi took the man into his mouth.

Thoorkook flung his head back, and let out a groan. He kept his hands to himself, knowing that a sudden move could result in an aggressive action from the larger man who was clearly still on guard. Not that Thoorkook was worried in the least. Despite their strange appearance and the taller one having fangs like a dog, he was a god, and would see to their deaths as soon as he was satisfied.

Quon grew aroused again as he watched Yun-Qi work the strange man. Yun-Qi could feel the supernatural power that flowed through this native male the moment he took him between his lips.

Quon moved behind the man, who didn't seem nervous at all by his action. The man's rear was plump and full. Quon pressed his body against Thoorkook, hugging him from behind, pressing his manhood against the man's cheeks.

Typically Thoorkook did the giving when it came to that, but he had allowed himself to be entered in the past. The one in front of him was doing such a good job, he knew if the man behind him made his way in it would not be long before he erupted.

Thoorkook heard the man behind him moan as he slowly pushed his way in. The sensation of being entered coupled with what was going on down front almost made his knees buckle. He put his right hand on top of Yun-Qi's head to support himself, and reached behind him until he had a handful of Quon's hair.

The threesome found a rhythm that worked for all, and within moments Quon and Thoorkook were arriving at the same time. Thoorkook's body shook and his head felt light as the climax brought on a high from top of his head to tips of his toes. He couldn't recall a time when sex had ever felt better. Maybe he would invite the pair to join him for a spell before killing them.

As the male grew flaccid once more, Yun-Qi could see the swollen veins in his penis still throbbing. He grabbed it, not wanting to bite it, but move it out of the way and reveal the actual prize he now sought.

Quon nestled against the man's neck He could feel the pulse in the artery that his cheek rested against. He slowly turned his head, licking along the vein. The man mumbled something, and Quon felt an arm slide between his stomach and the Aborigine's lower back. Then he felt that arm flex and trap the man's waist. Quon locked his right arm around the man's upper body and used his free hand to control his victim's head as his fangs dug into flesh and found blood.

Thoorkook could not believe the strength of the men who had him trapped between them. They were blood suckers. He thought they had gone extinct centuries ago. *Yara-ma-yha-who!* He screamed in his head. But they were something a lot more evolved than the four foot tall, red skinned, parasitical man-demon with a huge head and oversized toothless mouth. Those creatures dropped from the trees onto their victims and sucked blood from the head.

Thoorkook was strong as well, but by the time he gathered himself and realized what was actually happening, he felt his body grow weak. He struggled against them but could not break free. He thought if he transformed into the mopoke he could slip their grip and fly away. But first he must summon his companions.

Quon and Yun-Qi were sucking hard, as if in a competition to see who could get the most blood before their victim was drained. Just as the blood slowed to a trickle they could feel something happening. The next they knew the man's body seemed to melt away, and both men moved back. A dead bird fell on the ground between them.

"What the fu…" Quon started as he was tackled from behind. The dogs were all over him, biting into his flesh, ripping chunks of meat from his body. He managed to struggle to his hands and knees, kicking and punching the mad dingoes. His clothes and weapons were out of reach. Elbowing one of the mongrels that was on his back he made it to his knees. He grabbed and threw one dog and then another until he could spring to his feet and into the air.

Bloody and bruised, with bites covering most of his body, Quon looked down searching for Yun-Qi. Several dogs as well as a couple of other animals were biting at his mate. Yun-Qi was going from a run, to a crawl, then back to a run as the beasts caught him, he fended them off, then they caught him again. The situation was about to get worse as the half dozen hounds that had been attacking Quon now raced toward Yun-Qi.

He swooped down "Reach your arm up! I got you!" Yun grabbed for him, but something bit into his ankle and he went down again. Quon turned in the air and circled back. His partner was buried under a pile of the vile beasts with more on the way.

With one last gasp of strength Yun-Qi managed to throw several of the animals off him and make it to his feet. Quon slammed into him and grabbed his lover around the waist. A wolf and a dingo released their bite and fell to the ground as Quon soared skyward.

***

Thoorkook awoke surrounded by his animals. They were in one of the many dens they had in this region. He was still in bird form but with a thought he was once again a man. What the hell had happened last night was beyond him. A quick communication with his lead dog let him know that his attackers had escaped, though not unscathed. That was disappointing.

He would have to find them and destroy them, of course. He might enslave the smaller man for a while. The head had been delightful. Right now there was another issue to be dealt with. He could sense the change in his pets. Though the dingoes could survive without meat, they preferred it. All of his animals were craving meat tonight. Not just any meat—but human meat.

Thoorkook had a hunger as well. Actually—more of a thirst. It must be quenched. He knew of a nearby village that would provide exactly what he and his pack needed.

***

Quon and Yun-Qi had to feed twice during the night to heal their wounds completely. When they rose after sunset they felt powerful. While they had nearly been consumed by the crazed beasts, there was something in the blood of that Aborigines man that had caused a change within them. They had no idea what it was, but it was there nonetheless.

The pair had described what they had encountered last night to Huyen, their sorceress, who in turn described the proceedings to Tarka, the village Chief, and Jabiru, one of the elders. They told the age old tale of Thoorkook, and the sightings of him and his pack of devil dogs over the years. They were sure that was who Quon and Yun-Qi had met last night.

Huyen was fascinated by the tale. She had not met an ancient like herself in a long time. Her excitement was quelled when Quon informed her that they had killed the one named Thoorkook, but his animals still lived. She translated that to their Aborigines hosts, who looked at each other and laughed.

"What's so funny?" Quon insisted, furrowing his brow.

"Thoorkook has died a thousand deaths, yet he always returns," Huyen said, "he will probably be coming for your both."

***

They had feasted until they were stuffed. Two of his dogs had been killed, and some of the wounded villagers had escaped. He mourned the loss of his companions, then turned that sorrow into anger. Two more reasons those pale skinned blood suckers would die.

He was powerful before, but now he felt truly immortal. Not that anyone or anything had left him dead for long, but this was different. He felt stronger, faster, and discovered he could fly even while in human form. He would use that ability to scour larger areas and hopefully find his enemies quicker. They were dead men walking, regardless.

***

They had been on the hunt for many years, traveled to many places, always seeming to arrive a little too late. Gan had joined Biao and Yang-Bo over a decade ago. He had not been able to communicate with him, but he had seen Te and his captors through the eyes of the one he had unknowingly created back in

Me Linh, Vietnam, many, many moons ago. The one who had derailed him for almost a year, unable to control his feeding after taking his first human life.

Thankfully, because of the patience of Master Zhan, and the strength of Master Wei, he had persevered. It would have been easier on both of them to drive a stake through his heart, but they didn't. His first mission once he had regained control was to northern China then to the eastern Himalayas with Master Wei. Master Zhan never said it directly, but Gan knew he had paired the two together so Wei could keep an eye on him.

In Tarumanagara they had found a shipping company that belonged to two xiang shi that now traveled with the group. They had discovered the cluster that held their brother last set sail on a course that would take them east to Papuans. It took a little convincing, by use of force, but they had a small crew and a vessel and were on the high seas two days later.

Once again Papuans had been a miss. The ones they were after had sailed south to an unchartered land three weeks prior to their arrival. Three days later they were traveling again. They were all longing for Cai when they saw the beasts that lined the shore of their destination. Gan could communicate with animals, but controlling them the way Master Cai could was not one of his skills.

They sailed along the coast until they found a river that they took inland. There were plenty of crocodiles there as well, but most were not the size of the monsters on the beach. Once they found a decent cove to anchor, Gan flew them all, one at a time, including the crew, to a relatively safe spot far away from the bank.

This was a strange place to say the least, with an assortment of animals none of them had seen before. Gan could see Master Te through the eyes of Phuc. He had no idea where they were in these lands, but they were here. They were living amongst a tribe of dark skinned people who seemed to worship the female sorceress that led the group of mix and match demons.

***

Thoorkook had been searching for four days with no luck. The blood drinkers had thus far evaded him, but now he and his pack were heading north, into areas he had yet to check. They had left him alive and made him even more powerful. Though his new condition had a major drawback, incapacitation during the daylight, he had discovered some new abilities. Besides being stronger, faster and able to fly in his human body, he could change into many different forms now.

Thus far he had not been able to change back into a mopoke, but he had become a bat, a dingo, a wolf, a Tasmanian devil, and a quoll. In all forms he was quite a bit larger than his animal counterparts. After he fed in human form tonight, he had turned himself into a dingo and was running with the pack. They were going to find those Yara-ma-yha-who soon. They couldn't hide forever.

***

Biao and Yang-Bo were overlooking the village. They had spotted a couple of xiang shi among the native people, and what looked to be some of their human servants, but no sign of Te. Gan was busy flying the crew back to the ship in preparation for a hasty exit. They wanted to slip in, grab Biao's brother, and slip out with as little conflict as possible.

Then there were screams coming from the natives *"Thoorkook! Thoorkook! Wakara! Wakara!"* Some of the men grabbed arms to confront the threat head on. Others gathered the women and children and started herding them in the opposite direction.

Biao recognized the word run, *wakara,* but Thoorkook had to be a name for someone or something specific. Whatever it was, Biao figured they were about to find out. He wasn't sure if this distraction had just made things better, or turned them for the worse.

Quon and Yun-Qi sprung into the air. If those beasts were coming they had no desire to face them on the ground. The Aborigine warriors formed a tight band and held their spears at the ready. The crazed dogs tore into their ranks.

Te stepped out behind Huyen, but ahead of Phuc and Disung. Huyen had heard the name Thoorkook and could not wait to meet him. "Kill anything that is not ours, except the one named Thoorkook. He is mine," she ordered. Disung changed into panther form and headed into the fight. Phuc drew his sword and followed. Te stood there. He would have to focus on one enemy at a time if he wanted to avoid hurting their allies.

He took out one dingo, and then another, the dogs whimpering in pain as he destroyed their internal organs. Several of the warriors were down, others were trying to flee. Quon and Yun-Qi's servants were fighting hard, but a couple of them were in serious trouble. Te turned his attention there.

Biao could see Te, standing all by himself at the rear of the battle. He could also tell his brother was using his power for healing in reverse. It is not something he would normally do. *That black witch must have him under a powerful spell.* Biao hoped his presence could help Te break the bond she held on him and they all could make it out of this place alive.

Disung had just crushed the throat of one of the strange wolves when he sensed another like himself. He glanced over to see a black panther moving next to a large man. The pair were trying to get to Te without being noticed. Disung darted in that direction.

Biao was about five meters from his brother trying to decide if he wanted to knock him out and drag him off, or see if his older brother had the capacity to come willingly. He heard a crash behind him and turned to see Yang-Bo and another panther engaged in a fight. When he turned once more, Te was staring at him with an evil grin.

Yun Qi had been wounded by Thoorkook's spear, which was still stuck inside him. Quon had chopped the Aborigines demon's arm off with his sword, and now the two were fighting through the air. Yun-Qi was in agony, his stomach on fire where the wood shaft of the spear ran through it. He was ready to pass out from the pain, his weakened body plummeting to the ground. He slammed into the earth to the sound of bones cracking.

Then Eito and Masumi were there. Eito pulled the now broken spear from Yun-Qi's body, then hoisted the much smaller man into his arms. "That way!" Eito pointed his head east.

"What about the others? Master Quon?"

"We will come back, but for now we have to protect Master Yun. It is what Master Quon would want."

Huyen was about to throw a spell in Thoorkook's direction to help her pet vampire out when a tall Chinaman carrying two swords began racing toward her. She recognized him. He had been one of the one's with Te when she snatched her prize.

Biao was on his knees, one hand in the air pleading for his brother to stop. "Te, it's me! Please! Remember!" he yelled between gasps and groans, "It's Biao . . ."

This one was strong and kept making outrageous claims. This might require a laying on of hands to finish him. Te stepped closer and placed one hand on the top of the man's head and one on the side of his face.

Gan was fighting off the spell with a mental shield he had placed around himself. This witch was powerful—it would only be a matter of time before she broke through. Gan didn't know a lot about magic, but he could sense the spell she had cast reeked of death.

Yang-Bo had some scrapes and cuts, but was none the worse for wear. He had sent the other panther running. It was badly injured, but would heal. He thought about chasing it down and finishing it off, until he saw the scene between Te and Biao.

There was something in this man's eyes. It wasn't sorrow, or desperation. It wasn't rage either. It was unsettling. *How can this man look at me with love when I bring him death?* Te couldn't stand looking into those eyes a second longer.

Yang-Bo had shifted back into human form, hoping his teacher would remember him, and raced toward Master Te when the unthinkable happened. Master Te let out a guttural scream, you could feel his power vibrate through the night. That's when Master Biao's body exploded right in front of him.

Gan could see the one he had created, Phuc, approaching the sorceress from the left side. He was losing the battle, the spell threatening to break through at any moment. He reached out to Phuc with his mind. *Help me.*

He could see the man look his direction. There was a moment of recognition before the man looked back over at the witch. *Help me. I made you. If I die, you die with me.* Gan didn't know if that last part was true or not.

Phuc looked back and forth between his maker and Huyen. The man had gone to his knees and continued to plead to Phuc for help. *I can feel the bond between us, but I am also tied to my Queen.* He struggled between loyalty to Huyen and loyalty to his maker. *Will I really die if he dies?*

Phuc could feel the pain his maker was in as Huyen's spell began to spill over top of and around the man's shrinking shield. In a moment, if he did nothing, he would find out the answer to that question.

Bits and pieces of Biao's body covered Master Te and him. "Why? He was your brother!" Yang-Bo sobbed. Te stared at him with the evil eyes of a demon. That's when Yang-Bo felt the first stab of pain inside his body.

Phuc could feel Gan's life slipping away. So far he didn't feel any different. It was all just a bluff to turn him against his Queen. But then again, maybe it wasn't. *Decisions, decisions.*

Oh my, you are a powerful one. Maybe I should just subdue you and keep you around for a while. Huyen thought as she was deciding whether to drain the last bit of life from her victim or not. *Decisions, decisions.*

Thoorkook was reeling from the hard blows he had taken courtesy of the pale blood drinker, and the massive blood loss through his severed arm, Most of his pets were dead. The few that remained were on the retreat.

The last punch had sent him flying into some brush and rocks. He was dazed and hurting, but managed to switch into quoll form. While his body in this guise was twice the size of the furry, carnivorous animal itself, hopefully he could blend in to his surroundings and evade detection by his enemy until he could make his escape.

Thoorkook went to take a step and realized he was operating on three and a half legs. *Shit!* He managed to limp/crawl his way between two larger boulders. At that point he just laid still and waited.

Quon had taken his eye off his opponent for a moment to check for Yun-Qi and the others. He could see two of the servants were down, mauled so badly by the beasts their faces were unrecognizable. None of the others were within sight. He turned and swooped down on the area he had sent Thoorkook flying into. There was no sign of him, as if he had just up and disappeared.

Phuc leveled his sword and swung it hard toward Huyen's neckline. Her head flew up, flipping end over end. Phuc, even as her body was still falling, hacked away at her. By the time he was finished he had chopped her into a least a score of pieces. He would burn her body as soon as he could. If Huyen managed to reanimate herself he would be the first thing she killed.

Yang-Bo collapsed to the ground. The pain had subsided, but he could feel the damage Master Te had done. He could see his mentor standing there, staring at his hands in horror. "What is all over me?"

"Master Te, is it really you?"

"Yang-Bo, what are you doing here?"

"We came for you, Master Te." Yang-Bo looked into Te's eyes and could see that whatever fog he had been in, whatever evil had possessed him, was gone.

"Who is we?"

"Master Biao, Gan, and myself."

"My brother is here? Where is he?"

"I don't know," Yang-Bo lied, "there are still enemies about. We should make sure this place is safe, then gather the others and head home." Yang-Bo did not want to be the only one around when Master Te found out he had killed his own brother.

"Where are we?"

"Honestly, Master Te, I have no idea."

***

The sorceress was dead. Disung and Phuc disappeared. Yun-Qi recovered, and he, Quon, Eito, and Masumi were all that remained of their party in this strange place. Their ship wasn't due to return for ten months. With Thoorkook escaping them they could not stay where they were. If he happened upon them during the day the pair would be defenseless. Eito and Masumi would be no match for him on their own. They would die, then he and Quon would die.

They decided to head northeast, the direction in which they came when they first landed. It hadn't taken that long to sail from Papuans to here. Maybe they could fly it in a single night. Either way, the small village they had built up was no longer safe.

***

Thoorkook had switched back into human form after the coast was clear and found a wounded native that he fed on. It was almost unreal to watch his arm grow back as he drained the life from his victim. He searched the battlefield, and while he saw several dead with pale skin, none were the two blood suckers he was after. He would regroup and rebuild. The next time they faced each other it would be the last.

When he rounded up the remains of his pack, there were two dingoes, a wolf, and the devil that had survived. He would find a lair to wait out the day, then make a call out to the predatory animals around him. It might take a few days to get back his numbers, but then the hunt for the Yara-ma-yha-who would be on again.

***

Gan thanked Phuc for saving him, then immediately told his creation that if he ever saw him again, he would kill him. Phuc didn't understand how his maker could be so unappreciative. After being knocked through the air by a hard right, he got the message. That was fine with him, he was a free man, no sorceress or master to control him. He would make this new place his home.

Whatever beef the one named Thoorkook had with Quon and Yun-Qi was not his problem. They could deal with him themselves. He mulled over the thought of tracking them down and killing them himself during their daily rest. But then again, not his problem.

***

Thoorkook had drawn in seventeen dingoes over the first two nights. They weren't as blood thirsty as his wolf, devil, and two surviving dingoes, but they would do. He hoped to draw in a wolf or two tonight. It was a beautiful full moon set in a clear, starry sky. He would take whatever he added and be back on the trail of those pale *Yara-ma-yha-who*.

What heeded his call this time was quite the surprise. A pair of the largest wolves he had ever seen, three humongous dingoes, and an oversized Tasmanian devil came to him. They were the most incredible specimens he had ever run across. He himself shifted into dingo form and led them and the entire pack on a hunt. All the humans seemed to have fled the area, but a herd of kangaroos were close by. While they wouldn't sate his thirst for human blood, it would have to do.

After they had caught and ate their fill, Thoorkook led them to another lair east. He awoke that night to find six naked humans lying in a pile with his animals. The larger animals that had come to him last night were gone.

***

They reached the shores and anchored off, but stayed far enough away so they could avoid the large beasts that roamed the beach and surf. It would be Quon that made the test run to see if he could see land in enough time to make it before sunrise. If he could, then they would make their escape tomorrow night. If not, they would turn some locals into servants and start constructing a ship. All four of them hoped the latter would not be the case. That would take months, and the threat of Thoorkook and his crazed animals was all too real.

As soon as the sun was down, Quon kissed Yun-Qi and tore off into the night skies. He had a decent sense of time internally and if he didn't find Papuans halfway through the hours of dark he would flip around and head back. He was relying on his skills of sailing the high seas for years to guide him to his destination. Thankfully, at least at the onset, the skies were clear and the moon and stars were shining bright.

Yun-Qi and Masumi were in the lair they made as their temporary home cooking an animal Eito had killed earlier. The big man was out patrolling around making sure the perimeter was clear. The night was filled with the chirps of crickets and the scurrying of nocturnal animals. As dawn drew closer the songs of native birds joined the symphony of sounds.

As he walked back toward their hiding place he saw a huge creature descending from the sky. It looked like a bat, but there

77

could not be one that large, even in these strange lands. *Thoorkook!* He thought as he drew his sword.

The beast swung around and landed, hanging on a thick tree branch by its feet. Eito readied his sword to strike when the behemoth bat did a flip and hit the ground feet first, only it was Master Quon in its place. Eito lowered his sword and dropped to one knee.

"Master, forgive me. I did not know it was you. How?"

"That is a good question. I have felt something different, so has Yun, since we fed on Thoorkook. I wonder if that has something to do with this."

"What happened?"

"I don't know. I had seen the coast of Papuans and was heading back when I started thinking about how amazing it was to be able to fly. I have had that thought many times over the years. I pictured I was soaring like the eagle, how graceful they are in the air. Then I thought about the more chaotic flight of the bat. When I did, I felt a change. Suddenly, I really was the bat. Crazy."

"I can tell you that you are extremely scary in that form. If bats were really that big we'd all be in trouble. Do you think Master Yun can do it as well?"

"I don't know, but we shall find out. It was quite a rush flying like that once I got used to it. At first I almost crashed into the Ocean, but after that it was smooth sailing. Or flying." Quon was grinning from ear to ear. "Downside is that my clothes are shredded and lying somewhere in the drink out there."

Eito ate then took a nap until mid-morning while Masumi stood watch. They would be flying out tonight, Masumi on Master Yun and himself on Master Quon. This place was beautiful but so were many other places he had been. Eito couldn't wait to get off this oversized island. He was really excited to see his son again.

The masters were safe, but down for the day. Masumi took up a spot near them as Eito went out into the sunlight to look for tonight's dinner. He was also checking for any sign of Thoorkook and his pack of wild, blood crazed animals. All they had to do was survive the day, then they could put this all behind them.

There had to be something in the area that was making the wildlife uneasy. He had never had this much trouble finding prey. The quiet was almost eerie as he traipsed through the brush, crossbow at the ready. Then he saw them, two huge dingoes running right at him from his left. He leveled his weapon and fired, catching one of them in the chest. It went down yelping. He dropped the crossbow and pulled a dagger as the second one leapt on him taking them both to the ground.

The dog's mouth was clamped around his meaty right forearm rendering the dagger useless. He clubbed the side of the canine's body with his left fist. It moved out of range, shaking its head and ripping flesh from bone. The dagger fell from his hand as he screamed in pain.

Masumi could hear the cries of her husband's voice. She knew she should not leave the masters, but her man was in trouble. She grabbed a sword and ran out. He wasn't close, but the sounds of the struggle gave her direction. Whatever was happening, it was bad. She had to get there.

It seemed like it was taking forever to get to him. She leapt over a fallen tree and stopped dead in her tracks. The oversized dingo had ripped Eito's throat out and he lay there lifeless. The animal continued to chew on his body, gulping down chucks of it as it fed. "Nooo!" she screamed.

That got the dog's attention as it turned its head in her direction and bounded for her. Still in shock she had trouble moving, getting the sword ready to strike. Then a black blur came out of nowhere, slamming into the side of the dingo just before it got to her. It was a huge black panther. It had to be Disung.

Masumi stood there watching as the two beasts fought. It was clear Disung had the upper hand, and after a few moments he claimed victory, the dingo's blood soaking the earth under it. Disung turned his head away from her and spotted a second dingo with an arrow sticking out of it trying to limp away. The panther was on it instantly, ripping the wounded dog to pieces.

Masumi came out of her daze and ran to Eito. It was too late, her husband was dead. She wailed, tears flowing down her cheeks. Then a naked Disung in human form appeared.

He hugged her and urged her to be quiet. "There may be others. I am sorry about Eito, but we must go. It is not safe here."

Masumi continued to sob loudly. Disung scooped her up in his arms. "Which way to where Quon and Yun are?" Masumi didn't answer as she cried even harder and begged him not to take her from Eito. He would have to pick up her scent trail and follow it back to their lair.

Masumi finally stopped crying after about an hour, her tear-stained cheeks lacking color. For the past several hours she had just sat there hugging her knees, her body shivering like it was freezing even though the temperature in the shade was in the eighties.

Disung told her to stay put as he slipped into panther form and went out to check the area for the enemy. Those dingoes had been like him, part man and part animal. He was certain they were somehow connected to Thoorkook.

The sun was dropping but not fast enough. He had no idea what the plan would be when the vampires woke, but just having their strength would go a long ways to making him feel better, and maybe Yun-Qi could console Masumi. If nothing else the blood suckers could fly, so they could at least get far away from here. Soon Thoorkook and the rest of his pack were going to come searching for their comrades as well as them.

Disung went back to the bodies. He found a little ditch, which he widened, then drug the dead man-dog and dog-woman over and laid them in it. He covered them with dirt, rocks, branches and leaves. He hoped that would make it harder for others to find them. Eito was another problem entirely. He was huge, and because of his six foot seven or so frame, he was going to be hard to carry for the much shorter Disung. There was a creek nearby, maybe he could drag him to there and drop him in.

It took about twenty minutes to haul his body to the water, and only about thirty seconds for the crocs to start fighting over Eito's body. He'd tell Masumi he buried him and leave that part out. The sun was about to set by the time he was finished. It was time to head back, collect the others, and get the hell out of here.

Quon and Yun were awake when Disung got back to the lair. It wasn't true dark yet, so the xiang shi were confined for the moment. Yun tried to bring Masumi out of her catatonic like state while Quon got the story of what had transpired earlier from Disung. He could see the rage in Quon's eyes when he told him how Eito had been killed.

"Thank you for saving Masumi and watching over us," Quon said.

"We need to get out of here as soon as the sun sets. I have a feeling Thoorkook and his pack are close. Maybe we head to the opposite side of this place."

"I would love to stay and finish Thoorkook for good, but I have an even better plan than fleeing across this god forsaken place. We are flying to Papuans tonight. From there we will take a ship back home." Quon smiled. "That is unless you want to remain here?"

Te's heart was heavy. They had gone from one port to another on their return home, but this would be his last stop with Gan and Yang-Bo. He had been keeping to himself the entire trip since he learned it was he that had killed his brother Biao. The guilt and shame were almost too much to bare. He pondered ways to take his own life. One thing was for certain, there was no way he was going home. He could not face Zhan, Wei, Cai, and the others, if they were back. He would never be able to look them in the eye again.

As soon as they docked on the mainland, he would put up the strongest mental blocks he could muster and vanish into the countryside. They would never find him. That's even if they cared to come searching after the atrocity he committed.

Te decided he would travel, healing as many people with infirmities as he could. He would use his gift to save as a way to drown his ability to kill. He would never let that part of him loose upon anyone ever again. If he could have found a way to use it on himself and end this existence he would have.

***

Gan and Yang Bo had gone to barter for food. Te was going to the local stables to see if he could obtain a horse for the long trip back to the monastery. They were to meet back at the docks in an hour. Almost two hours passed and there was no Te. The two scoured the city for him, checking in both the local stables and many other places of business. Three more hours passed. Gan took to the skies flying above the city and all around the surrounding area. He had reached out with his mind numerous times and found no trace of his healing master.

Gan's frustration grew. They finally found Master Te only to lose Master Biao to death. Now Te was gone again. He and Yang Bo hung around for another week searching for Te. *Has that sorceress returned to life and taken him captive once more?* Gan thought as he let Disung climb on his back and they flew off, heading home.

Part 2

Merciless

How do you know we can trust him? He is the most merciless man I've ever met. He killed his own brother." Jia-Li, one of the first female human servants created by Ju-Long, stared up at her tall, muscular, Raksasha lover. Balavan saved her from the chosen ones from China who were pursuing her master. She had not seen or heard from Ju-Long, or her twin sister, Li Na, in decades. She often wondered if they were still alive.

Balavan was still captivated by the beauty of his Chinese angel after over forty years together. They had seen a lot, been through a lot, and survived a lot. Yes, this man who had taken them captive was known as the *Scourge of God* by his enemies, and he had killed his brother Bleda. But he offered safety and anonymity for Jia-Li and himself. They had been on the run for way too long, being chased around India by a couple of the chosen ones, a man named Ling and his partner Naina.

Then there were conflicts with other Raksasha whose territories they traveled through. They had lost the two others, both human servants, who escaped the Caves of Ajunta with them, along the way. The human they now served planned on killing Balavan and taking Jia-Li for himself. Balavan had been able to convince him otherwise.

After single handedly taking out twenty armed men, and surviving a multitude of sword and knife wounds, Balavan impressed this leader so much that he offered him a job training his warriors in the art of hand to hand combat. He had never seen such moves before and was anxious to make his already powerful hordes even more deadly.

"Do not fret, my love. We will remain with them until the time is right, then make our departure. You must admit the last few months have been nice. This is the first chance we have had to breathe in a long, long time." Balavan lifted Jia-Li's five foot delicate frame up into his arms.

"But I fear his madness grows. To kill your own brother just so you don't have to share power? What will he do to us when he no longer finds us useful?"

Balavan supported her easily, each of his huge hands cupped on her ass. Jia-Li's legs were wrapped around his torso. "Let me worry about that." He kissed her forehead. "I have an exit strategy if things go south. Trust me?" Jia-Li nodded.

For the first two years after leaving Ajunta, Jia-Li politely shunned his advances. She was loyal to Ju-Long. Balavan in turn stayed celibate during this period, trying to show her he could wait an eternity to be with her. When she finally relented, it was actually her that attacked him. Since that night they made love almost daily, often multiple times. They remained monogamous the entire time, and Balavan wanted it no other way.

The cover over the door of their tent opened and one of the soldiers came in. "Sir, King Attila requests your presence."

"Inform the King I will be there right away." Balavan gave a slight bow as he set Jia-Li down.

"Both of you, sir. Yourself and the mistress."

Balavan and Jia-Li looked at each other for a moment. He could see the concern in her eyes. "As the King wishes, so shall it be."

Balavan walked hand in hand with Jia-Li into Attila's tent. The couple knelt before him and awaited his command. "Rise and be seated." The King cleared his throat. Jia-Li kept her eyes lowered as she sat. Balavan looked at him, but not directly into his eyes.

"There are others like you in this world, yes?" Balavan nodded. "How do I kill such creatures?"

Jia-Li looked up, fear in her eyes, before immediately lowering them again. Balavan spoke up, "I believe, per our original agreement, I never had to answer the question as to what would kill me."

"You mock me!"

"No, Sire, I merely remind you of our agreement. Your Majesty has so much on his mind I merely thought you might have forgot." Balavan lowered his eyes.

"Well, I do not ask how I kill you, but how to kill them!"

"The methods are one in the same, your Highness."

"I see. So how do I kill her?" Attila spat looking at Jia-Li. Balavan gazed up at his king with malice in his eyes. "I bet she is a lot easier to kill than you are."

"With respect, my King, also part of our agreement was that Jia-Li would never be harmed." Balavan bowed his head again. What he wanted to do was leap upon this evil man and rip him to shreds.

"Do not throw my words back at me. I do not wish to harm her, or you, Balavan. I merely wish for an answer. If I don't get it, I will start by chopping your head off, ripping your heart out, and burning your body. If you recover from that I will quarter your body and have it taken in pieces to the farthest corners of my empire. Shall I go on? If I want you dead, you will be. There are a growing number of your kind that are putting my domain at unrest. I must eliminate this threat." Attila got up and walked toward Balavan, drawing his sword. "I am all too aware that the sun is not your friend. You avoid it at all costs. I would hate to have you chained down under clear skies when it rises next."

"Wood."

"What was that?"

"Wooden weapons. Metal has no real effect—unless you behead us. Wood will injure us—wood through the heart kills us."

"Very good, Balavan. And the sun?"

"Will burn us to ashes."

Attila was furious. Balavan had seen that look in his eyes before. He was glad Jia-Li was not here to see it this time. The King's eyes struck fear into most men, and he used that to his advantage. "That coward Theodosius thinks he can just ignore payment and go unpunished? By the time I am finished he will be begging to just pay the six hundred and sixty pounds of gold we agreed upon." Attila spat.

"We will march on the Romans, destroying all that cross our path. Constantinople will fall by my hand." Attila was known for killing the men and enslaving the women to be sold to the wealthy. Any male survivors were given an ultimatum—join the Hun army or die. "Ready the men. Send word to the other camps. We ride west at dawn!"

The others stood, as did Balavan. "I know my role, your Majesty. I will ensure things here run smoothly in your absence."

"Not this time, Balavan. Your gift of flight will come in handy on this trip. We will ready a mode of transportation to protect you during the time of the sun."

"And Jia-Li?"

"Bring her. She has proven, though merely a woman, she can take care of herself."

Balavan bowed before turning to exit. This move west might be their opportunity to go back on their own. The King had treated them well, but Jia-Li yearned to leave, to once again look for her sister. That would probably mean finding Ju-Long as well. That was something Balavan did not want. Once reunited would she go back to her master and forget about him? That was a question he did not desire an answer to.

***

Balavan had flown far ahead to spy on the capitol of the Eastern Roman Empire. He had not made it back before sunrise and had to hole up for the night. Now, with the main horde in sight, he had news to deliver to his King.

"Balavan, you had us worried. Especially poor Jia-Li. I almost brought her to my bed to comfort her." Attila laughed.

"It was farther than I thought. The sun came up before I could return." Balavan went to one knee in front of him.

"Of course. That nasty old sun."

"I have gathered information for my King. I think he will be quite pleased."

"Rise and deliver this message. Have the Romans heard of my coming and killed themselves to save me the trouble? It would be just like those cowards." Attila grinned as he twirled the ends of his moustache.

"Constantinople has been hit by an earthquake. The people there are scrambling to rebuild its walls. They are weak and ripe for the taking."

"Then we move forward." Attila stood, drawing his sword and pointing it skyward. "There, where I have passed, the grass will never grow again."

***

They had pillaged all the territory around Constantinople. The walls of the capitol, for the most part, had been resurrected. There was a gathering of troops being readied to defend the city. Attila was prodding the edges, testing the resolve of the Romans in their attempt to defend this place.

He dismounted and wielded his sword like the master of it he was, issuing death to the last remnants of this pathetic Roman brigade. Attila was covered in the blood and flesh of his enemies when a light rain started to fall. It was cool and refreshing after the heat of battle. The only thing really left to do was gather the spoils and prepare for what came next

Attila rallied much of his army to this place. They would overwhelm and crush their opponent, taking their capitol for his own. By the time the sun sank into the western sky two days from now, his enemies would know who was in charge.

"King Attila," A female voice called for him.

"Who calls me, child?"

"My name is Lalita. I am here with my master. We represent Theodosius II. We have come to negotiate on his behalf."

"And why would I need to negotiate? You may return and tell that coward he can surrender all, or I will simply take it from him by morning's light."

"I beg you to reconsider." Lalita knelt, still a safe distance from Attila and his men. "I assure you his offer is substantial."

"We had an agreement. He ignored it, and now he shall pay! I can't believe he sent a woman to do his bidding!"

"I am not alone."

"You have no army behind you. You spoke of a master, but I see no one else." In an instant Ju-Long disarmed him and had Attila by the throat. His Hunnish wasn't great, but the xiang shi knew how to make a threat.

"I am right here, asshole!" Something grabbed Ju-Long from behind. He released the Hun's neck to defend, but felt himself flying through the air, launched by a powerful creature.

Attila coughed, sucking in air and gathering himself. "I have one of those too, bitch!"

"Balavan?" Lalita asked.

"I do not wish to fight, my lady."

"You know these people?"

"Yes my Ki..."

"Little late for that, monk!" Ju-Long had flown full speed into Balavan and tackled him to the ground. Ju-Long was stronger, but for only the second time in his existence he wasn't the better fighter. When they finally stopped skidding across the wet soil Balavan was on top pinning Ju-Long's arms down.

"Please, Master. I do not wish to fight. I am under oath to protect the King. Please just let us go our separate ways."

"I made you! Your allegiance is to me!"

"I have no choice. They will kill her." A soft, sad look came over Balavan's face,

"Her who?" Ju-long wasn't waiting for an answer. Balavan had lost focus for a second and he was going to take advantage. He thrust his hips upward and tossed his opponent off him. Ju-Long was on his feet first and delivered a hard uppercut to Balavan as he too tried to stand.

Lalita tried to move in, only to find a bevy of recurve bows, nocked and ready to fire, pointed at her. They were accurate and a staple of the Hun army. They could launch arrows that achieved speeds great enough to pierce armor from one hundred yards away. She was going to be a spectator for the moment.

Balavan ate a right, a left and another right before he recovered and caught a kick headed for his abdomen. He gripped the leg tight and spun hard, sending Ju-Long flying through the air for a second time.

One of Attila's captains asked, "Shall we kill the intruders, my King?"

"Not yet. This fight is turning into such fun. I want to see how it ends." Attila retrieved his own sword, but was now insulated by many of his warriors should there be another attempt on him.

Ju-Long was back on his feet, bleeding from the side of his head where it had smashed into a rock. His sword was drawn as he stalked toward Balavan.

"If you kill him, you will be forced to become his replacement. You will serve me just as you now serve Theodosius."

"That is where you are wrong, Hun. Ju-Long serves no one. I know no master, I am my own god, and like you I am merciless to any who defy me."

"Oh, I like that quality. Someone throw our friend a sword. Let's keep this fight even."

Balavan caught the sword just in time to parry off a strike from Ju-Long. The clank of metal echoed through the night, the swords dancing at unbelievable speeds. If it were the long staff they were fighting with, it would be advantage Balavan. With the sword Ju-Long was equal, if not better.

Balavan blocked Ju-Long's sword downward and delivered a roundhouse left to the side of his master's head, knocking him sideways. Ju-long hit the ground, then countered with a leg sweep putting Balavan on his back. Both men bounced up simultaneously, but Ju-Long had his blade in better position. He drove it through the chest of his surprised combatant.

Balavan placed his hand over Ju-Long's and the hilt of the sword that ran through him, preventing his opponent from pulling it back out. He brought his sword up, but Ju-Long was ready and caught his arm by the wrist.

"Just give up. I will end it quickly. As good as you are, you are no match for me, Balavan."

"Master! Please don't!"

Ju-Long looked to his right. "Jia-Li? My Jia-Li!" He shoved hard and sent Balavan onto his back, the sword still stuck in his opponent.

"Now, my King? Shall we kill them now?"

"No, captain. This is getting far too interesting. The plot thickens."

"Master, how I have missed you!"

"And I you."

"Balavan saved me during the attack on Ajunta. He has protected me ever since as we searched for you."

"And now you have found me."

"Where is Li-Na?"

Ju-long shook his head. Jia-Li began to cry, tears joining the rain drops on her face that beaded and ran down her cheeks. She slumped to her knees, wrapping her arms around her master's thigh. "I am so sorry Jia-Li. It was the chosen ones. I will make them pay in time. Her death will not go unavenged."

"How long has she been gone?"

"Over forty years."

"I want to be with you when you face them. I want their blood," she pled, looking up at him.

"And you shall have it. But I must deal with Balavan and this other idiot first." He nodded in Attila's direction.

"Can't Balavan come with us?"

"I thank him for keeping you safe, but he must die tonight for his defiance. There can be no mercy."

"I love him, Master."

"What?" Ju-Long said, anger in his voice. "You have slept with him?"

"Forgive me. The first two years we were both celibate, but we didn't know when, if ever, we would find you."

"Whore!" He backhanded her, sending Jia-Li into a mud puddle that was forming.

Balavan was back on his feet, a sword in each hand. He was weak, and would be until he fed. "It's me you want Ju-Long. Come get some."

"Oh, your fate is sealed."

"Lalita, please help," Jia-Li called out in desperation. "You have the Master's ear, as well as his heart. Reason with him. No one else has to die here tonight. I have already lost my sister, please don't let him take my love from me as well."

"Nothing will deter me from ending this pathetic monk's existence."

"There might be one thing that does."

"Don't worry. You are next."

"You do realize that I have over a hundred marksman with their bows aimed at you and your lovely, Lalita was it? I say the word and they fire."

"No, wait. Please, my King. She was originally his human servant. He made her. When he dies, so shall she," Balavan begged.

"Well, it appears we have arrived at a crossroads. What shall we do?" Attila snickered.

"If I may," Lalita started, "we can come to an agreement that will serve all involved."

"And how is that?"

"Theodosius is offering twelve hundred pounds of gold as a peace offering. It is nearly double the original agreement."

"And in return?"

"You and your army return home and leave Constantinople be."

"And?"

"Ju-Long kills Balavan, we take the woman, and you never have to see us again."

"Well, to the gold offer, tell your coward Emperor it will cost him twenty one hundred pounds of gold to keep his little palace."

"Are you mad? That is over three times the amount!" Ju-Long spat.

"And he shall pay thrice the amount for his ignorance and arrogance!"

"Done," Lalita answered, drawing a look of rage from Ju-Long.

"As for Balavan, he proved his worth to me tonight, I don't think I will allow his death."

"The girl?" Ju-Long growled.

"She can choose if she wants to go with you, or stay with Balavan."

"Come, Jia-Li. You are free to go and your lover will live."

Jia-Li mumbled something Ju-Long could not understand. "Quit sobbing and let's go!"

"I want to stay, Master." Though she merely whispered it, he heard her words loud and clear. Ju-Long made a move toward her.

"I would think twice about that," Attila threatened.

"Come, Ju-Long, let us take our leave." Ju-Long turned and walked toward Lalita, staring down Balavan as he passed.

"Had we met under different circumstances we might have been the greatest of allies."

"Or the bitterest of enemies."

"True. I am not one for sharing. Just ask my brother," Attila chuckled.

"Know this," he began as he reached Lalita's side, "if we ever cross paths again." He looked at Balavan, and then Attila, "I will kill you."

"Know this," Attila answered, "if my gold, in full, is not here by mid-morning, I will take Constantinople by storm. I will find you wherever you are hiding, and see to your death while you are trapped by the sun."

India, 410 AD

Ling ran his hand up and down her arm. Naina was lying with her back to him on their oversized bed. "He doesn't look good. This may be his last days." Marcos had been sick since they came back home from the west coast of India after the battle on the beach with Ju-Long. Her adoptive father had already lived a long life when she and Amal were born. Naina wished her brother were here now.

From what she understood, Marcos had been on his deathbed before their birth, and with their mother and father dying shortly thereafter, something had changed in the old man. The aging process reversed and he looked like a middle aged man again. When the twins reached their teen years, the aging process started back. The last ten years had really been bad.

"He has been through a lot. Your father is a strong man. He may come through this and surprise us once again." Ling leaned in to kiss her on the cheek. He noticed that unlike most nights she wasn't crying. "I love you, Naina."

"And I you. Maybe it is just time. He has suffered a lot lately. It kills me to think of losing him, and tears me apart to watch him suffer like this."

"I am here. I will be your rock."

"I know, Ling." She rolled over to face him. Her breasts pressed against his chest always turned him on. Actually, just lying naked next to her turned him on. *Who am I kidding? Just seeing her smile, watching her breathe—turns me on.*

"Excuse me." She frowned. "Something seems to be jabbing me in the tummy."

"So sorry. He has a mind of his own."

She could feel him flexing it against her. "Persistent little fellow, isn't he?"

"He's just knocking. Can he come in?" Ling smiled.

"Well, I don't think he is going to be able to make his grand entrance through my belly button." Ling rolled them over until he was on top of her, He was short, but so was she. Ironic, because her twin brother Amal was over seven feet tall. Their bodies matched up almost perfectly.

"You are my goddess." He leaned in and kissed her mouth deeply. "Your lips are like wine," he whispered as he kissed her cheek, then her neck, "I love the taste of your skin." Ling looked into those incredible eyes. "Your beauty takes my breath from me."

They went through seven of their favorite positions from the Kama Sutra. Well, technically her favorite positions. Ling didn't care, he was just happy to participate. They finished with Naina collapsing on top of him, their bodies covered in sweat.

"Are you hungry?" Naina asked.

"Famished."

"Want to grab some fruit and walk down to the stream?"

"Sounds wonderful."

***

The next day, after sleeping in until the afternoon, they awoke to find Naina's father in the kitchen eating a snack with Chanta, their cook, and lately Marcos' caretaker when Ling and Naina were away tracking down demons. She wasn't much better off than Marcos. Today they both looked fresher. "Good morning."

"You're feeling better, dad?"

"Much."

"I am so happy." She leaned over and gave him a hug and a kiss on the cheek.

"Paan?"

"What?"

"Paan, Naina. You could use some paan." She covered her mouth. Ling laughed as he reached into a basket on the table and tossed a piece of the nutty breath freshener wrapped in a betel leaf. Chanda always had some made up. He popped a piece into his mouth as well, just in case.

Naina kept her hand over her mouth as she chewed. "I was so worried I was going to wake up today and . . ."

"I am not dead yet. Don't count this old man out too soon."

***

One week passed, then two. Marcos' health kept improving. Surprisingly, so did Chanda's. They each had more pep in their step, and had better color to their skin than they had in years. Naina didn't know how it was happening, but she was grateful.

One night, after a session of lovemaking, Ling crept to the kitchen to grab a snack. He could hear some soft moaning before he rounded the corner. At first he feared Chanda or Marcos had had a spell and he would find them on the floor. What he found was Chanda bent over the table, dress pulled up over her waist, with his father-in-law pumping away behind her. He backed out before either of them noticed.

When he returned to the bedroom empty handed, Naina questioned him. "Was there nothing?"

"Of course not. I just thought we might pick some fresh fruit off the trees outside. Take a walk to the stream. It's a beautiful night."

"That dumb look on your face tells me there is something you are leaving out. What is it, Ling?"

"Nothing. You just don't want to go into the kitchen right now."

"Why? What's wrong? Is it dad? Is it Chanda?"

"Kinda both."

"What are they doing? Are they ok?" Naina was on her feet and heading toward the door. Ling stepped in her way.

"They are fine. I don't know if *my mind* will ever be right again."

"What?" She paused. "No? They couldn't be! Not at their age!"

"They could. They were. It is an image I may never get over."

"Where?"

"I really don't want to talk about it." Ling pounded his fist against his forehead. "The table."

"Gross! I may never be able to eat there again."

"Who are you telling?"

***

Naina and Ling took off that next morning to check out a coven of Raksasha terrorizing an area inside the border of Nepal. This group was mostly female, having just two males. There were a dozen blood suckers total, according to reports. Heading in this direction reminded Ling of their original trip over the Himalayas from China into India. Biao, Xiong, Jie and himself, the fearsome foursome.

They were all spread out now. Biao had returned home. Last he heard his brother was with Gan and Yang-Bo searching for Te. Jie was married to Nyimi, living with their Sherpa friends, and the couple was expecting their third child. Xiong was with Naina's brother Amal, still tracking Ju-Long. No one had heard from them in a long time. It all seemed like yesterday. It all seemed like a thousand years ago.

The couple were in the proximity of the Rakshasas' territory as night fell. They would try to find one of the blood parasites and track them to the lair where they spent their days. Then, after the sunrise, there would be the staking. Sometimes that was easier said than done. While the majority of vampires were incapacitated from dawn until dusk, there were some that could remain awake during the day, though they too had to avoid sunlight.

The evening was a hot and humid one. This time of year, in this area, it was either raining or hot, with very little in between. Ling was looking for the home of the gentleman who sent the letter advising them of the infestation. It was a possibility the demons had moved on. Better to confirm a recent citing than to wait around for something that was already gone.

He knew the man's name was Aanga and he lived on the outskirts of town in a modest home. It had a large yard set next to a creek on the south edge. In front of the house were two large Gum trees that semi-concealed the domicile from the dirt road that passed in front of it. It sat somewhere along the southwest edge of Nepalgunj. Thus far they had not come across it, but they still had ground to cover.

***

Sonam, a tall, thin, handsome male that Dahla had turned to satisfy her occasional man craving, came running in. "Queen Dahla, Queen Karhla, the Raksasha hunters are near. I have spotted them just outside the city limits."

"Are you sure it is them?" Karhla asked.

"They travel at greater speeds than any human could. They are not one of us."

"Go round up the others and get everyone back here immediately."

Karhla and Dahla were a part of a group of Yak Nomads when they were turned. It was actually Karhla's brother-in-law, Lopsang that crossed them over. He thought he had created the perfect partners to carry with him for eternity. Lopsang did not choose to take his own pregnant wife and their small child, but instead two women he had desired for quite some time.

Karhla was short and thick in all the right places. Her face was the girl next door variety of beauty. Dahla was tall with a gorgeous body and the face and hair of an angel. Lopsang's plan would have been perfect, except Karhla didn't like men, especially him. She had a crush on Dahla as well, and wasn't about to share her with that piece of shit.

They kept him around until they learned all they could from him about survival in their new form. Then they brought a third girl into the fold. She was young, pretty, and a virgin. Amirita was the distraction. While Lopsang was preparing to pleasure himself with the young beauty, Karhla shoved an arrow into his back, through his heart, and out the other side.

Since then they had kept an eye on their former tribe, especially Karhla's sister and young niece and nephew. They had actually fought off a couple of smaller covens, and destroyed several lone Raksasha that got a little too close to her family. Her once wandering people were now firmly planted not far from here. Funny how your lifestyle can take a turn after you meet the things that go bump in the night.

"Dahla, you take Amirita and head toward Kathmandu. When all is safe here I will come and get you. If things go bad I'll get myself out and we'll have to move on."

"I don't know how to get to Kathmandu!"

"I'll give Amirita some directions. If you were as bright as you are beautiful you'd be leading this group, not me. But you are gorgeous, and you taste so good, who gives a fuck."

***

Naina spotted the house and the couple made a dash for it. They could see a candle lit inside, but there wasn't anyone around. The wooden shutters on the front window were open, so Ling slipped inside. Naina continued to search the perimeter. Ling could see a foot at first, and then found the rest of the body. It was drained of blood with a hole in the chest where the heart had been removed.

Then came a yell from outside. It was Naina's voice. Ling hopped back through the window and ran toward the sound of fighting. He rounded the corner to find one Raksasha down, head removed, and a second one on top of Naina, who was taking lefts to the face while holding the blood suckers right arm with her left hand and her right wrapped around its throat. He put an arrow through its left shoulder and loaded another as he moved closer.

The vampire howled in pain as it sat up trying to pull the quarrel out. Ling put a second one through its chest and a third through its eye all within the span of a few heartbeats. Naina tossed the already rotting corpse aside.

"Are you okay?"

"Right temple is pounding and I'm sure I'm going to have a nasty bruise." Naina rolled her tongue around her mouth, then spit out some blood. "All my teeth are still there. That's a win."

Sonam had already found the others and sent them back to their lair. As he approached the location where he figured he would find the last two he ran into a fight in progress. Both of the women were killed. The chosen ones had found them. He needed to get back and warn the others.

Ling saw something off to the left dart away. It was a human form, but it was not human. "Can you run?"

"Yes."

"This way."

Sonam could hear the footsteps of those chasing him. They were gaining ground. He still had a little ways to go, but if he could just hold enough of a lead they would have the numbers. Sonam dared not look back, even though he could feel they were almost upon him. He let out a loud cry hoping his friends would hear it and head this way.

Karhla shushed the group. "That is Sonam. He approaches and I bet he is being pursued. Let us face those who seek to end our existence and destroy them!"

Ling dove on the back of the Raksasha running away from him. The demon was tall, but Ling leapt high bringing the stake he had in his hand up and over the top of the vampire's shoulder, driving it into its heart.

"Here comes his friends," Naina yelled, her bow already out as she covered her man. She fired into a female taking her down. Ling took out a second with his bow a moment later. Naina sunk an arrow into a third before the other three Raksasha were upon them.

The male tackled Ling, while the two remaining females circled Naina, who had switched to her sword.

"Too bad. This is going to be such a waste. She looks good enough to eat, but I guess we will just have to drink her, Diki," Choden, the larger of the two women said.

"Yes, Choden. I'd love to have that pretty little mouth buried between my legs."

"You both want this? Well, who is going to be first?" Naina didn't wait for an answer as she jumped to her right and sent the smaller one's head sailing through the air with a single, severing blow. The larger one caught her wrist as Naina spun to face her. She snapped it and Naina cried out in pain as her sword fell from her hand.

Choden flung Naina sideways through the air. She looked around to see Tenzing, the only male remaining in their coven, fighting the other chosen one. *Where is Karhla!* Choden scanned the area, but her leader was nowhere in sight. "Karhla!" She felt something sink into her back and looked down to see an arrow protruding through her breast.

"You should have broken my left wrist why you were at it, bitch." Naina released a second arrow and plunged it in next to the first. The Raksasha fell to the ground, her body decaying instantly.

Ling had sliced up the vampire pretty good, but had not been able to behead the demon so far. The creature turned its head and saw its partner fall. Ling moved to take a swing at its neckline only to meet empty air as the Raksasha flew skyward. He took a quick look around before rushing to Naina, who was holding her right arm, screaming obscenities.

***

The lovers returned back home three days later. Naina's wrist and forearm were splinted, but she was on the mend. When the demon tossed her after breaking that wrist, Naina barely escaped slamming head first into a tree. It had been a close call, too close. They had destroyed eight of the proposed twelve Raksasha. They knew the one male had escaped. They never saw the other three.

They entered through the front of the house and began calling for Marcos. Neither he nor Chanda were anywhere inside. Naina had a moment of panic. They had only been gone a week, but she feared the worst. The couple dashed out back looking for her father. There were a couple of younger people splashing around down by the stream. Naina ran toward them. "Hey! Hey you in the creek, have you seen my fa . . ."

"Naina! You're back."

She stopped immediately, staring with her jaw agape. "What the hell?" Ling said as he came up beside her. Marcos and Chandra were in the stream, buck naked. Buck naked and looking like they were in their twenties.

"Dad? What? How?"

"You don't know how already? You remember that I told you my aging process reversed so I could take care of you and your brother after your parents passed?"

Naina nodded looking away from her father and Chanda. They were in the water waist deep, but Chanda's big boobs were staring right at her and Ling. It was a little awkward.

"Well, that same thing is happening again."

"Why?"

"Because you are pregnant, Naina."

"Pregnant?"

"How?" Ling asked, his eyes wide.

"First the man puts his penis inside the woman's vagina . . ." Chanda started.

"Got that part, thanks. I mean how do you know? We've been trying for five years with no luck. Is it possible, Naina?"

She looked at him and shrugged her shoulders. "I guess, maybe."

"Maybe nothing. You are pregnant. I don't know how many you have total over your lifetime, but you are going to start with two." Marcos smiled.

They were celebrating their birthdays as well as those of their eight children. Their first set of twins, Marco (not to be confused with Naina's father, Marcos) and his sister Mahika were thirty two. The set of girls, Shehani and Sona were twenty four. After learning of the death of Ling's brother Biao, and the second disappearance of Te, who wandered off to be alone after discovering he had killed his own brother while under the spell of a black witch, the set of boys that were now sixteen inherited their uncle's names.

The youngest boy, Jie, was named after their dear friend who passed away the year before their son was born. Then his sister, Chanda, was named for the woman who had been mom, grandma, and nanny to all of them. All of the children were born in sets exactly eight years apart.

After the birth of the last set, Marcos and the elder Chanda had started the aging process once again. The youngest ones were eight today, and Naina's father and Chanda had gone from being perennially twenty five—to in their thirties during that time period. Not too bad considering Marcos was approaching two hundred and Chanda was nearly a century and a half old.

The eldest twins were opposites in size. Marco was short and athletic built like his parents, and had their gift for speed. Mahika was nearly six feet tall and was nothing but corded muscle. She was beautiful like her mother, but intimidated most men. They had spent four years in China being trained by Ling's brother Wei in hand to hand and weapons tactics. For the past twelve years they had been helping defend India from all manner of evil, both alongside and occasionally without their parents.

While their gifts had nothing to do with speed or strength, Shehani and Sona had also spent two years in China training with Wei. The next six years they were in Kathmandu studying with an ages old sorceress. These two were identical, not only to each other, but their mother. Shehani's gift was magic, which required discipline lest you be lured into the dark arts. Sona had the same talent as her uncle Amal—telekinesis. It was coupled with mind reading and the power of suggestion. They had just returned from that journey, but the pair would be leaving in a week, along with their eldest brother Marco. They were going to track down their uncle Te, if he was still alive, and try to get him to come back.

Biao and little Te would be heading off to China to train there. Biao was strong, and huge, like his uncle Wei. He also inherited speed from his parents. Little Te was just like his namesake uncle. He was a healer, but could also use that power to destroy. Mahika would be traveling there with them to ensure the teenagers safety. She would remain with them for the entire four years before coming back here for four years, then taking the youngest two to Wei to be trained as well.

While still young, Jie and Chanda were showing signs that just like their uncle Xiong, they were both going to be fast and strong. The young girl and her brother were constantly competing with each other, whether it be racing, wrestling, or performing some feat of strength. They were also the daredevils of the family, constantly pushing the limit and their luck. Except with papa Marcos. He could get them to listen when no one else, including Naina, could.

Naina and Ling also had a mission. A small coven, that they had first started chasing forty three years ago, had rebuilt and reared its ugly head several times since then. Every time Ling and Naina ended up destroying the majority of the Raksasha, but missed out on the two or three that made up the nucleus. This time they were purported to be near the southern coast. There was always some evil to fight, and no shortage of blood suckers.

The couple had taken on many over the years, but this pesky group was a grudge match for them, and whenever, wherever they popped up, this coven became the priority.

"I have overheard talk that the King will be poisoned tonight."

"By whom?" Balavan asked.

"Some of his captains are being paid quite handsomely by Emperor Flavius Marcianus Augustus to kill Attila. The Emperor has refused payment to Attila since he took over, and fears retaliation by the Head of the Huns. From what one of his liaisons was telling the captains it will be beneficial to all with Attila gone, and they will be rich enough to never worry or want again."

"Damn Jia-Li. What do we do? And why is Marcian doing this now? He sent his soldiers across the Danube last year and defeated the Huns on their home turf. Coupled with the famine and plague that erupted in northern Italy, Attila accepted a bribe to return to the Hungarian plains. Why is he still seen as such a danger?"

"Marcian wants insurance that the Huns will never return. He doesn't trust Attila, and who would?" she sighed. "Let them kill him. Then we will take our leave. He is the most atrocious man I have ever known."

"True, but he has saved us more than once, and protected and provided for us for a decade. We have wanted for nothing."

"Balavan, do you know why several years ago I chose you over Ju-Long?"

"I would hope because you loved me."

"Of course. But at one time I also loved Ju-Long. He was my master. There is not a bond much stronger than that." She paused, reaching her hand up to touch the side of his face. "I chose you because you know mercy. You are a xiang-shi, a Raksasha, a blood drinker, a demon—yet you still know mercy."

"It is that small fragment of the monk left in me. I know that my soul is gone. I know I am damned to hell, but that small part is what keeps me from being merciless."

"And it is that small part that makes me love you so much." She leaned in and gently kissed his lips. "But tonight, when the time comes, I need you to show no mercy for Attila.

***

The King and his brand new wife, Ildico, sat at the head of the table. A feast to celebrate their union was underway. Balavan and Jia-Li sat together on the left side of the King, several others between them and the newlyweds. They both wondered if Attila's food was being brought to him poisoned, or was one of the others responsible for planting it while they dined. It didn't really matter, Jia-Li was just curious.

"It's the wife," Jia-Li whispered in Balavan's ear, "she is the agent delivering the poison. Ildico just slipped something in his drink." The pair kept an eye on her. Attila was drinking heavily, and every time his glass was refilled, his bride slipped some more in. They watched her do it six more times. Then, with her husband good and drunk, she whispered something and he nodded yes, slapping her ass as she stood, then staggering to his feet to follow behind. They were definitely heading to his chambers.

Balavan and Jia-Li waited for a while, then excused themselves and headed out the other end of the hall. Balavan could remain awake during the day, but they would not be able to leave until sundown. They went to gather a few items before taking off.

"I'm going to take real good care of you, my King." Attila laid across the bed as she removed his boots and his pants. Ildico went over to the small table and poured him another glass of wine, slipping a larger dose of the poison in with it. She helped him arrange some pillows against the wall as he sat up. "Drink, my King, while I pleasure you." She grabbed his limp penis.

"You swill have ya work out cut for ya. I am verily drunk," he slurred, chugging the wine down and tossing the cup aside. His head was swimming and there was a slight pain starting in his stomach. He pushed her head away and tried to get up. Attila fell to the floor, holding his belly and coughing like crazy. He stared up at Ildico, who seemed to be smiling. It was hard to tell as his eyes wouldn't seem to focus.

"Get help, bitch." He tried to get to his hands and knees. "Now!"

"There is no mercy to be found here. A message from Emperor Marcian—*Go fuck yourself.*" She laughed as she walked out of the room.

The path out that would have them meet the least resistance and help conceal their departure led down the hall right past Attila's chambers. Typically that hall had some sort of sentry patrolling it, but tonight, with the feast, it was empty. Balavan heard a pleading voice as they passed the doorway to the King's quarters.

"Help." Then coughing. "Please help."

He stopped. Jia-Li grabbed his arm. "We need to keep moving."

"Who's there? Help."

Balavan took three steps with Jia-Li. "Please. I don't want to die," the voice cried.

Balavan pulled away from Jia-Li. "I can't." He paced toward the room. "Watch the hall."

"Balavan . . ." He ignored her as he continued on.

Attila heard steps coming toward him. "Thank you." He was on his side, coughing up blood. "Who is it? My vision is gone."

"It is Balavan, my King."

"Balavan. Always there when I need him."

"I believe you have been poisoned, Majesty." Balavan knelt beside him. "I believe it was a conspiracy between some of your captains, your wife, and Emperor Marcian."

"I will kill them all!" Attila went into a coughing fit, blood flying out of his mouth.

"My King, the only way I can save you is to turn you."

"Then do it."

Hunnic Empire, Early 454 AD

He stayed with Balavan and Jia-Li for several months learning all he could about this new existence and discovering his new powers. Funny, when he had been perfectly healthy and asked Balavan to turn him years ago, the vampire told him he did not know how. Attila forgave that lie. Balavan had shown mercy upon him when he was on his deathbed. It was also one of the reasons he had to part ways with his savior. Balavan had mercy. Jia-Li, though unhappy Balavan saved him, had mercy. Attila was merciless.

He flew back to his homeland and was there to exact revenge on those who betrayed him. He smiled as he landed outside his former palace. He knew that his people were already in disarray. None of these cowards were strong enough to lead. He didn't care about his empire anymore. He would wipe those who tried to rule it now from the annals of history.

I'm back.

Attila had no idea which of his captains betrayed him, so he would kill them all. Then he would find that wretched bitch Ildico and give her hers. Attila took out three of his former guards as he entered the area. All three were half drunk and useless as sentries. That was something he would have never allowed during his reign. If this was a sign of the shape of things, then the rumors that the empire was in decline were true.

Disgusting.

One by one he took out the traitors. Some, asleep, he ripped out their hearts while clamping a heavy hand over their mouth to stifle their brief screams. Others he crept up on and snapped their necks. He originally planned on killing those who were in charge.

He changed his mind and decided to kill all he happened upon during his search. Mercy was for the weak.

Those who saw him as he came were so terrified they couldn't find the voice to scream. Attila killed thirty-five by the time he walked through the door of his own chamber. There was an orgy going on between six of his former captains, Ildico, and two other women. Everyone was oblivious to his presence.

He killed the first two men, one sodomizing the other, before anyone realized he was there. One of the women looked up and screamed. He grabbed the man on top of her and twisted his head off, blood spewing everywhere. Then Attila stomped on her neck, silencing her. One of the men scrambled off the woman he was on. Attila grabbed him by the throat, crushing it.

The remaining men, who had been filling his wife, were on their feet and reaching for swords. He picked the woman up by the hair and threw her into them. As they all fell to the floor, Attila retrieved one of the swords and began hacking away, their screams and pleas for mercy like music to his ears. By the time he was done, the two men lay in one big bloody mess.

Attila looked around and saw that Ildico had fled the room. "Run, bitch! I am coming!" It took him mere moments to catch her. He pinned her naked body against a wall face first. "Did you miss me, my dear?"

"They were going to kill me. I had no choice!" She sobbed. "I love you."

"Lying whore!" He grabbed her hair, tilting her head to the side and exposing her neck. "I would give you a message to give to the Emperor, but you won't be around to deliver it," Attila hissed in her ear.

"Please, spare me! I don't want to die!"

"Neither did I. Thanks to a friend, I didn't. You and Marcian will not be so lucky." He bit hard into her neck as she screamed. Annoyed by the sound of her voice he ripped her throat out, but continued drinking. He heard footfalls and the yells of men running toward him.

"You won't be coming back, slut!" Attila punched through her back and ripped her heart out. As he turned the pair of soldiers stopped in their tracks. They both had a look of terror upon their faces as he killed them and picked up their swords. Toting one in each hand, Attila killed until there was no one left to kill.

Drenched in blood he realized that several of his captains were missing. They were probably out among the other camps. He would have to pay a visit to all of them before heading for Constantinople and his final act of revenge.

Island of Gangra, Paphlagonia, 454 AD

Te came to respect and even like the man he was conversing with once again. The discussions were always fascinating, and his friend was very staunch in his beliefs. Though they were far different than the Buddhism he was raised in, there were some similarities in beliefs between Dioscorus' religion and his. The good in men, the love for your neighbor, and the need to do right were all things the men agreed on.

Actually, they seemed to be far more agreeable than Dioscorus of Alexandria's Coptic Church and the Catholic Church of the Roman Empire. Dioscorus had been the twenty-fifth pope of the Coptic Church before his exile to this island. He was denounced by the Council of Chalcedon (ordered to convene by Eastern Roman Emperor Marcianus) in 451 and banished here to live out his days.

While Marcianus appointed Proterius pope, many still saw Dioscorus as the church patriarch. Te saw dissention between differing religious factions in his homeland. It often led to bloodshed. He was still stunned by fact that two churches, so alike, believing in the same God, could be in such discord. The Copts' were persecuted, and even executed by the believers of their sister church. The cruelty, stubbornness, and evil that could be man continued to astound Te.

The Copts did not hide from their persecutors, but openly promoted their beliefs in defiance. Many became martyrs, and none of them feared death over their beliefs. They saw it not as the end, but the beginning of their new existence.

Te believed that the god Dioscorus followed was indeed real. His friend performed many great works and led people to his

Christ even after being defrocked. His prayers often led to the sick being healed, which he explained was not him, but his Savior at work. Despite all he had been through, Te's friend seemed to still have rock solid faith. It was something Te admired, as he often questioned his own beliefs and existence. Especially after Biao's death.

For whatever reason, Te was able to open up to Dioscorus, revealing his struggles, especially the part where he had killed his own brother. His friend prayed with and for him, counseled him as he once counseled young monk apprentices.

"There is evil at work. Just as my God has His emissaries and followers on this earth, so does Lucifer. You were unprepared to deal with such power, for you knew not my Jesus. You did not kill your brother, the devil did."

"Even so, I was the vessel he used to do it. It is unforgivable."

"No, Te. My God is a loving God. All you have to do is accept him as your Savior, acknowledge that he died for your sins, and ask for forgiveness."

"And that's that?"

"Then you have to follow Him, and let the past go. You cannot achieve happiness until you forgive yourself. You cannot receive love until you love yourself. Let Him wash away your sins and make you whole once again."

"How?"

"Just repeat after me." He led Te in a prayer that asked for forgiveness and invited Christ into his 'heart', as Dioscorus explained it.

"I don't feel any different."

"You lack faith. That is all. You must believe in order to receive."

"How can I believe in something I can't see?"

"By feeling His Presence. He is all around and within us. You must open up and let Him in."

"I don't know if I can."

Dioscorus shook his head and smiled. "Te, you have been given the gift of healing, correct?"

"Yes."

"And the people you heal, can they see your talent at work?"

"No."

"Yet they can feel it working in them, no?"

"Yes."

"Just like you can reach inside the body and mend what is broken physically, my God can do it spiritually, emotionally. Your mind is suffering, your soul in torment, and all that is stopping you from getting better is your willingness to believe it can happen. That my God can make it happen."

That was one of many conversations they had. Not all of them were about religion. Sometimes they discussed art, music, and life in general. Te told him about his home, his other brothers, and their mission. Dioscorus had never heard of xiang shi. He knew that Satan was at work in the world, and demons did exist, but he had never run into this particular variety.

Now Te sat by his friend, having what could very well be their last talk. Dioscorus was terminally ill. He wanted so bad to lay his hands on his friend and take away the infirmity. Dioscorus refused.

"The Church I serve is known to many as the Church of the Martyrs. My death, with my final breaths professing my love for Jesus Christ, will inspire many to do the same." He cleared his throat. "The path for me starts fresh with my passing. Yours is still ahead, on this earth. You must resume your mission. You must someday return home and reconcile with your family. I don't believe your brothers have ever stopped loving you. I don't believe they have ever stopped believing in you. Continue on your path, my friend. I don't believe we simply met by chance."

"You believe we were predestined to meet?"

"No. But my God does work in mysterious ways. Blessings, trials, and tribulations are thrown in our paths.

However, it is our choice as to how we deal with every situation. The Lord will guide us and protect us, but we have been given the free will to choose for ourselves."

"I believe he helped bring us together so I could witness to you, and you could learn of His love and mercy. I believe that having my God on your side will only make your ability to fight evil," he coughed, "even stronger. That is if you choose to believe."

"And his protection is from what? Stuff that happens?"

Dioscorus laughed. "Shit doesn't happen on its own. People happen. Sometimes the choices we make affect us. Sometimes they affect others. And of course, the decisions of others can have a positive or negative impact on us. Everything in life is a choice, either ours or someone else's."

"Your words weigh heavily on me. I have much to contemplate tonight. You should rest. I will see you in the morning."

"God willing and the creek don't rise."

***

Te tossed and turned well into the night. Just as he was finally drifting off a cold breeze swept through his room. It was way too hot, and his room had no windows, for it to happen. It felt as if a presence had dropped by to say farewell. He shot up out of bed, dressed, and rushed over to where Dioscorus slept.

Before he entered the room he knew his friend had departed. He wanted to lay hands on him and try to resurrect his comrade. Dioscorus had made a choice, and he needed to make the choice to respect it. He knelt beside the bed and lowered his head. "So long, my friend. May heaven accept you with open arms."

He wiped away a tear as it threatened to roll down his cheek. Memories of Biao, happy memories, filled his mind. "Tell my brother I said hello, and I love him."

124

***

He had no idea where Ju-Long was. Hell, he barely knew where he was. Te did know the direction home was in, but he wasn't ready for that yet. He would get back to the mainland and head south. He had a book, The Book of Dioscorus' God with him. He would travel, study the teachings of this Christ, and continue to heal all he could as he worked on healing himself. Where he was headed he was unsure, but for now he was headed south.

The coven was larger than ever. Naina and Ling had to be a lot more cautious this go round. When the hunt truly began there were thirty Raksasha. They had taken out ten before they suffered a setback. Ling had the femur in his left leg snapped and they had to sit for over a month while he healed. It would have been nice if their son Te were close, but he was in China, so Ling had to heal the old fashioned way. Thankfully, they recouped at a faster rate than a normal person, but a broken femur took a while regardless.

By the time they caught the coven again, they were up the west coast nearing the place they battled Ju-Long over fifty years ago. The group added four more, putting their number at twenty-four. As always they were a mostly female group. This time there were five males, the largest number Naina and Ling had ever encountered with this coven.

They had the element of surprise on their side, the vampires didn't know they were back. Hopefully they could reduce their number before the demons realized they were there. They had no idea where the den was, but hopefully tonight they could track someone back to it.

"There. Across the creek." Naina pointed. "That is one of them. I recognize her. She is the one that broke your leg."

"Sure as shit. Do we lay back and tail her until she returns to the lair? Or do we snatch her and make her talk?"

"The sun has only been down for an hour. I don't know if I have the patience to wait it out. She might not head back until dawn," Naina whispered. By the time they heard the noise behind them it was too late. The wooden staffs smacked into their heads simultaneously.

***

Naina awoke to the sound of moaning beside her. She could see a tall, gorgeous, naked female hovering over someone. She turned her head further to see that the man the woman was riding was her husband. He was chained by the wrists and looked like hell. "I am so sorry," he mouthed, a tear sliding down the side of his face. Naina could feel her anger grow. Not at him, but at this bloodsucking bitch she had never seen before. She tried to get up, but she was chained down by her wrists and ankles as well.

"Get away from my man!"

"Oh, you're awake? Your husband was wonderful, so fully of energy. Let's see if you stack up to him."

"I will fucking kill you!"

"You are in no position to make threats or talk shit." Dahla stood. "Karhla, would you care to join me?"

"In a minute, love. Get her warmed up for me."

Dahla leaned over Naina's body and pressed her left breast against her captive's lips. Naina opened her mouth and took it in. "That's right, lover. Just like that," Dahla cooed. "Mother fucker!" She shot up, blood running down her stomach. "She fucking bit me! She bit my fucking nipple off!"

Naina turned her head the opposite direction of Ling and spit out a hunk of flesh, blood and tissue. A strong hand grabbed her hair and twisted her neck around until she was looking straight up at the face of another female Raksasha she had never laid eyes on.

"I'd hate to bust all those pretty little teeth out." The woman's breath was hot and smelled like fresh blood. Their faces were in opposite directions, so when Naina spat a second time the blood and saliva went into the vamp's eyes.

"You are a feisty little cunt!" Karhla said as she wiped her face with her left hand.

"Dahla, go somewhere until you have finished whining. It is quite annoying."

"Get your boob bit hard and see how you like it!"

"Go drink some blood. You'll be fine. Now go!"

"Kiss my ass!"

"I'll bite it later."

"Fuck you."

Dahla stepped out into the chilly night air. Raksasha or not, there was a burning sensation where her nipple had been. Karhla was right though, as usual, a little blood would take care of that. She just needed to find a victim.

"Over here." A female voice called from behind her. Dahla turned and felt three thuds as something slammed into her chest. She looked down to see three arrows buried in her as she fell.

"Mine got there first," Marco proclaimed as they scanned the area.

"Hardly, eldest one. I don't care how fast your bow can make it travel, the two I sent with my power beat it by a mile," Sona replied with a smirk.

"Mom and dad are in there, in Buddha knows what condition. Focus on what's important," Shehani said, a little disgusted with her siblings. They walked up to the large home and began to investigate.

"The windows are all boarded shut. Shehani, can you quietly magic us an entryway?" Marco asked.

"Easy." She turned the handle of the door in front of her and opened it. "Tada!"

"Smartass," Sona replied.

"Dumbasses." Shehani smirked.

"No matter how much you two look like mom, you are without a doubt your father's daughters."

Marco led the way as they entered the home, his recurve bow armed and ready. Sona had an arrow in each hand. They came upon a room that was sunk down, with a small balcony partway around it. There were over a dozen vampires in the room, most of them engaged in some form of sexual activity.

"I got the man on mom," Marco said.

"I got the bitch on dad. If I don't throw-up first."

"I'll take the ménage a trois in the far corner. I can't risk hitting mom by going after the women trying to smother her." Shehani was preparing a knock out spell. They would have to stake the vamps to finish them. She couldn't use a spell to cause death, for it always opened up the doorway for the dark side to creep in.

Two arrows sunk into Tenzing and he fell forward onto Karhla. Amirita slumped on top of the man she was on. Karla used Tenzing's body as a shield. She scooted to the back exit. Karhla saw three of the other vamps fly into the wall and fall lifelessly to the floor. Two more arrows hit Tenzing's dead body. He was growing slippery as he rotted from over fifty years of death.

"The balcony! They are on the balcony! Kill them!" Karhla yelled. She shoved Tenzing's body away and crashed out the back door.

The twins and Marco were facing eight Raksasha, two males and six females. *Kill the demon beside you.* Sona sent the thought toward four of the vampires on the right. Two of them turned on each other. Two kept coming. Her power of suggestion worked on the weak minded and newer Raksasha. Two out of four wasn't bad. She flung her energy out and threw the other two across the room.

Marco got one before another one jumped on him. With the bow knocked from his grip, he tried to hold off the demon's fangs with one hand, while digging for a stake with the other. Shehani froze two Raksasha with a spell, one of them in midair three feet from her. She staked them both and looked to the corner to see the three she stunned earlier still out.

Sona loaded her hands with arrows again and sent them into the two she flung across the room as they got up. She walked over to the two vamps that were fighting and handed the one on top a wooden stake. "Here ya go. Try this."

"Thanks." She took it and drove it into the other Raksasha. Sona then drove one into her.

"You're welcome."

"A little help over here!" Marco retrieved the stake, but the vamp caught his hand and pinned it down. Sona lifted the demon into the air, still holding her brother. *Let him go!* Marco dropped to the floor with a thump, the impact knocking the wind out of him.

With the Raksasha pinned to the ceiling, Sona took the stake from Marco's hand and drove it up into the demon's chest. Blood and gunk fell from its body onto Marco. "There you go."

"Yeah, thanks. I think." Marco wiped his face with his sleeve.

Shehani was staking the last three blood suckers as Marco rushed to his mother's side. "Are you okay, mom?"

"Yes. No. Maybe. I don't know." She began to cry.

"Sona, look around for a key to these shackles."

"Can someone get this putrid corpse off me?"

"Sorry, dad." Marco pulled the woman off Ling. "Gross." The vamps flesh peeled off her arm as he drug her.

"How did you find us?" Ling asked.

"We were in the southern part of China when Sona got a feeling in the pit of her stomach. She could actually see your leg was broken. We started heading this way. We were close when you started out again, but because you were healed she lost sight of you. Then when you got captured by the coven, she could see you again. When we ran into some Raksasha, we knew we were on the right track."

Ling's shackles snapped open. A moment later Naina's did as well. He rushed to his wife, who was still crying. "I am so sorry, my love. So, so sorry."

"Did you get them all?"

"How many were there?" Shehani asked. She had used a simple spell to free her parents from their restraints.

"Twenty-four total." Ling answered. Marco looked around the room getting a body count. "We got thirteen in here. How many did we encounter outside, girls?"

Sona thought for a moment. "Nine before we got here. Then the one I killed just outside the house."

"You mean the one I killed."

"That's twenty-three." Shehani did the math.

"Please tell me you got the bitch that was planted on my face!" Naina's crying was turning to rage.

"She got away. I fired two arrows at her, but she used the guy that was on you as a shield."

"Damn it. She was the queen! Fuck, fuck, fuck!"

"We will go track her down, mom." Marco looked at his sisters,

"She's long gone by now. I'm sure she has the ability to fly." She turned her face into Ling's shoulder. "Just take us home. All of us."

Karhla was furious. She had flown around the outside of the house and found Dalha's body, her perfect beauty now grisly remains. She hoped her coven had killed them all, but she wasn't going back to find out. In the end she would see them dead, but not tonight.

Attila spent a little over two years combing his former kingdom until he was sure every last traitor, and then some, were dead. He had killed thousands. Now it was time to take out the last one. After that he would head west, explore new places, have sex with exotic women, and live forever.

It was a pity Marcian was ill and already on his deathbed. Thankfully, the coward had not died before he got here. Attila killed several guards on his way in. He could have easily snuck by them, but what fun would that be?

He wasn't sure what room he was looking for, until he spotted two Roman soldiers posted in front of a set of double doors. The corridor was dimly lit, and Attila was almost upon them before they even noticed he was there.

"Halt! Who goes there?" the guards challenged.

"Just an old friend here to see the Emperor."

"His Highness is not taking visitors at this time of night. How did you get in here?"

Attila drew his sword and stabbed the one talking through the throat before burying a dagger into the other man's forehead.

He opened the door and walked into the room. It smelled of death, and was empty save Marcian lying asleep in his bed. Attila was surprised there was no nursemaid at his side. There was a bell on the stand beside his bed. As if he sensed someone near, the withered old man's eyes opened as Attila stood looming over him.

"Are you death, come to take me?"

"I am death, but not the angel of death you seek."

"Well," Marcian coughed. "Whatever form of death you are, please take me and end this suffering."

"Aren't you the least bit curious as to who I am? Let me lean in closer so you can see my face."

"You can't be." Marcian's eyes grew wide. "You are dead."

"Technically, yes. In reality, no."

"And you have come to exact your revenge?"

"Yes. I am glad I got here in time. I wanted to be the last thing you saw before you died."

"Then do it. It will actually be the only merciful thing you have ever done." Marcian went into a wheezing spell as he grew more and more excited.

Merciful. The word left a bad taste in his mouth. "But I have had a change of heart."

"So you are not going to kill me?"

"I wouldn't want to deprive you of a single moment of suffering. Seeing you like this actually brings joy to my heart."

"But, you wanted to be the last thing I saw before I died. That could take weeks. Certainly you don't want to wait that long."

"Oh, I will be the last thing you see." Attila clamped his left hand over Marcian's mouth, and used the thumb and index finger of his right hand to gouge the old man's eyes out. When he removed his hand the Emperor let out a shrill scream.

"Damn you! Damn you to hell! You truly are the *Scourge of God!*"

Attila moved over to the window. The soldiers were coming, and it was time to take his leave. *I am the Scourge of God—and I remain merciless.*

Eastern Cape Region, South Africa, 446 AD

Te sat with the young girl who was still shaking like a leaf. Her mother had fallen victim to an impundulu overnight. She had seen the demon drain her mother's blood, so terrified she couldn't move or scream for help. The blood sucker turned to her afterward and winked, stating he would be back soon to collect her.

The girl's older brother did most of the speaking. Tumelo was seventeen years old, tall, with a thin but muscular build. Te had known him for several weeks, first meeting when the young man came to him with a broken arm. Tumelo was bright, articulate, and had an easy smile. Today he looked as scared and uneasy as his little sister.

"What does this monster look like?" Te asked. During his travels in this exotic, untamed, beautiful land he had heard tales of bat like men who hung from their clawed feet in trees and drank the blood of their victims, biting them with their iron teeth. There were also the human looking blood drinkers who had glowing green lights that shone from their ass and their armpits. He would have paid to see that. Thus far he hadn't run into any of the various blood suckers the natives spoke of.

"It is always the same. He appears as a handsome young man, one that women cannot seem to resist. Once they are in his sights and under his spell they are almost defenseless against him. The one he serves makes sure he is well fed while he goes about doing his masters bidding." Tumelo answered.

"Master?" The face of Ju-Long popped into Te's head. "What does he look like?"

"She. His master is a witch, he is her familiar. The impundulu is passed down from generation to generation, mother to daughter. He could serve the same family for centuries."

Witch. The word left a bad taste in his mouth. He didn't remember everything, but he got flashes of the evil things Huyen, the dark sorceress, made him do under her spell. It made him sick to his stomach. It also made a long dormant rage begin to build within him again.

"How do I find this impundulu and his master?"

"She reportedly has a lair along the coast. No one knows for certain where it lies. Any who have gone that way have never returned."

Te reached inside the collar of his robe and pulled the chain that hung around his neck over his head. On it was a Coptic cross that his friend Pope Dioscorus gave him over a decade ago. "Take this and your sister, find a safe place to hide. If the demon shows up again before I get back, hold this up and point it in his direction. It should ward him off."

"Don't leave us."

"I must."

"Why" Where are you going?"

"To the beach."

"Seriously?"

"To hunt down a witch."

***

She spotted the tall, pale skinned stranger long before he got close. Obviously, he wasn't from around here. His hair was long and straight, with a scraggily unkempt beard that touched the top of his chest. The man was lean, not much to look at, but she could sense there was something different about him. Something other than the color of his skin.

"Jomo,"

"Yes, my Queen?"

"We have some unexpected company headed our way. Be a dear and go see what he wants. He appears to be looking for something. I don't think he is going to like what he finds much."

"Yes, my Queen."

Thema watched as her handsome young servant went to greet this foreigner. *Just what exactly are you?*

Te saw the man coming toward him across the beach. The boy wasn't just handsome, he was gorgeous. He was sure it was the impundulu, and somewhere close was the witch that controlled him. Thoughts of his brother, the carnage that he had made of Biao under the spell of the last sorceress he had encountered, filled his mind with painful images—and his heart with hate.

The thought of the little girl, terrified after losing her mother to this blood sucker, only served to fuel the fire in him. It was all he could do not to turn this demon inside out right there. But that might scare his real target off, and that witch was one dead bitch.

"Greetings, my friend. Welcome. What brings you to my coastal paradise?" The young man was charming, and Te could feel him trying to probe his mind. Years of blocking Zhan, who was far more adept at mental manipulation, made it easy to shut out this amateur mind bender.

"I am merely traveling after being shipwrecked south of here. I have no idea where I am, or where I am heading. You are the first person I have run into in days." Te answered.

"Well, I am Jomo. I am sorry to hear your vessel sunk. The ocean can be a very unforgiving place. Were there others with you?"

"A score of men."

"Where are they now?"

"Drowned, or eaten by some sea creatures. I was the only one that made it to shore alive."

"My condolences." Jomo shook his head. "Are you hungry? You look exhausted."

"Starving, and I don't think I have ever been this weary," Te replied.

"Come, let me share a meal with you. My place isn't lavish, but it is near. You can rest, regain your strength, and I can point you in the right direction, depending on where you want to go."

"Your hospitality is much appreciated."

"You speak and understand our language very well. It is almost as if you are from here."

"I am well-traveled, and I am a student of cultures and languages. Thank you for the compliment."

"You are welcome," Jomo replied with a smile. "And your name is?"

"Te. You can just call me Te for short."

"There is a difference?"

"It's a joke. My brother Ling always loved to introduce me like that."

"Well, walk with me, Te." The pair walked up the beach.

"Do you live here alone?"

"Just me and my aunt."

"Doesn't it get lonely?"

"We enjoy the peace and quiet. The serenity that surrounds us is part of the charm of our little patch of paradise."

"She won't be upset with you bringing me to her home?

"We like the quiet, but we still enjoy company. We haven't had any in quite a while."

Thema was doing her best to peek inside the man's thoughts. He was shielding better than any average person could. There was something about him. Maybe, whatever he was, she could gain control and use him to her advantage. She fixed her hair, pulled the front of her dress down to expose the cleavage between her dark, smooth breasts, and went to meet Jomo and their guest.

Like Huyen, she was beautiful in this guise. Maybe it was really her, or maybe she could take different forms like the Ngai sorceress. Not that it mattered, she would die just the same. He had to be careful and wait for the opportune moment. Together they might be too powerful for him to attack at the same time. If he could get them separated, preferably with him and her alone at first, things would be easier. He had no idea if this bloodsucker was as strong and fast as the xiang shi, but she controlled him, so he was betting she was the greater threat.

"So, Te is it." She asked. "What is it you do, Te?"

"I worked for a shipping company for a while, before striking out on my own."

"Was it your ship that wrecked off our beautiful coast?"

"How did you know the ship I was on wrecked? I don't remember telling you that."

It caught the witch by surprise. He hadn't told her directly, that was true, but she knew everything Jomo knew the instant he knew it. She had slipped and she was aware of it. "My nephew whispered it to me as we came up to the house." She tried to cover. It was a lie and Te knew it, but he nodded as if that is how she found out.

"No, I was merely traveling by ship. I am not in the shipping business any longer. I love to travel, but quite frankly I hate to work. I do what I must to get where I want to go, but I much prefer to just enjoy life and all its splendor."

"So you are a man without a home?"

"I am a man without a country. The world is my home, and my hell."

"Interesting. Jomo said you were hungry?"

"Yes. Very."

"What would you like?"

"I am not picky. I would eat whatever you have to offer with gratitude."

"Jomo, would you be as kind as to fetch our guest some fresh fruit and dried meat?" The young man stood and walked out of the room without question. *Perfect,* Te thought.

"Is there a stream close by I could bathe and hand wash my clothes in? Fresh water is so much better than the salty sea for that, in my opinion."

"I have even better. We have a place outback where a stream comes down into a pool from a small waterfall before continuing on. The water is crisp and clean, and while a man of your height wood have to sit, the water from the fall will run right over you. It is quite refreshing."

"Sounds wonderful."

"Would you like me to take you there?"

"Indeed." He gave a slight bow. "If you wouldn't mind."

"No problem at all."

The two walked out the back and down a path away from the house. Thema reached over and grabbed Te's hand as they approached the water. "It is not often we get a guest, let alone a virile man like yourself, around here."

"It is probably even less often that I find myself in the company of a woman so beautiful."

"Flattery will get you everywhere."

"May I kiss you?" Te had never kissed a woman before and really didn't know where to begin. However, he would use his power to sooth to make up for his lack of experience once their lips met.

"I wouldn't say no if you tried." She smiled. Te leaned down. Thema was at least five ten, but he was upwards of six eight. She tilted her head slightly to his right, so he tilted his slightly to his left. He wrapped his arms around her in a gentle embrace as their mouths came together. Her tongue slipped between his lips and his eyes went wide. Luckily hers were closed so she didn't see the shock on his face. *Wasn't expecting that.*

Te gathered himself and slowly started to pour his power over her. He could feel her body relax as she melded against him. When they broke she was a little breathless.

"That was the most amazing kiss I have ever received. My body is tingling all over. If the kiss is that good, I can't wait to see what else you can do." Te smiled down at her, then leaned in once again. He let more of his healing gift trickle into her. He could feel how lost she was becoming from his handiwork.

He pulled her in tighter, one arm around her lower back holding her to him, the other hand he placed behind her head. She reached up and caressed his cheek. That's when the energy changed. He clamped her mouth to his hard, painful even to himself. She struggled against him, her nails raking the side of his face as he twisted and tore her heart to shreds, his kiss stifling her screams. Within moments she went limp in his arms. Even then he continued to ravage her internal organs. He wanted her to have no chance of survival.

Then he heard Jomo yell in the distance. "Thema!" His voice was desperate. "I am coming, my Queen! Hold on!"

Te carried her lifeless body over to the pool and dumped her in. Then he waded in and submerged himself underneath her.

Jomo saw Thema floating face down and jumped in the water pulling her face up until it was above the surface. Then he felt hands grab him by the ankles, yanking him down into the pool. The hands let go and he tried to surface, only to find them clamped around his throat a moment later.

He couldn't think, his brain was being scrambled and pain racked his entire body. His vision went, he stopped breathing, and then he felt the world slip away.

Te surfaced and sucked in a deep breath. It took him a moment to settle himself. *Definitely not a xiang shi.* He walked over and sat down under the waterfall. *She was right, this is refreshing,* he thought as he watched their bodies float in front of him. It was time to find Ju-Long.

Part 3

When in Rome

Amal and Xiong stumbled upon a small den of xiang shi, another mini mess left behind by Ju-Long. Thus far they had yet to catch up with him, always a little late when they were able to pinpoint a location on the demon, which wasn't very often. There were six in this little band of blood suckers, all men.

"We wait til daylight, then stake them?" Amal asked.

"It's the easiest way."

"It's also boring."

"Boring is good. So is easy. It's not like we don't have time."

Amal stood, stretching his seven-foot plus frame and letting out a yawn. He was a little over a foot taller than his Chinese partner, who was six-two. Xiong was using a small dagger to shave the dark stubble off his face. He was okay with having hair that now fell to his knees, but he was not into the mustache and beard look. Like Ling would say, we *are much too pretty for that.* Xiong chuckled to himself.

A horse and rider blew by them, heading right into the area the Raksasha were in. The rider obviously had no idea of the danger that lie ahead. "Well, looks like boring is out!" Xiong jumped to his feet and began running in that direction. Amal levitated and followed.

Orrin and the others heard the hoof beats of a lone horse coming to them. They had already fed, but there was no harm in a snack being delivered right to their door. He stood, as did the others, awaiting the fool who had chosen the wrong path home.

An arrow rang out, followed by a second. Orrin saw two of his comrades fall before any of them knew what was happening. A female rider emerged from the trees, sending a third arrow into the man next to him. The rest of the vamps leapt for cover. The woman, a tall figure in the saddle, switched to her sword and dismounted. She seemed even taller on the ground, easily six feet two with long, flowing black hair and a light olive tinge to her skin. The woman was as gorgeous as she was deadly.

Orrin watched as the other two vamps jumped from behind the rocks they hid behind, launching themselves at her. She side stepped right and sliced one in half as he came down. It was a crazy sight to see both his upper and lower body separated yet flailing. The end with the head was cursing bloody murder. The woman whirled around slicing through the neck of the second demon, his head flying one direction as his body fell to earth.

Orrin took off away from the woman and their camp.

Xiong, though in awe of what he had just seen this woman do, spotted the large xiang shi jump from his hiding spot and begin to run. He tracked the demon for a moment, then let the arrow fly. It hit its target and the creature fell face first.

Amal saw the arrow fly from Xiong's bow, then watched as a second later the woman spun around and sent an arrow into his partner's shoulder. The beauty was reloading when Amal used his telekinesis to lift her skyward. "Easy now, young lady. We are . . ."

She released her bow and shoved her right hand toward him. Some sort of energy blasted Amal in the chest, sending him sailing backwards. She fell twelve feet to the ground, rolling as she hit and coming right back up to her feet.

"Stop!" Xiong yelled, "We are friends!" She had retrieved her bow and had a fresh bolt knocked in and pointed at him.

"Who are you?"

"I am Xiong, from China," he panted, "my friend is Amal, from India. Have you ever heard of those places?"

"Of course, idiot! Why are you here?"

"These xiang shi started in my country, then spread to his. We are after the original one, Ju-Long."

"What is a xiang shi?" Her voice wasn't soft, but softer than one would imagine considering her build and ferocity.

"Basically a blood drinker."

"Ah, a Vrykolakas."

"I take it that is your word for xiang shi?"

"Yes."

"Any chance you can help me get this arrow out of my shoulder?"

"I haven't decided whether I am putting a second one in you yet." She re-aimed her bow.

"Please," Xiong pleaded.

A smile crossed her face. "I suppose I don't need to kill you just yet." She turned and shot the arrow into the top half of the demon on the ground trying to pull himself together. It pierced the creature's heart and it went silent. "That was annoying."

"What is your name?"

"Meagan." She ripped the arrow from Xiong's shoulder.

"Damn it!" Xiong grunted, "That hurt!"

"Quit whining. Men are such babies. Hold still." She placed her hand over the wound. He could feel a warmth flow over him, just like when Te healed someone.

"Wow. How many gifts do you have?"

"Many."

"What gift sent me flying into a tree and knocked me out?" Amal came walking up holding the back of his head.

"I can push energy with my hands. I am not sure what you would call it."

"Ouch, might be a good moniker." The three laughed.

"So how old are you, young lady?" Xiong asked.

"Older than you, child."

"I wouldn't bet on that? Xiong replied, rubbing his shoulder. It felt perfectly fine. "I am a shade over one hundred."

"Come talk to me when you hit a thousand."

"No way!"

"Way."

"What are you?" Amal asked. "I met someone your age once. She was a succubus."

"They are still around? I haven't seen one of those in nearly five hundred years."

"Well, there is one traveling with Ju-Long, the Vrykolakas, as you call them."

"Interesting. Many of the lesser demons began to disappear when the Light came. Some have crept their way back recently. Then these blood drinkers began to appear. Much more human-like than any blood suckers I ever encountered in the past."

"Whoa, slow down. The Light came? What's that?" Xiong asked.

"He is the Son of the God of Gods. You do not know of Him?"

"Nope," Amal answered.

"I suppose His Word hasn't reached the Far East yet."

"Interesting. Does His Word exist in written form?"

"Yes, Xiong. It is called the *Codex Sinaiticus*."

"Where would one find such a book?"

"You are in the heart of Christian territory, Xiong. It should not be hard. Just go to a church."

"Christian?"

"Yes. During his time on earth his name was Jesus Christ. His followers are known as Christians."

"What happened to Him?" Xiong was more than intrigued. History and religion were two of his favorite topics.

"He sacrificed his mortal body to pay for the sins of mankind, then ascended back to heaven to be with His Father."

"So what about you? What are you?" Amal asked. He had never met a woman this tall. She was a little taller than Xiong.

"I was born into a tribe of warrior women known as Amazons. It was near the tail end of our reign of power. I was given gifts that

I thought were to overcome our enemies, but found I was anointed with them to fight evil in any form."

Amal was totally distracted by her beauty as she spoke. "And what are these boobs you have?"

"Boobs? Do the women where you are from not have breasts?"

"Breasts? I didn't say breasts."

"No, you said boobs. Same thing."

"I said gifts." Amal looked away from her cleavage. They weren't huge, but were proportionate to her body and definitely eye catching.

`"You said boobs, Amal," Xiong chimed in with a laugh.

"Well, I meant gifts." Amal was blushing. "Besides the 'Ouch' one, what are your gifts?"

"I have superior speed, strength, and the 'Ouch' thing."

"You healed me." Xiong added.

"I can heal myself and others, to some extent."

"Can you use that healing power in reverse? You know, to do damage."

"No." Meagan thought for a moment. "I don't think so. Why would anybody ever do that?"

"My brother Te is a healer. He can use that power in reverse. He abhors that side of his power."

"I can imagine." She shook her head. "If I can, I don't want to know about it."

They went back to the humble abode Meagan lived in and spent the night. When Xiong and Amal awoke, she was already up, sharpening her main sword. "Breakfast is outside, hanging on a tree or bush, or hiding under some foliage. Sorry, I'm not a house wench, and I don't wait on men. Not sorry."

"We are more than capable. We appreciate the hospitality you have shown us. We will eat and be on our way." Xiong bowed.

"Where are you headed?"

"It is a place called Crete. I believe it is an island south of here."

"That would be correct. What business do you have there?"

"Supposedly it is where Ju-Long is headed."

"The Vrykolakas?"

"Yes. He and his succubus girlfriend. And whoever else might be with him."

"The succubus. I haven't killed one of them in centuries. I might just tag along." Meagan smiled. "Plus I have an old acquaintance down there I haven't seen in a while."

"A boyfriend?" Amal asked.

"He is a man, and we are friends—most of the time. Jealous?"

"Not hardly."

"Afraid his is bigger than yours?"

"Not likely," Xiong laughed.

"You've seen it?"

"It's a long story, but yes." Xiong lowered his head, knowing what was next.

"Show me. Or are you too shy?"

"Here we go," Xiong grumbled.

Amal stood, his head nearly touching the ceiling. "You sure you're ready for this?" He smirked.

"Whatever. I bet I've seen bigger." Amal dropped his pants.

"Oh, my!"

An hour later they were headed down the trail. Meagan seemed to have trouble making eye contact with Amal since the *unveiling.* She spent most of her time looking straight ahead, or looking Xiong's way as she answered his unending questions about the Light, her life, and the island they were headed to.

"So, this Jesus was crucified, by his own people? The Jews?"

"Yes. Well, the Jews and the Romans"

"Why?"

"Greed, power, fear . . . the fact that they did not believe he was the Messiah. Why doesn't really matter. He was born in human form to die for mankind. If you believe in that kind of stuff."

"You don't believe? Are you Jewish?" Xiong's mouth was agape.

Meagan laughed, "No. I serve what the Christians call Pagan gods. I serve the gods of Mt. Olympus."

"Who are they?"

"You really don't know much about gods or religion do you?"

"I know Buddhism, Hinduism, Taoism, Daoism, Animism, and the teachings of Confucius. Heard of them?"

"Not really. I see your point. The Greek gods are Zeus, Hera, Apollo, Poseidon, Athena, Ares . . . just to name a few. They had various powers that allowed them to rule over us, with Zeus being king of the gods."

"You said had powers? They are no more?" Amal chimed in. Meagan stared ahead as she answered.

"They are still around, I think, but they have been silent since the Light came as well."

"Yet you still follow them? And do not believe in the Christian God?"

"I did not say I did not believe in the Christian God. Their God is the same as the God of the Jews. The difference is Christians believe that the Jesus the Jews crucified, or caused to have crucified, was the Son of God."

"Wow. So you do believe then?" Xiong asked.

"Yes. No. Maybe. There is something to it though. There is too much evidence for their not to be."

"So..."

"So how about we give all questions a rest for a while. You are exhausting."

"Who are you telling?" Amal laughed. "You haven't been on the road for seventy years with him."

"Hahaha," Xiong answered. Meagan looked over at Amal and smiled, then immediately turned her head. Amal could see the blush creep up her face.

Yeah, she's into me.

Island of Crete, 468 AD

Ju-Long had finally beaten the behemoth into submission. It had knocked Lalita completely out, killed his two human servants, and its partner had eaten chunks out of three of his xiang shi warriors before they were able to drive it away. Everyone was either injured or dead—except him.

He had never seen such creatures. They were tall, hairy, and muscled like the Yeti, but their fur was dark brown and black. They had the head of a bull, with huge horns. Their body was humanlike, but their feet were the hooves of a beast. Their blood was thick and delightful, but held no magical quality like the dragon or the monk named Zhan. He called his three injured men over to feed as he went to check on Lalita.

She was fine, just unconscious. Nothing a little energy transfer wouldn't cure. He knew exactly how to wake his love. He pressed his lips to hers and poured power into her.

***

After last night's fiasco, Lalita was ready to head to Rome. The couple had never left the cavern they were in, obviously the lair of the two Minotaur's. Lalita knew what they were, but had thought they were extinct. Actually, she didn't know there had ever been more than one.

They were awake all day, on watch for the dead one's mate to return. The one they killed had been female, so they discovered later. They drug it to the back of the cavern and left it there before dawn.

The pair revisited many of the places Lalita had been when she was younger. They lingered, sometimes for years, in some locations. When you had eternity, time just didn't matter much. But it was time to go to her first home. They had been here for a month. Rome was calling. She only hoped the presence that drove her out years ago wasn't still strong enough to prevent her return. Damn the Light.

Argus hoped the locals were right. He hoped the Minotaur couple was in this cavern. He had followed many dead ends in the past. If he could take these two down it would make nineteen off his list. This had been his mission for a long, long time.

Night had fallen as he arrived. He crept up on the cavern, a sword in each hand. His chiseled six foot body made him look like what he was—dangerous.

A roar behind them sounded like the beast's they had fought last night. *Did I miss a secret back entrance?* Ju-Long thought. He drew his sword. "Stay here, I got this."

As he moved down the tunnel his night vision was excellent, partly because he was xiang shi, but also because of the Yeti he had fed on and killed decades ago. He could hear the creature breathing even before it came into view. Once he saw it he realized it was the female he thought they had killed last night.

"You may have survived last night, but I will make sure you never see another dawn." Ju-Long prepared to take a swing at the beast's massive neck. The Minotaur dropped to its knees.

"Master," it uttered in its rough voice. Ju-Long hesitated.

"What did you say?"

"Master."

Is it even possible? Have I created an entirely new species? A smile crossed his face. "That's right. I am Master." His grin grew wider. "What do you crave?"

"Blood," it snorted, "and flesh. But mostly blood."

"Rise and join me, my child. I will introduce you to the others. They are not master, but I don't want you to hurt them."

"Yes, Master."

Argus heard the roar and knew he was in the right place. *Time to take care of business.* He moved slowly, covering the last few feet between him and the entrance. He would go in if he had too, but preferred to fight them outside in the moonlight. He clanked his swords a couple of times and yelled into the cavern, "Come out you cowards. Come get your dinner if you dare!"

"Who the hell is that?" one of the xiang shi asked, looking at Lalita.
"I have no idea. You three, go check it out."

For a split second Argus got confused as to how humans were exiting the lair of a Minotaur and not screaming and running for their lives. Then he realized they weren't actually human. He chopped off one of the demon's arms at the shoulder and drove the other sword through a second one's chest. A punch landed on the right side of his face and he staggered sideways, nearly falling.

His one sword was still stuck in the second one's chest, and he used his free hand to block a kick from a third man. He could see the fangs on this one. "Blood sucker? Where in the fuck did you all come from?" Argus ate a hard right from the one-armed demon and fell to the ground, quickly rolling back to his feet.

The trio of Vrykolakas circled him. *How in the hell do you kill these things?* A sword through the heart didn't do it. He stepped to one arm and took off his head. The vampire crumpled to the ground. Without turning he adjusted his grip and drove the sword into the demon coming up behind him. Argus pulled it back out and whirled around cleaving the blood sucker's head from its body

The remaining vamp jumped on his back and established a rear choke on him. *This fucker is strong!*

Ju-Long, Lalita and Agnes (they found out the female Minotaur's name), stepped out of the cavern. "Doesn't look like the boys are faring too well," Lalita said, "shall we give them a hand?" Two of them were down, never getting back up, and the last one was being pummeled by a muscular figure with dark hair,

"Argus!" Agnes growled.

"You know this man?" Ju-Long asked.

"He hunts and kills my kind. He has done so for hundreds of years. We should go."

"Argus?" Lalita asked. "The last of the Spartan's, Argus?"

"The same."

"Yeah, Agnes is right, we better go." Lalita looked a little spooked.

"Both of you are afraid of a single man?"

"It's a little more than that, Ju-Long. He is like the chosen ones. We may fight and win with the three of us, but I can assure you one of us will not make it. If the Amazon bitch he sometimes runs with shows up, it could be even worse."

"I fear not, but to protect you and my new pet, we shall go. Agnes we are about to find out if you can fly."

"Ju-Long! Master! Help me!" The Vrykolakas underneath him yelled. It was the demon's last words as Argus stabbed the beast in the throat again and again until it was a bloody mess. He stood and turned, scanning the area. He could see two smaller figures and one larger one with huge horns flying west. *What the hell?*

Argus cleared the cavern just to make sure it was empty. A Minotaur's den was one of the nastiest, unclean places on earth. Even after all these years of hunting them he still felt sick to his stomach, sometimes for days, after he came out of one. He cleaned his weapons then went to a small stream nearby where he cleaned his clothes and himself.

"Hey, old man." Argus recognized the voice even though it had been decades.

"What brings you to Crete, hag?"

"Is that any way to speak to a lady?"

"If you're a lady, then so am I."

Meagan stared at him as he came up out of the water. He was nothing but muscle, with a thick black beard and moustache to go with his shoulder length black hair.

"So why are you here, Meagan?"

"Business."

"The kind that requires my assistance?"

"There are a couple of men I'd like you to meet."

"You know I can usually sense when you are coming. I did not this time."

"I had a harder time locating you as well, but I found you."

Argus got halfway dressed, most of his clothes were still wet, then picked up his weapons and the rest of his gear. "So where are these men?"

"Over checking out your handiwork, the three dead Vrykolakas."

"These are the most extraordinary blood suckers I have ever encountered."

"Agreed. Come with me, my friends know a lot more about them than I." Meagan turned and walked away.

After giving Argus the run down on xiang shi, their strengths and weaknesses, Xiong let him know about their mission. "So we are after the original one of his kind and his succubus girlfriend. We were given information that they might be headed here."

"You said his name was Ju-Long?" Argus asked, then continued before getting the answer. "The last bloodsucker I killed yelled that name, begging for help. No one answered his cry, but in the aftermath I saw two human figures flying west with one of the Minotaur's."

"Ju-Long can fly." Xiong looked over at Amal "and Lalita can levitate and move herself through the air with the gift she gained from drinking your blood. It could be them."

"Minotaur's can't fly," Argus stated. Amal and Xiong both looked at each other.

"What is it you two?" Meagan asked.

"Ju-Long may have created a new monster."

"The Minotaur has always been a monster, Xiong. That is not new."

"Yes, but now it will be stronger, faster, and more blood thirsty than ever."

"And it can fly," Amal added "What can you tell us about the Minotaur?"

"Short or long version?"

"Short." Amal answered.

"Long." Xiong immediately requested. I have never heard of the Minotaur before, but Meagan told me you were the last of the Spartans? I have read a little on them. How old are you?"

"I hope you got a year or two. Once he starts asking questions they are unending, and my friend has stamina." Amal shook his head.

"My name is Argus Calazans. I am the bastard son of the prophet Calazans. My mother, Mycanae, was young when she gave birth to me, and died shortly thereafter. My father did not claim me so I was taken in by a Spartan couple. At age seven I began my training, as all Spartan boys do, to become a soldier in the Spartan army—the most elite fighting force the world has ever known."

"I was fifteen in 371 B.C. when Sparta fell. I continued to train with a group that one day intended to reclaim our lands. It never happened, but it was readily apparent that I had greater speed and strength that any of my fellows. I also had some gift of vision, surely from my father. Those skills would serve me well as I hunted down and killed the remnants of some very nasty creatures, including the Minotaur's I have been after for almost eight hundred years."

"And this creature, the Minotaur, how did it come about?" Xiong asked.

"There was a King, King Minos, who asked Poseidon to send him a snow white bull."

"Poseidon is one of the gods of Olympus?" Xiong asked.

"Yes, god of the seas. Poseidon sent the bull, the Cretan Bull, to Minos. King Minos was to sacrifice the bull in honor of Poseidon when he was through with it. He betrayed his part of the bargain and kept the beautiful bull. King Minos instead sacrificed another bull believing it would pacify the god." Xiong was all ears, while Amal sat rubbing his temples. Meagan knew the story as well as Argus, so she busied herself sharpening a dagger, and stealing glances at Amal.

"Poseidon was not fooled or pleased. To punish Minos, Poseidon caused Mino's wife Pasiphae to fall deeply in love with the bull. She sought out the craftsman Daedalus and had him construct a wooden bull, left hollow inside, so she could mate with her beastly lover. And thus the Minotaur was conceived."

"Pasiphae tried to care for her offspring, but he soon grew too large and ferocious. Being the unnatural creation of a woman and a beast, the Minotaur had no natural source of nourishment, so he began to devour humans. Minos, after speaking with the Oracle of Delphi, instructed Daedalus to build a gigantic labyrinth to house the Minotaur. The architect erected it near Minos' palace in Knossos."

"Periodically the Minotaur was fed humans, sacrificed by the Athenians in retribution for the death of Minos and Pasiphae's son Androgeos. When the third time of sacrifice arrived, the Athenian hero Thesus came forward to be one of the 'volunteers' to enter the labyrinth. With the help of Minos' daughter, Ariadne, he was able to slay the Minotaur. Thesus and Ariadne later escaped together."

"That is some crazy shit. But if there was only one Minotaur, and it was killed by Thesus, where did the other ones come from?" Xiong puzzled.

"Before the Minotaur was defeated, an evil wizard entered the labyrinth and placed a sleeping spell upon the creature. Over the next two weeks he snuck in thirty women he had control over and mated them with the Minotaur. He hid the women away until they birthed the abominable offspring. The Minotaur was dead by then, but his children were very much alive."

"There were thirty-three of them total—three of the women bore twins. Nine of the mothers died during child birth. Six more were dead within months due to complications. In the end, all the rest were eaten by their offspring."

"I have hunted down and killed seventeen of these beasts. Sixteen remain."

"So if there were two here, and you saw the one escape with Ju-Long and Lalita, where is the other?"

"I didn't catch it earlier. What did you say the female's name was?" Argus asked.

"Lalita."

"And she is the succubus?"

"Correct. You know her?"

"She has used many names over the ages, but that is the guise she was under when we met a hundred years before the coming of the Light."

"Did you try to kill her?" Amal asked.

"Quite the opposite. I had no idea what she was until it was too late. She nearly killed me."

"So you had sex with her?"

"I did not say that, Amal."

"But you did. That is how she sustains herself. Trust me, I know."

"You slept with her?"

"Yes. Only once by choice. The other dozen or more times I was a prisoner."

***

By the time dawn was on the horizon Amal and Meagan had fallen asleep. Xiong and Argus were still talking, neither of them tired. "So there are seven of you brothers, born seven years apart exactly?"

"There were seven. Only six of us remain."

"What happened to the one that is gone? If you don't mind me asking?"

"He was killed while looking for our brother Te. It was an evil sorceress that caused his death. She was slain during the battle as well. One of our apprentices, Gan, traveled a long way to find us and let me know. It took him almost three years to locate Amal and I. Biao and I were the two youngest. We were very close." He left out the part that the sorceress had used his brother Te to kill his brother Biao.

"I am sorry to hear that. So is the rest of your family still in China?"

"Not all. My eldest two brothers, Zhan and Wei remain there, along with a middle brother Cai. Nobody has heard from Te in years, and Ling is in India with his wife Naina, Amal's sister, At least that is where everyone was last I heard. It has been years."

Screeches sounded and they looked over to see two small wildcats running away from the xiang shi's bodies as they burst into flames. Argus laughed. "Shit!" Xiong shot up and ran in the direction of the cats.

"What's wrong?" Argus asked, already on his feet and chasing after Xiong.

"We gotta catch those wildcats!" Xiong leapt over a log. "If they ate the flesh of those demons we are going to have even more problems on our hands!"

They spent a good part of the morning looking for the cats with no luck. "They are like ghosts," Argus said, "I have only seen their kind twice in all the times I have been on this island."

"Too bad my brother Cai isn't here."

"He is the one that communes with animals?"

"Yes."

"Well I don't know about you three guys, but I am starving." Meagan walked up with a goat over her shoulders. She killed it when she realized they were never going to find those stupid felines.

After overindulging on lunch, then starting back at the cavern and being led by Argus as he tracked the other Minotaur east during the afternoon, Xiong hit a wall. "Guys, I am exhausted."

"Yeah, I'm running on day three with no sleep. Let's set up camp and call it for now," Argus said with a yawn.

"I got some sleep earlier. I'll take first watch," Amal announced. There didn't seem to be any rain or foul weather approaching, so camp was simple. Within the hour Argus and Xiong were fast asleep, and Meagan laid down. She was lying on her side with her back to him. Her shoulders tapered down to a narrow waist that ran into the beautiful curve of her hips. Her backside was amazing, not big or small, but just right—like her boobs. Those long legs showed muscle tone, but also had a softness to them that was so enticing.

The thoughts he was having stirred his groin, but also reminded him that he had not urinated in a while. Amal stood, his stare lingering for a moment on her body, before he headed for some trees to the left.

"Whatcha doin'?" He heard Meagan's voice behind him.

"Just had to take a leak. I'll be done in a minute."

Meagan saw the Minotaur standing five feet away, staring at them. It noticed her staring at him and took a step forward. She shot out her right hand sending a blast of energy into the beast. It flew backward with a low groan.

"What the hell was that?" Amal tucked himself away.

Xiong and Argus zipped by them. "Nice," Xiong said.

They caught up to and killed the Minotaur. Xiong, who was slightly faster than Argus, had gotten to it first. It tossed him through the air like a ragdoll, but provided the distraction needed as Argus drove two swords through its heart, then used them in a scissor motion to lop the beast's head off. By the time Amal and Meagan got there it was over.

Night had fallen and Argus was ready to head home for a couple of days. He offered them a place to stay if they wished. They were on the move almost immediately.

"So what was the big deal about catching those cats earlier? We searched like crazy, but you never said why," Argus said.

"When an animal consumes the flesh of one of the xiang shi, it becomes infected and turns blood crazy. Human blood crazy. Anyone they attack that survives after that becomes infected as well. They become part human, part animal, and part demon. They can shift between human and animal form."

"Shifters?" Meagan asked.

"Shifters?" Xiong was puzzled.

"Ones who can shift from human to animal. They are considered a lesser demon. Not particularly strong, but they can take several different forms. Haven't seen one of those in a few centuries."

"Not exactly," Xiong continued, "these creatures are quite strong and fast. They can only take the shape of the animal that created them. Not all are bad, and they still possess a soul. We have a few friends who have been attacked and are stricken with this curse. They fight alongside us."

"Interesting." Argus nodded. "So we may be looking at a new enemy, or ally, emerging in Crete?"

"I am afraid so."

"I have a question."

"Yes, Meagan?"

"What if our friend back there consumed some of the Vrykolakas' flesh? Then attacked a human, and the human survived?"

"The Minotaur?"

"Yes."

"Then the problem is even worse than we thought." Xiong shook his head.

The foursome spent the next week combing the island for attacks by feral cats, or victims of a Minotaur. They found a small camp near the coast on day two. Five men were dead, ripped apart, much of their bodies consumed. It was definitely the work of Argus' arch enemy. The question was were there any survivors? And if there were, where were they now?

By the end of the week they had investigated two separate reports of attacks by Cretan wildcats. None were fatal, and one of the cats had been killed. Both of the men, who were pretty clawed up, healed in less than a day. The whereabouts of either man were unknown. They merely disappeared from their respective villages overnight.

In the meantime Amal and Meagan were side by side, often hand in hand, all day long. It was more than just physical attraction, or the fact that the sex was amazing (they made love twice), but they found a kindred spirit within the other. Meagan's personality matched Amal's stride for stride. She was witty, sarcastic, restless yet easy going, and like his sister Naina, Meagan didn't take shit from anyone.

All this did not go unnoticed by Xiong. He and Amal left their siblings behind in India because love had come for both Ling and

Naina. He could see some of the same things happening between Amal and Meagan. He was sure that either she would be traveling with them, or he was about to lose his friend Amal. Then what would he do? He actually spent more time with Amal than his own brothers. He wouldn't hold his friend back from love, but things would be so weird without Amal by his side. Together for damn near seventy years. Together through thick and thin, fighting back to back and surviving so many impossible situations during that time. Xiong's heart ached at the thought of it. He would find out soon how it all turned out. Regardless if he had company or was solo, it was time to get back on Ju-Long's trail. His mission remained the same.

"Will you stay?"

"Will you go?" Amal responded.

"Answering a question with a question?"

"Meagan, I have been with Xiong forever. I promised I would help him see this through. I am falling hard for you, woman. I have never been so torn in my life, not even when I left my homeland."

"I will go. I will go to be with you. I have fallen for you. All these centuries and I have never needed anyone like I feel I need you."

"What about Argus?"

"We were lovers, never in love."

"I have never felt what I feel with you, Meagan. I don't know what to do, how to proceed. Do we get married? Do we settle down and have kids?"

"We do whatever we want to do. There are no rules, there are only opportunities. I don't want to change a thing right now. There is no time-table, no fixed agenda—just us, doing us."

"That's one of the many things I love about you. Maybe that is why you have waited centuries. Maybe that is why I ended up here. Maybe we were just meant to be."

"Can we make love?"

"Holy cow, Meagan, am I just a piece of ass?"

"Are you serious?"

"Hell no!"

"You sure you want to do this?"

"Like I said, I have a couple of leads on some Minotaur's along the way."

"I feel like I'm abandoning my best friend, just slipping off in the night like this."

"We left the note. If he truly wants to follow he will catch up in no time. It's not like we can fly."

"Do you think he will?"

"You're handsome and all, but you're no competition for Meagan, so don't make it one. That's why we leave exactly the way we are, Xiong."

"I suppose you are right."

"I know I'm right. Whatever decision he would make would tear him up inside, so we take the onus off him and make the decision ourselves."

"Thank you, Argus. I would say you are wise beyond your years, but you're pretty damn old."

"They're gone."

"What?"

"They're gone, Meagan."

"Both of them?"

"Yeah. They left a note."

"Why? What did it say?"

"That they didn't want either of us to have to make the decision to stay or go, and they definitely didn't want us to stop pursuing our discovery of each other."

"Wow!"

"So now what?"

"How about we start with a bath in the creek and some breakfast. Somebody made me all sweaty last night, and I am ravenous." Meagan smiled.

"Sounds like a plan."

"I believe this is the one you seek, Odoacer."

"That is either King or Emperor Odoacer," the German warrior stated indignantly.

"You are neither to me. I could just kill and kill until one of you speaks. Instead, my precious Lalita has negotiated a deal with you that you will now honor."

"Or?"

"This one at my feet will not be the only barbarian that dies here tonight."

"You dare threaten me, Ju-Long?"

"Oh, it is not a threat, Odoacer. It is a guarantee."

"Gentleman, let us not have a dick measuring contest. I am sure both of you are well endowed." Lalita looked at Ju-Long "I know he is. We have brought you the one you have asked for, this Orestes, who rules Italy in his son's name, whom we have also brought as a bonus, your Highness. All we ask is you honor your promise and release the male Minotaur you hold to us."

"Ah, my diplomatic lady. I am afraid that the Minotaur is quite invaluable to me. You just brought him his next meal in that weak Orestes."

"Kill me, but leave my son be, Odoacer."

"You will speak only when spoken to, Orestes," the new King spat. "But fear not, I am not a child killer. Your son is safe."

"I also hope you aren't seriously breaking our deal, Odoacer."

"I will pay you handsomely in gold, but I'm afraid I am taking the Minotaur off the table, my lady."

Lalita crossed the room in the blink of an eye and snatched Odoacer by the throat. "Let's get one thing straight, my partner is actually the nice one, I'm a real bitch. You will have the Minotaur brought here to us right now or I will crush your neck before one of your warriors can do a damn thing about it. Am I clear, your *hind ass*?" The grizzled barbarian had a look of fear in his eyes.

"He . . ." Odoacer rasped, "is a two day ride from here. I had him moved to a new hiding place after I made the deal with you."

"So you had no intent of following through with your word? Maybe we are on the wrong side, Ju-Long. Maybe it is Orestes we should be helping."

"No, I will have him brought here. Please."

"You really think I am going to have the patience to wait two days?" Lalita hissed in his face. "You will send one of your men with Ju-Long to where the Minotaur is being held. Once he has been handed over to my lover and king, I will set you free. If I haven't heard from my man in two hours, you die. If anything happens to Ju-Long, you die." She tightened her grip.

"O. . . K."

"Ju-Long, take Agnes and one of Odoacer's men and go fetch her prize. I will await your call."

"And leave you alone with this vermin and his men? I . . ."

"I will be fine, lover."

"You had better be, or I will return and kill everyone here." He drew his sword and plunged it through the heart of the man on his right, then beheaded the one on his left. "That was just in case anyone here questions my resolve and ability to do just that."

Ju-Long sheathed his sword. "Which of these ingrates is going with me?"

"Theos, go with him." Odoacer ordered, able to breathe a little better as Lalita loosened her hold. "Who is Agnes?"

"She is our Minotaur, and she is lonely."

"Which one of you is Theos?" Ju-Long asked. An average sized man, with the scars and look that told the story of years of battle, stepped forward. "I hope you aren't afraid of heights. We are about to fly, and if you piss or shit yourself while I am carrying you I'll drop you and circle back for someone that can hold their mud." The two made their way to the door.

"Now that they are under way, next order of business. The boy."

"I said I was no child killer."

"Yes, I know, but I want more for him than that."

Odoacer glared at Lalita. "What would you have me do for him? I will not raise the child."

"What is your name, boy?" Lalita asked.

"My full name, ma'am?"

"Yes."

"Flavius Manyllus Romulus Augustus."

"I'm going to go with just Gus, is that okay?" The boy nodded.

"Good. Do you have relatives here?" The young man shrugged.

"We have relatives in Campania, the southern part of Italy," Orestes answered for his son.

"Wonderful. Odoacer, you will see the boy has a pension and is well taken care of. You will have him escorted to his relatives there. If a hair on the child's head is ever harmed by you or your men, I will know, and I will come back and kill you." She lied about that part. Her powers, while many, didn't include the ability to know that.

"You do not believe me to be a man of my word?"

"Like the one you kept on our previous deal with the Minotaur?"

Odoacer coughed. "I was merely seeing if you were open to a bribe of gold. Of course I desired to keep the Minotaur. He is a very powerful and a rare weapon. But I am handing him over now that I know your reason for wanting him."

"That and the hand around your throat." Odoacer shrugged. "What are you waiting for? Give the order and have the boy taken to his family."

"I will send them in the morning."

"No, now." Lalita slowly tightened her grip. And you will have all your remaining men leave this room. They can guard the doors from outside, and make sure no one enters."

"I do not trust her, my King," one of the soldiers said. In a flash Lalita crossed the room and snapped the man's neck, then resumed her choke hold on Odoacer before the King could move an inch.

"Now, Odoacer, or I kill you and then every man in this room!"

"You heard the lady. Organize a party to take the boy to his family. The rest of you out!"

"What of the prisoner, your Highness?"

"Orestes stays. If he walks out either of the exit doors, kill him. As for now I have use for him before he dies," Lalita hissed. Cautiously, not taking their eyes off her, the men backed out of the room, young Romulus Augustus in tow.

"Now, for the last order of business. I have not fully fed tonight and I am starving. You both are going to enjoy this." She glanced at Orestes. "You're going to be dead in the end, but you will die with a smile on your face." Lalita took her hand off Odoacer's throat and began patting him down for weapons. She took two daggers off him, then moved over to Orestes. She knew he was unarmed, Ju-Long having relieved him of his weapons earlier in the night.

"Stand and disrobe."

"You can go ahead and kill me! I wouldn't touch you if you were the last woman on earth, witch! I don't care how beautiful you are, I will not corrupt myself in your demon flesh!"

"Oh, you are going to do as I ask." Lalita put her hand on the side of his face. For a moment he looked up at her defiantly, but Lalita pushed her power through him and she could sense the swelling in his groin. The look of need replaced the anger in his eyes. "That's better. Now strip for mama." Without turning around, Lalita yelled back at Odoacer. "You can stop trying to ease your way to the side exit. Disrobe and get on your hands and knees."

Odoacer considered making a mad dash for the door, then remembered her speed. Instead he hesitantly did as she asked.

"Come, Odoacer. Let us play."

Lalita put her clothes back on, staring down at Orestes' dead body. He did in fact have a smile on his face.

"That was incredible. Orestes is dead?"

"Yes. And I must leave you now. Ju-Long has let me see that the male Minotaur is in his possession."

"Are you ever coming back?"

"It would be unhealthy for you if I did. If and when I see you again I'll probably kill you." Lalita began strolling toward the door. "Oh, and if I were you, I'd have Orestes beheaded and his body burned before sundown tonight. If you don't it might end up coming back to bite you in the ass. Literally."

Sicily, 478 AD

The first time Ju-Long saw one he huddled away from it like a frightened child. It didn't seem to have any ill effects for the humans who had these all over their places of worship. Lalita explained that the cross was a symbol of the Light and the power of their mighty Christian God. Ju-Long could stand in its presence now without cowering, but he could not go near them, or enter a building where they were present

He had experimented a little using a human servant to place the cross on the bare skin of a newly created xiang shi. It burned and smoldered as the vamp screamed in pain. Then there was the 'Holy Water' test. This was blessed water coming from a pool used to baptize followers of this Christ. It also melted and burned the flesh of his kind when the two came into contact.

He did not like being around one of their churches either, the grounds surrounding it brought violent pains to his stomach whenever he neared them. He didn't particularly care to be anywhere close to a *Codex Sinaiticus*, a book telling the story of this Christian Savior and the God that sent him.

Over time he noticed that he was not always anxious in the presence of one of the teachers of this religion. Sure if they were wearing a cross or carrying the Book he was uneasy, but some were weak. They were weak because they did not practice what they preached. Granted, he could sense the strength some of these men held, but others gave off an evil aura almost as thick as his.

After a year in these 'Christian' lands, testing boundaries and limits, he found that if he caught one of the weak teachers without a cross, or carrying the Book, he could make a meal out of them. It became a game for Ju-Long and Lalita. She would lure them in and feed on their life force via sex, then Ju-Long would finish the job by sinking in fangs before ripping their hearts from their chests.

He had dealt with religious believers and leaders before, including the Buddhists from China that still pursued him. While they had gifts, he had never run into a belief system that could give ordinary men such power. That is, if they truly believed. Ju-Long could see how this Light's actual physical presence could drive Lalita and other lessor demons into hiding four plus centuries ago. This God, whoever or whatever it was, was powerful.

Lalita stared across at Ju-Long. There was something weighing heavy on her lover's mind. She had seen him like this before, but it had been a long, long time. "What is it?"

"What is what?

"C'mon Ju-Long, you know what I am asking. What's wrong?"

"I do not like feeling powerless against something."

"What do you feel powerless against?"

"This Christ and His followers." Ju-Long rubbed his temples.

Lalita walked over and wrapped her arms around him. "Listen, lover, already their faith and obedience is lacking. They grow weak, even as their numbers rise, most of them are still slaves to the flesh. Man wants to be good, but he enjoys being bad." She kissed his neck lightly. "Already, even those ministers who profess the faith to non-believers, wane in their beliefs. Some of them seek power and status far more than they pursue salvation."

"Even so, their cross holds me at bay, and their buildings won't allow me to enter." Ju-Long pushed her back gently, shaking his head. "I can't stand the feeling that there is something more powerful than I out there."

"The Spirit in the air today pales in comparison to the power that was wrought on us when their God took human form. Their God may be pure, but man is easily corrupted. If the Light were still here, we wouldn't be." Lalita ran a hand down his chest. "Greed, personal power, sex and other pleasures of the flesh are what mankind turns to in the end. It has been for thousands of years, and will continue to be for thousands of years to come."

"Think about it. Sure, some of these people have been converted, but they are also prisoners of their former beliefs. Do not think the Vandals have abandoned their precious Oden. Or the Greeks have totally forsaken their Zeus? This place, the hub of Christianity, is all a melting pot of cultures, beliefs, and foreigners. Not just the Vandals influence the area. You have Ostrogoths and Visigoths marking territory, as well as the people who once were the Hunnic Empire. Over time this too shall pass. I have seen dynasties disappear, empires crumble, watched religions fail time and again. Even if the Light never truly goes away, His ability to hold the attention of man is not limitless."

"Besides, there are many places that the Light has not touched yet. China and India know little to nothing about this God and His religion. Yet we exist in the Roman Empire, where Christianity abounds, and still we survive."

"I suppose that is true. Still, I must find a way to overcome the power the symbols of this religion have over me. I will not be brought to kneel at any cross, or to any god, whether they are from heaven or hell."

"Ju-Long you are among the most powerful creatures on earth, can't that just be enough?"

"No."

"Believe me, there are things out there that will always be more powerful than us. The Light is just one of them. But that does not mean we cannot rule the dark on this plane."

Ju-Long put a finger to his lips to hush her. *People are here. I can't believe I missed it and they got this close. Our servants are dead. The warriors are armed with bows and spears. One of them is a chosen one.*

How many?

Too many.

Where are the Minotaur?

They are holed up in a cavern until nightfall. They didn't make it back here before dawn.

How long until sundown?

About an hour or so.

What do we do now, Ju-Long?

You need to blast through the roof and make your escape. The sunlight doesn't affect you.

And just leave you lover? I don't think so.

Lalita, please. Go and find the Minotaur. He placed an image of their location as well as the directions to get there in her head.

They won't be able to help until the sun is gone. You could be dead by then!

I will be fine. Ju-Long grabbed a sword off the table, then drew another from his belt. *Now go!*

The home they had taken over had two stories. Lalita headed to the second floor to make her escape. They had been living there for several months, and Ju-Long had a secret underground passage built by his servants. He hoped they would have trouble finding the hidden entrance, and he could hold them off using the close quarters to take away their numbers advantage and only have to worry about a frontal assault.

Ju-Long headed for a small room between the living room and kitchen. He sheathed one of his swords then lifted the hatch to the tunnel and jumped in, pulling it closed behind him. Once he was three feet into the tunnel it turned pitch black. His superior vision adjusted and he could see far better than any of his pursuers ever would. Advantage Ju-Long.

Something blasted through the roof and shot off into the sky. No way was the figure that took off Ju-Long, there was way too much daylight left. Xiong was sure of two things—one, Ju-Long was inside, and two, he knew they were coming.

"I believe that was Lalita," Argus said, referring to the figure that blew through the roof. "That leaves Ju-Long and the Minotaur."

"The fighting inside is going to be close quarters. What do you think?"

"We will take a half dozen of the best warriors in with us with a backup team of six ready if we call for them. The rest of the men will surround the house and kill anything not us that comes out." Angus pointed to the front of the structure. "You take three and enter from the front, I'll take three and circle around back." Xiong nodded. "Give me about five minutes to give the orders and get my team into position"

The tunnel actually went several hundred feet into an empty field behind the house. Ju-Long could escape from the hatch at the other end, but only after the sun went down. The passage was wide enough and tall enough for both Minotaur to pass through it side by side. To the right of the hatch was a recess which ran six feet back and four feet wide. He would hide there until the enemy was close.

Xiong and Argus met in the middle of the home, neither encountering anything until they met each other.

"Second floor?" Xiong questioned.

Argus stomped the floor, but it was solid, no dungeon underneath. "I'll check upstairs. You and the others scour the place again."

Xiong nodded and went about going room to room again, this time checking the walls and floors for any hidden escape route. Argus headed cautiously up the ladder to the second floor. He doubted the Minotaur's would be hiding up there. The ceiling on the first floor didn't look that sturdy.

The upper story was just one large room. The windows were completely covered, but the evening sun came through the hole in the roof. It was obviously Ju-Long and Lalita's chambers. Argus methodically checked the room. It was unoccupied. *Where is Ju-Long? Where are the Minotaur?*

He could hear one of the men downstairs. "Xiong! Over here! I think I found something." He could hear feet scuffling to where the voice was coming from. Argus moved back to the ladder and dropped down to the first floor, arriving at the trap door the man had discovered about the same time as the others.

"Would have been a damn good time to have brought a torch," Xiong commented.

"There must be an exit somewhere outside. Two of you go outside and alert the others to be on watch," Argus ordered. "Xiong and I will go first, the rest of you will follow."

"Sure you don't want me to guard the rear? Ya know, just in case?" Xiong smiled.

"Let's go, China doll."

"Ouch."

Ju-Long could hear the men enter the tunnel. Hopefully they would take their time getting here in the pitch dark. He had already heard one of them saying they wished they had a torch. He could feel that the sun would be down in about an hour, but at the moment that felt like an eternity. If he ever was in a situation like this again he would make sure to have a few quick to set traps to slow down his pursuers.

The group moved cautiously, but there was no doubt they would reach him before night fall. As he listened to their footsteps slowly draw closer, a plan began to formulate. Ju-Long drew on his rage and began calling the storm.

The rain began slowly. Ju-Long focused harder and he could hear the winds pick up, as well as the first rolls of thunder. The power he stole from the Naga long ago back in his home country was still his, it had not betrayed him over the years. He knew the chosen one, or chosen ones would be in the tunnel. As he continued to call the torrent, he stepped out of the recess and walked several feet down the tunnel.

Ju-Long began pushing the wood beams that supported the walls and ceiling. With any luck his pursuers would either have to take time digging through the rubble, or turn back and head the other direction to get out. Even with his great strength the beams were not easy to move. This made Ju-Long's frustration grow, which was bad for the beams but good for the storm, which was now torrential outside, water streaming in through the hatch.

"Do you hear that?"

"The rains? Yes. There wasn't a storm cloud in sight earlier," Argus answered.

"No." Xiong stopped. There is grunting up ahead." They both listened. "Minotaur?"

"No. I would be able to smell them. There is something down there though." A few more loud groans echoed through the corridor, followed by a cracking and crashing sound.

"What the hell was that?" Xiong exclaimed.

"That was the tunnel caving in up ahead. Whatever is down here doesn't want us going that direction," Argus answered. "Back the other way, now!"

Ju-Long pushed the hatch open and jumped back into the recess. It was dark outside, the sun hidden from view. He only caught a brief glimpse before the wind snapped the hatch shut again. Drawing his sword Ju-Long leapt upward, blowing through the trap door and flying into the stormy skies. He could see men hunkered down under trees, some crawling on the ground trying to make it back to the house.

Ju-Long focused on the winds, already so strong it was raining sideways, and pushed an enormous gust toward his former domicile. He kept it going as the structure started to rattle and boards began to fly as they were ripped away. Ju-Long would flatten the structure, trapping the chosen one and his men inside the house.

Xiong reached the tunnel exit to the house first and climbed out. The house was shaking, they needed to get out quickly. He turned and reached down, grabbing the first man's hand and pulling him up. He had three men out when the ceiling came crashing down on him.

Argus felt some of the earth above him fall on his head and shoulders. He was bringing up the rear after quickly checking the other end of the tunnel and finding it completely blocked. Some of the men let out yells. Something bad was happening ahead.

Far to the west Ju-Long could see that the sun was still up. He needed to go north toward Rome where he and Lalita would rendezvous. He knew sooner or later he would lose the cover of the storm, and if the sun still shined he would be trapped once more. Ju-Long, having expended a lot of energy already, felt the thirst call to him. As he looked down on the leveled house he decided it was time to feed.

The escape hatch was covered by heavy debris, leaving everything in the tunnel pitch dark. The men were panicking and the upper body of someone, he believed it was Xiong, was hanging from the opening unconscious, his legs trapped by layers of heavy wood. Getting out of this mess was going to be no easy task. Argus could touch the boards blocking their exit, but just barely. "Damn this!"

Ju-Long landed near a cluster of trees where five men were seeking some form of shelter. He killed three of them before they even knew he was upon them. He drove his sword through the chest of the fourth and pulled the fifth one in close, sinking fangs into his neck. With his thirst sated Ju-Long calmed. The skies remained dark, but the wind and the rain slowed.

"Vampiro! Vampiro!" Several of the warriors shouted as some charged him with spears in hand.

Stupid humans, running to their death! Ju-Long smiled as he drew a second sword and went to work.

Using a battle axe, and the spears the other men carried, Argus and a couple of the warriors were able to lift and slide some of the debris out of the way. Eventually there was enough room for one of the smaller warriors to climb out, followed by another. Pushing and pulling they managed to make space for Argus and the others to work their way topside.

The rain and wind had slowed considerably. Argus ordered the others to stand guard as he moved the boards that trapped Xiong. His friend was breathing but still out cold. Once Argus had him freed it was apparent Xiong's right leg was broken. The three men who had been out of the tunnel when the roof collapsed were dead, and looking around there was no shortage of bodies lying lifeless in the surrounding fields.

The light rain hitting Xiong's face began to rouse him. He winced as he tried to sit up, pain stinging through his right leg.

"It's broke. We need to reset the bone and splint it." Argus said.

"You know how to do that."

"I've had to reset more than one over the years, and not just my own."

Ju-Long was a safe distance away observing. There was a thought to swoop in and kill the rest of them. There were only seven men, a wounded Xiong, and the Minotaur hunter he had seen in Crete. That is what caused him to pause. Lalita had described the man, Argus, if he recalled correctly, as an extremely lethal adversary. The sun was nearly down. He was neither intimidated nor foolish, the chosen ones day would come, but for now he must reunite with his love and his powerful pets.

Apennines Mountain Range, Near Perugia, Italy, 478 AD

They had spent some time in Rome, but it was not a good place to keep Minotaur's hidden. They were traveling into the mountains to find their pets a lair, secluded enough to keep them out of sight, but close enough to a settlement for feeding purposes. The plan was for Lalita, Ju-Long and their four human servants to return to Rome once the beasts were settled.

They came upon a cave that looked promising. There was still hours before daylight, so if this one didn't work out they would still have time to look around. Anders (Agnes' mate), a huge male Minotaur at nearly ten feet tall, went into explore the potential dwelling. The mouth of the cavern was huge, at least twenty feet high and thirty feet across. As he stepped into it he could smell something living inside. Whatever it was, it was about to become dinner.

Brontes caught a whiff of the foul beast that had invaded his private abode long before he saw it. Whatever it was, he hoped it tasted better than it smelled. He picked up his club and went to meet the intruder.

Ju-Long, Lalita, and Agnes were flying around checking for trouble and keeping an eye out for the human servants who should be arriving on foot soon. They heard Ander let out a loud snort, followed by the sounds of a struggle. As Ju-Long went to land, his enormous pet came flying out of the cave.

Agnes landed, rushing to her love, whose face was bloodied. He was alive, but knocked out. Ju-Long drew his sword, wondering what type of creature had the power to do that to

Ander. He could hear the grunts and feel the vibration of the heavy footfalls heading out of the cavern.

What emerged was monstrous in size. The strange looking man-like creature with one eye was at least sixteen feet tall. It carried a huge club, but from the look of it the behemoth didn't really need it. Its shoulders were like boulders—biceps enormous. The giant had a broad chest, thick with muscle, and legs like tree trunks. Its belly was plump enough to show it was well fed. *What the hell does that thing eat?* Ju-Long thought.

"It's a cyclops!" Lalita yelled, still in flight.

"What the hell is a cyclops?"

"Go for the eye Ju-Long! Drive your sword through it!"

Brontes wasn't expecting to be greeted by more unwanted guests. He let out a roar that shook the air. "I will kill you all and feast on your flesh!" He charged the puny human on the ground, keeping an eye on the woman in the sky. The man jumped into the air, coming for his face with a two hand overhead grip on his sword.

Brontes swatted him hard with his empty left hand, sending the man sideways and into some trees. About that time the woman landed on his right shoulder, plunging a dagger into his neck. The pixie flew up and out of reach as he went to grab her and squeeze the life out of the bitch.

Lalita had hit a large vein in the gargantuan's neck. Blood was spurting out and the smell intoxicated her. Such power. She had heard of these beasts, but thought they were extinct long ago. To taste that liquid would be divine. Her blood lust had her lost for a moment, until she met the business end of the club and sailed through the air, pain racking her body.

Agnes turned to see her mate's attacker bleeding from the neck. Ju-Long and Lalita were nowhere in sight. Her body, shaking with rage, wanted to destroy the giant. She lowered her head and went charging toward her one-eyed enemy.

The cyclops saw her, but a moment too late. She rammed headfirst into its belly. One of her horns penetrated, but snapped off as she fell backwards, reeling from the impact. She managed to roll to her right as the beast came down hard with the club in its right.

Brontes roared in pain as he pulled the horn from his body. Blood ran from the wound, but nothing like the amount gushing from his neck. He dropped his club and clamped his hand over the wound, trying to suppress the bleeding. He staggered for a moment as the blood loss made him dizzy. For the first time since fighting the Titans he considered running. It might be the only way to survive this night.

Ju-Long was hurting, and he had no idea where his sword went. What he did see, and smell, was the rich powerful blood that would cure his ills. Both Minotaur's were down, and he couldn't see Lalita, but the cyclops was hurt. Ju-Long put both arms out in front of him, fists clenched, and flew as fast as he could toward the giant.

He caught the behemoth square on the jaw, his hands exploding in pain. Ju-Long let out a scream as he turned in midair and watched the cyclops fall to the ground. He knocked it out cold, and now he would bathe in its blood.

The xiang shi went right for the wound in its neck. The blood rained on him and he shuddered with the power it brought. Covered in the warm liquid he brought his mouth down on a part of the puncture and drank heavily. By the time he came up the blood had slowed to a drip.

Ju-Long looked down and saw Agnes feeding on the inside of its left leg. Ander drank from the wound in its belly, but was also eating the flesh of the cyclops. "Ander, no. We will drain this abomination dry, but we will not destroy its body." The Minotaur snorted, but quit chewing and went back to sucking the blood from the giant.

"Where is Lalita?"

"I am right here." She popped up from the other side of Brontes' neck, her face smeared with blood. "Wow! What a rush!" She giggled as she stumbled backward and fell on her ass.

"You drunken whore!" Ju-Long laughed. "Let me help you up." He stepped onto the Cyclopes neck and his back foot caught as he went to step down. He landed face first in Lalita's lap.

***

The human servants arrived about an hour before dawn. The rough terrain delayed them. Carlo and Georgio were brothers, two years apart. Carlo was slightly taller at six feet three and a little leaner at one hundred eighty pounds. Georgio was only six feet, but stout at two hundred ten pounds. Both were handsome, though Carlo was the prettier of the two. The brothers had dark hair, Carlo's about shoulder length while his younger brother's was short.

Karah and Vianca were not related and had never met before. Vianca was tall, almost six feet with long jet black hair. Her olive skin was smooth and soft, her body thin, but curvy in all the right places. Karah, four years older than Vianca, was five two with big breasts and a big derriere. She was like a shorter version of Lalita, though not as beautiful.

The four stood watch just outside the cave entrance. Ju-Long had Agnes and Anders drag the cyclops deep into the cave. The two Minotaur rested between the giant and Ju-Long. He and Lalita were closer to the mouth, but well out of the sun's reach which had come up hours ago. The pair had napped a little earlier, but were up discussing what they would do if the Cyclopes rose at sundown as a Vrykolakas.

"Are you sure you will be able to control it?"

"I am marked as master of whatever I create. You see how the Minotaur listen."

"Yes, Ju-Long. But not everything you have bitten has seen you as master."

"And what have I bitten that does not bow before me?" He stared at her, studying her face. The answer was right in front of him. "You. You would not be controlled, but you have become obedient. Most of the time. When you feel like it." They both laughed. "If it does not obey, then I will kill it. But if it does . . . what a weapon. I will have three special surprises for the chosen ones when we meet next."

They spent the afternoon and early evening talking. Well, mostly Lalita talking as she told the history of the cyclops, the Greek Gods, and the battle with the Titans. While they fought on the side of the gods against their relatives the Titans, the cyclops did not fear the gods. They honored Zeus for freeing them from their imprisonment, giving him his weapons of thunder and lightning. Generally though, they just disregarded him.

"So, if they will defy gods, why will this one listen to you?"

"Because his blood is linked with mine."

"And mine. And Agnes'. And Ander's. What if he latches on to one of us as master?"

Ju-Long laughed. "Preposterous. It will be dark soon. I am going to go greet my new creation the second he rises."

"Shall I come with?"

"I will not put you in danger if things go bad. It will have to get through me and both Minotaur to get to you." Ju-Long kissed her on the forehead. "But fear not, I shall return."

Agnes, whose broken horn had grown back after feeding last night, and Ander were still dead to the world, figuratively and literally. Ju-Long continued past them to the chamber where the cyclops was held. The giant is ice cold, no sign of life at all. *It is early yet.*

How much blood is something this size going to need? Ju-Long wondered. It only took one human per Minotaur, but they consumed the body as well. Even eating the human, this thing could probably do four a night. Agnes walked in, followed by Ander. Both were armed with battle axes.

"We came to ensure your safety, master. What would you have of us?" Agnes asked.

"Go and be with Lalita," he answered, "I will be fine." The couple gave a slight bow and headed toward the mouth of the cave, but neither of them looked happy about it.

Ju-Long waited. And waited. Apparently the cyclops was not going to rise. Frustrated, Ju-Long headed to the entrance. It was time to eat and explore some more.

Lalita was glad to see him walking to her still in one piece. He shook his head no and she knew the cyclops did not rise.

"Let us go and feed. Then we shall return and rid your new home of its carcass," he said, looking at the two Minotaur. He ushered them all out of the cave, gave instructions to his servants, and headed for a nearby village.

Carlo and Vianca were on watch while Georgio and Karah did their thing somewhere off in the trees. It would be his and Vianca's turn next. There was a huge groan that echoed through the cavern, followed by heavy foot falls. The pair drew their swords.

Brontes wasn't sure how he was still alive, but he knew he was hungry. He had always had a taste for flesh, but now the need for blood masked that. His wounds weren't bleeding, but he could still see the hole in his belly and feel the cut on his neck. He didn't know what awaited him outside, but he hoped it wasn't a repeat of last night. He could smell something human. It smelled delicious.

Carlo moved cautiously forward, waving at Vianca to get behind him. Vianca watched in horror, unable to even scream. The one-eyed giant grabbed Carlo so fast, flicking his sword away before he even had time to react. She winced at the sound of bones crunching as the cyclops bit his head off. Then the behemoth seemed to register that she was there. She turned to run but felt her bones being crushed as its free hand caught her and clamped shut.

Georgio begged for one more round, but Karah heard something coming from the direction of the cave. She moved until the entrance was in her line of sight. She didn't see Carlo or Vianca anywhere. They both dressed and began moving back to the cavern.

Ju-Long dropped the young woman he had just drained. The look on his face was one of puzzlement and rage. "What is it?" Lalita asked.

"Something just killed at least one of my servants. Get our pets!" he yelled as he took off skyward.

Brontes sucked the blood from the neck of both humans after biting their heads off. He was just chewing up the legs of the woman, his powerful jaws and pulverizing teeth turning bone onto powder. The meal was good, but he was still hungry.

He could hear a female voice outside yelling "Carlo, Vianca?" His victims must have been her friends. He sniffed the air. Brontes could smell a man approaching with her. He smiled. *I love it when dinner is delivered.*

Ju-Long got there in time to see the cyclops appear to swallow the last of his human servants. It wiped its blood smeared mouth, then snarled as Ju-Long landed in front of him. The giant went to reach for him and Ju-Long sidestepped, chopping its forearm with his blade. The monster howled in pain.

"I am not a meal! I am your master! You will kneel before me or die a true death!" Ju-Long reinforced the message as he invaded the giant's mind. It studied him for a moment with a look of uncertainty. "I said kneel!"

Pain shot through Brontes head and he went down on one knee. "Please." he groaned, falling forward on his hands and knees from the intense throbbing in his brain.

"What is your name?"

"Brontes," he replied.

"Well beast, I am Ju-Long, but you will refer to me as master. I have turned you into a more powerful creature than ever before. I made you, and I can end you. Your only hope is to pledge allegiance to me."

Brontes was prepared to do anything to stop the agony ripping through his head. "Yes, master."

"Yes to what?"

"You are master, and I am your servant." Even through the pain he could sense something that actually tied him to this man.

"That's better."

Brontes took several deep breaths as the pain in his head stopped abruptly. "Thank you, master."

"How do you feel?"

"Still hungry, master."

"Yes, and I have no more human servants for you to devour."

Lalita and the Minotaur's landed, causing Brontes to stand and back up a few steps. "Do not fear, Brontes. They were enemies to you last night, but now they are allies."

"Yes, master."

"I'll be damned." Lalita shook her head. "You do have him under your control."

"You doubted? Ye of little faith," Ju-Long tsked. "Come, our Brontes needs more food. Then we will explain to him what it is he has become."

***

Ju-Long and Lalita hung out in the mountains for a week, teaching Brontes all he needed to know. Brontes could get by on four humans per night, but he preferred six. The first cave where they found their cyclops was the main home for Brontes, but he had several caverns throughout the mountains. It was a good thing, because they needed to move from place to place to avoid being tracked down, and as not to completely decimate the food supply in any one area.

Tonight he and his woman would head back to Rome. The Minotaur would stay with Brontes. Ju-Long had created eight human servants to guard them by day. He gave implicit instructions to the cyclops that he was not to eat them.

"We will create a few new servants once we are back in Rome. Then we can explore the city you called home five hundred years ago, at our leisure."

"Until the chosen ones find us again."

"When they come calling next, my love, we will draw them here and finish them with our pets. There will be no more running for us."

Florence, Italy 481 AD

They traveled by ship to Sardinia and come up empty. Next was Corsica, where they found no trace of Ju-Long or the Minotaur. Heading back to the mainland they made berth in Genoa. They found no enemies, but were told by travelers that there were creatures in the mountains, two that resembled bulls and one giant, that were eating humans.

They traveled to Florence checking all points in between. They heard more stories about the terrors that lived in the mountains, and actually ran into a few Vrykolakas, or vampiros as the locals here referred to them. Only one of them even knew who Ju-Long was, and he had not seen him in half a century. While that one was more than willing to answer their questions, in the end they staked him just like the others.

Xiong and Argus had been traveling on their own since Sicily. They needed to move quickly, too quickly for mere humans. The hope was to gather a small force of willing men to help them once they located Ju-Long. The pair sat in a tavern talking to a man in his mid to late forties. He had been living on the outskirts with his wife and three sons when they were attacked.

He had been heading back to his homestead after helping his brother in law do some repairs to his barn. He was running late and night had fallen. In the distance he heard screams. It sounded like his wife. Kasan urged his horse on, thinking a band of thieves had hit his place. Then he heard grunts and snorts that were not human. *Is it the monsters of the mountains I have heard tales of?*

The voice of his wife, Arianna, had gone silent. He could hear one of his boys yelling. It was Massimo telling his younger brothers Santonio and Terzo to run. A loud roar shook the night air, and then came the eerie quiet. He had his steed at full gallop.

When his house came into view he could see half of it had been demolished. A colossal figure was disappearing into the tree line.

Kasan dismounted and began searching for and calling out for his family. There was no answer. All that remained were torn, bloody garments his wife and sons had been wearing. He fell to his knees and wept. He remained there, sobbing until the sun came up. His entire world had been stolen from him in one night. That was when the drinking started, and it hadn't really stopped in the two weeks since then. He hadn't even returned to his home the entire time, living on the streets for the most part and using coin he had squirreled away over the years for alcohol and the little food he ate.

"Will you give us directions to your place?" Argus asked.

The man hiccupped and let out a belch. "I'll do ya one better. I'll take ya there." The man stood, then staggered sideways into the wall.

"Maybe you should rest and let us go." Xiong knelt down next to the man who was now slumped on the floor. "Kasan? Kasan?" The man had passed out. "So what now?"

"We get a room and get some rest," Argus replied.

"What do we do with him?"

"Drag him with us."

They slept for several hours, waking up when they heard their drunk friend start coughing and complaining about needing a drink. Argus filled a cup, helped Kasan into a sitting position, and handed it to him. Kasan took a huge gulp, then immediately spit it out.

"That's disgusting! What did you give me?"

"It's called water, and you need to drink it." Argus scowled.

"Where's my wine? That's all I need to get right. My head is killing me."

"No wine until you get us to your place. Then we will give you all you need," Xiong added, pushing the cup back up to the man's mouth.

"What if I refuse to move until I get a real drink?" Kasan protested.

Argus crouched down until his face was mere inches from Kasan's. "That would be a tragic mistake on your part," he growled, grabbing the cup and refilling it from his water flask. "Drink up, butter cup."

Being jostled around on the horse made his head pound even harder and his stomach do somersaults. He wretched his guts out three times, the last ending in dry heaves, during the ride. He felt like death and in some respect he wished he was.

"Is that your place up ahead?" Argus asked.

Kasan lifted his head and squinted into the morning son. His eyes were having trouble focusing, but he could tell it was his home. Or at least what was left of it. "Yep."

The three men dismounted. Xiong and Argus went looking for clues as to what had happened here and what did it. Kasan waited until they moved away, then grabbed one of the flasks on Argus's steed. He put it to his lips and sipped. *Water.* He dropped that one and grabbed another. *Wine!*

"These are unmistakably Minotaur tracks," Argus stated.

"Well, what in the world made these?"

"A giant."

"Those things are real?"

"I thought they had gone extinct, but apparently I was wrong." Argus replied as he watched Xiong step into one of the giant's tracks.

"Unreal. This thing makes a Yeti look small. Hell, it makes my brother Wei look like a dwarf."

"They are incredibly strong, just like their size would suggest. While not the brightest of creatures, it has deceptively quick hands and with its long strides it easily outruns any human."

"Why would something this size run from humans?" Xiong asked.

"Not from, after."

"Oh." Xiong continued to study the huge footprint. "Have you ever met one?"

"Long ago. It was a mountain giant, even larger than this one."

"There are different types of giants?"

"There were several different giants back in the day. Or so legends say. They typically ranged in size from a dwarf giant at ten feet tall, to a mountain giant that can reach up to thirty feet."

"No shit. Wow. What happened to them?"

"Gods, heroes, and man. Not to mention different clans of them were at war with each other most of the time."

"Well, we may have another problem."

"What's that?"

"What if Ju-Long turned this thing, just like he turned the Minotaur? It will be stronger and faster than ever before." Xiong looked at Argus.

"Then we are in for one hell of a fight."

They found Kasan knelt down, sobbing into a garment. There were two empty flasks in front of him. It was his wife's dress, and he clutched it as if somehow it would bring her back.

"Kasan?" Xiong whispered, "Kasan?" The man continued to weep, not acknowledging Xiong's presence.

"Kasan?" Argus patted the man on the shoulder. Kasan grabbed his hand and held it.

"I am sorry, Arianna. I failed you. I failed our sons," he wailed.

"Kasan, snap out of it!" Argus took him by the shoulders and shook him. Kasan cried even harder, wrapping his arm around Argus' waist in a hug.

"Father, forgive me, for I have sinned."

Argus looked at Xiong and shrugged. "What now?"

***

Travel over the next three days was slowed by Kasan's withdrawals as they dried him out. He was still sick and irritable, but he was coming around. Xiong had seen his eldest brother Zhan go through this a couple times about a century ago. It wasn't pretty or fun.

They traveled south along the mountains and ran into a couple of settlements and a small village that had also been hit by these monsters. Everyone had lost some or all of their family, just like Kasan.

However, the nights had been quiet recently, suggesting the beasts had moved on. Where they were, and in which direction they were headed was a mystery. "Do we keep moving south? Double back north?" Xiong asked. "Damn, I wish Amal was here. He could fly around and scout for us. It might take us months or more to find them in these mountains."

"Then we will have to search for months. Hell, it's been over a decade since you and I joined forces to hunt this Ju-Long and his slut. We have been close a few times, but come up empty. If we become impatient we are more likely to make a mistake. If you make a mistake with the things we pursue, well, that could be our very last mistake."

"I know, Argus, but while we have been searching for a decade, I have been chasing Ju-Long for a century! It is so frustrating! When does it end?"

"End?" Argus chuckled. "End? It doesn't end. I have been hunting Minotaur and other evil creatures for close to a millennia. It never ends. Good will never completely conquer evil and the dark will never totally extinguish the light. Only the end of times, or our own death, will release us from this fight."

"That is depressing. What is the point? I figured that once I found and defeated Ju-Long I would be able to get on with my life."

"That's your problem, my friend. You are waiting for one thing to happen so you can move on. Don't wait. Get on with your life now. Your tomorrow is no more guaranteed than anyone else's."

"You mean abandon my mission?"

"No. I have been on a mission since before your great, great, great, great, great, great grandparents met and did the nasty. I am still on the mission, but I am also living. Maybe not the traditional husband, wife, home and family life, but my life. You, Xiong, are just existing."

"Don't you desire a normal life?"

"What is normal? For me, this is. I don't want to be tied down, or have to watch loved ones die. I travel, I fight, I drink, I enjoy the company of women, and I come and go as I please. I live life on my terms. I just happen to fight evil along the way because I enjoy it." Argus stretched and let out a yawn. "What is normal to you?"

"I don't know. This is all I've known."

"Do you enjoy any part of it?"

"I guess. Yes, I do enjoy seeing new places, meeting others like yourself, fighting the bad that threatens our world."

"Then like me, this is your normal. Now just add life to it."

"So how do I do that? What secrets can you share with me? I don't see you doing much *living* since we struck up together."

"The reason you don't see it is because you have an ideal in your head of what life is supposed to be. Life is what you make it. You have to live life in the present, and you can't make *moments*—but you can enjoy them when they come to you. Does that make sense?" Argus asked.

"So basically I need to slow down and let life come to me?"

"No, Xiong." Argus shook his head. "Figure out the things you want or enjoy and go after them. However, don't be so blind on your path that you miss the beauty that surrounds you. Don't miss the *moments* because you are so focused on the mission."

"What if I can't?"

"Can't never could. I thought you said you Buddhists were positive thinkers."

"We are, but how do I have *fun* with all the chaos going on around me?"

"Wow, you really are a special case. For me, sometimes the chaos is the fun. But as I said, think about things you have enjoyed and do them. Don't wait until the 'mission' is complete, live in the now." Argus patted him on the shoulder. "Believe in and love yourself first and foremost or you will never experience life at its fullest."

"But what if I have lost the faith I once had in me? What if I no longer believe in me?"

"How can you not believe in you?"

"We had Ju-Long three times and couldn't finish him. Each time I was out early on. The first time I was knocked out by Ju-Long before I ever got a shot in. The second time he put an arrow in my heart that nearly killed me at the onset. You were with me when I broke my leg."

"And yet you are still alive."

"Yes, but only because others saved me."

"And how many times have you saved another? It hasn't happened in a while, but I've had my ass handed to me a couple of times. Meagan has saved me more than once."

"I just don't know."

"Well, I know this, you should start drinking, and we need to get you laid."

Lalita walked into the room and everyone and everything seemed to stop. Ju-Long was already there, admiring her himself as she entered. It was one of many formal dinner parties they had attended since settling in Rome three years ago, rubbing elbows with the rich and elite, the powerful and the beautiful. It was how Lalita had lived for centuries before Ju-Long came along.

She taught him to feed off the sexual energy in a room like this (and the energy was usually thick enough to cut with a knife) completely undetected. He would draw it from a woman's hand as he kissed it, pull it from her body as they danced, and steal it when he brushed them as he walked by. A little here, a little there and soon his hunger was sated. The first few times he struggled to contain himself, wanting the instant gratification of a full feeding.

More than once Lalita had to drag him somewhere private and calm him, generally by feeding him through sex. Now, he was a pro at it. He didn't want to feed like this every night, but he could. He could actually make it several days without drinking blood, but he rarely skipped more than a night. There was nothing more fulfilling than consuming blood, except maybe taking it in while indulging in other pleasures of the flesh.

This method allowed them to mingle and play without being discovered. It almost always ended with the couple taking on some new partners and stealing more energy, leaving them filled and their human counterparts alive, but exhausted.

Lalita was far better at this then he was. She could just pull the energy out of the air around her, or from the lustful gazes of both men and women as they gawked at her. Sometimes Ju-Long had to fight the erection he would get from just watching her do this.

Tonight she had on her low cut black dress that showed enough cleavage to be considered obscene, except in the circles they ran in. These people might shun a woman dressed like her on the street, calling her a whore, but in here she was greeted like a queen. Her hair was braided and tied up in a bun, her silky smooth, creamy tan skin was flawless. Her face required nothing, but she did wear red lipstick on her full lips. The only thing he loved more than having those lips on him, was having himself inside the other set she had.

The slit up the left side of the dress ran to just above her waist, exposing her gorgeous long leg. It flashed a little of her bottom when she turned one way, and a lot of thigh when she turned the other. She fed and fed as one man after another held her hand and kissed it. Some, but not all, were fortunate enough to get a hug and a peck on the cheek. They lined up hoping they would be the one.

The women were in waiting as well, some kissing her or giving her exposed hip a squeeze as they unwittingly supplied energy to her. She eventually made her way to Ju-Long. By now, everyone knew they were a couple. They also knew that couple liked to play. The goal was to be one of the ones who played with them. Word had gotten around that the sex was mind blowing.

By the time she reached Ju-Long her body was radiating with the sexual energy she had collected. "Good evening, my love." She planted a kiss on his cheek as he wrapped his arms around her.

"I want to ravish you right here, right now, in front of everyone," he whispered in her ear.

"I'd bet they would all love that show." Lalita turned her head and blew gently on his neck. Ju-Long felt the energy tingle from there down to his groin.

"Have you chosen for tonight?"

"I believe I have found one. This one is a first timer here. Some of these people must be supporters, because he is not hiding what he is.

"The man of the cloth, over in the corner?"

"You spotted him already?"

"Hard to miss the cross he is wearing. How do you plan to get around that, my queen?"

"I brought back-up." Lalita looked in the direction of Capri. She was a sight to behold, long jet black hair, and at five feet ten she was an inch taller than Lalita. Built quite differently than her master (Lalita had made this one especially for Ju-Long), she was slender with smaller breasts, narrower hips, and a firm, round rear that was much less pronounced than Lalita's.

She was escorted by Renzo, another of their human servants. For a man he was breathtakingly beautiful. Six foot two, well built, with long dark hair tied back in a tight ponytail. The pair, who had never been here before, were absolute head turners.

"I see you have let the children out to play tonight, my love."

"I fear we may be becoming a little too comfortable here and getting complacent. I thought it might be time to start bringing extra eyes to watch our back."

"I am not concerned. These people, the ones who hold the power, worship you like royalty and trust me because I take care of their 'problems.'"

"Yes, they do. But should they discover what we are and how you take care of their 'problems', they would turn on us in a heartbeat."

"You worry too much, my dear."

"And you don't?"

"No. And once I have dispensed of the chosen ones, there won't be anything to even concern me at all."

"Ju-Long, there is a reason I have survived over a thousand years, and a reason you still need me in your life."

"I will always need you, Lalita."

She took his hand and placed it on the center of her chest, his fingers catching the material of her dress—sliding it to the side until her nipple was exposed. "There, that is better. Let's finish working this room." She smiled.

"Such a tease." Ju-Long grinned.

Capri approached the man as instructed. He was short, only about five-five, and slender. He wasn't much to look at, and his beady eyes reminded her of the pervert uncle who groped her as a child every chance he got. Were it not for her older brother looking out for her, her uncle would have done far worse.

She led him back to a side room as Lalita ordered and had him cornered, talking sweetly to him as he stared at her breasts. "Forgive me, father, for I have sinned. And I want to sin some more. Can you help me, father?" The man was sweating and seemed unable to speak. Capri wrapped her hand behind his neck and pulled his face into her chest. "Please, father. I need you to bless this body."

She pushed him back by the shoulders. "Why don't we make you a little more comfortable, okay?" Capri asked, lifting the silver chain holding the cross up over his head. She laid it on a table beside them, then untied the sash around his waist and pushed his robe back. He was completely naked underneath. She wondered if that were common among his type, or if he was just prepared for what he was expecting to get tonight.

To her surprise, his penis was flaccid. Usually the men she had been with before were rock solid by this point.

"Where is your boyfriend?" The man looked around nervously.

"Oh, don't worry about him. We are very open in our relationship." At that moment, as if on cue, the door opened and in stumbled Lalita, with Renzo draped on one side, and a middle-aged, but attractive woman on the other.

"Oh, my! What are you playing with over there Capri? May I have a taste?" Lalita smiled as she stepped away from her two companions. The woman reached after her, but Renzo pulled her back and locked his lips on hers. Lalita spotted the cross laying on the table. She put a hand on the man's chest and instantly his manhood went rigid. She finished removing his robe and laid it on top of the cross, hiding the offensive object from her sight.

The door popped open again. Ju-Long entered, carrying a young lady, probably in her early twenties. She had huge bosoms and was plumper than what he usually went for, but she was beautiful. "You are so strong." The woman giggled. "Are you going to tie me up and have your way with me?" He walked her over to a large couch and laid her on her back.

"Oh, I am going to do things to you that are going to make you squirm, squeal, and beg me for more," he said as he ripped open the front of her dress and watched her enormous boobs fall slightly toward either side.

Lalita was bored with the little man. He was putting in the effort, he just wasn't good at it. She occupied herself by watching Ju-Long take the big girl. She felt the so-called priest climb up from between her legs as if he would mount her. Then she felt the pain. She screamed as her flesh burned. The bastard had planted the cross just below her neck and between her breasts. "Die demon!"

Ju-Long was across the room in an instant ripping the man off Lalita. Capri grabbed the priest's hand that held the cross and crushed it. Once that dropped to the floor Ju-Long bit into the man's neck. "Vampiro!" the two human women in the room shrieked.

Renzo had gone to Lalita's side and the middle aged woman who had come in with him and Lalita made a dash out the door screaming bloody murder. Ju-Long dropped the lifeless body to the floor and helped a sobbing Lalita to her feet.

"It hurts so much!"

Ju-long spotted the larger woman who had fainted on the couch. "Take her to that woman so she can feed. I will deal with any who enter."

"We need to go, Ju-Long," Lalita pleaded.

"I will kill them all!"

Lalita grabbed his arm and pulled him toward the window. "Woman!"

"Not now, lover!" she answered as they crashed through the window.

Two naked people streaking through the air and two running just below them through the city drew some attention as they flashed by and over the people on the streets. Within minutes they reached their huge home just on the outskirts of town.

"Damn it, Lalita! I wanted to make it rain blood inside there before we made our escape!"

"And had we lingered we might have had the whole city down on us, including a garrison or more of the army. Now we have a head start to make our way out of here."

Ju-Long sent a message to their other human servants to begin loading the wagons with their treasures. The packing was underway when they walked in. The foursome went through the front of the house, Ju-Long barking orders on what to grab and what to leave, as he dashed toward the back door and out to the pond. Lalita joined him as Renzo and Capri went to dress and help with the loading.

The couple dove in the water, quickly washing the blood off Ju-Long, Lalita helping him with his long dark hair which was matted with the coagulated liquid. "This was fun while it lasted." She sighed.

"You need to feed. Is it still hurting?" The skin where the cross had touched her was charred or missing, the tissue underneath raw. He kissed her lips and she drew from him. The pain eased and the wound improved but did not go away. "You must need blood as well, Find Renzo and drink from him. I will continue to get us ready."

Lalita gathered his hair and began ringing the water out. "Where to now, my King?"

"We will send the servants south with our belongings, except Capri and Renzo. They will come with us as we head to the mountains to collect our pets."

"South? You have a destination in mind?"

"Carthage."

"Any particular reason?"

"Nope. You rather go north?"

"Doesn't matter. I've never been to Carthage. Works for me," Lalita answered, squeezing down the ponytail she held one last time. They exited the water together and headed inside.

They dressed for comfort, unlike the finery they were wearing when they started the evening. "What do we do about the others?"

"Others?" Ju-Long questioned.

"The other Raksasha we have created around the countryside as a buffer and warning system against the arrival of the chosen ones? Do we let them know that we are leaving? Do we gather them to take with us?"

"I will reach out to them with my mind and let them know we are heading to the mountains. If they wish to join us they may. I don't really care. They are merely fodder as far as I am concerned." He exited their private room and headed to check on the servant's progress. Once he had them on their way he would contact the 'Newborns' as he referred to them.

Lalita joined him after feeding on Renzo and doing a walkthrough of their home to ensure the servants hadn't missed anything important. The wound had in fact healed after taking in some blood, but it left a nasty scar. She switched clothes to hide the hideous cross shaped mutilation.

"You all will take turns driving the horses, stopping for nothing but food and water until you reach the southernmost tip of Italy. If we have not met up with you by then, seek passage by sea to Messana, Sicily. Travel across the island to Agrigentum. Wait there until we arrive, or a full week. If we haven't met up with you by then, something has turned to shit," Ju-Long instructed.

"At that point, proceed to Carthage by boat. There you will see about acquiring us a home close to the city but secluded enough for privacy. If one is not available, find a parcel of land and begin construction. I will contact you through our mental link to give the specifications of how I want it built."

"How we want it built."

"But of course, my love." Ju-Long smiled. "Now get moving, who knows when the hostile natives are going to come calling at our doorstep."

Ju-Long started reaching out to the south. He couldn't find a single one of his creations in that direction. He turned east and came up empty again. *Where are they? Have they migrated without letting me know?* He scanned north, starting on the other side of the city and reeling in toward his current location. Nothing. Nothing until he was almost back to their front door. Then he could sense one of his females. She was scared. Someone was with her, and she was afraid of him.

At first he thought the voice was in his head, but with the look Lalita gave him, Ju-Long knew she heard it, too. "Come out demon, spawn of hell. Allow me to send thee back to where thoust belong."

"Who the hell is that?" Ju-Long asked.

"I have no idea." Lalita shrugged. "But I am getting a bad vibe."

"I will not be intimidated. If this man wants me, he is going to get me, to his demise."

"Ju-Long, wait," she pleaded, but he was already heading out the front door. Renzo and Capri followed, with Lalita reluctantly falling in behind them.

When Ju-Long stepped out the front door he saw a huge man, a giant, holding the tiny Jina with one hand. He wasn't the scary one though. There was something emanating from the other man, maybe six feet tall with curly brown hair and a thick moustache and beard that sent a chill through the vampire. Maybe it was the two large crosses he held, one in each hand, which was causing Ju-Long anxiety.

"I have dispatched your 'children' save this one. She has been kind enough to bring me to thee."

"I am sorry, Master," Jina sobbed. "He promised to set me free."

"And I shall deliver on my promise right now." The giant pushed her to the ground in front of the man speaking. "Thy soul was set free when that abomination made thou what thou art. I now free the shell that remains from this evil existence." He touched the top of her head with the cross in his left hand. There was a huge flash of light that blinded Ju-Long and the others for a moment. When he could see again, Jina was reduced to a pile of ash, and the man and his enormous companion were marching toward him.

"Face me, demon! Meet thine end!"

Lalita grabbed Ju-Long by the arm. "We need to go."

"You may be right." Ju-Long wrapped an arm around Capri as Lalita did the same with Renzo. The two launched themselves skyward, bolting northeast and not looking back.

Apennines Mountains, 481 AD

Xiong was tired. How in the hell could it be so hard to locate a sixteen foot tall one eyed giant and two Minotaur? Even in these mountains. It was like they were constantly late to the scene, and the damned things kept changing directions and moving from the west side to the east side of the range. These were not like the Himalayas back home, but they were still mountains.

Argus never seemed to tire, though when he did sleep he slept soundly and awoke hungry, but refreshed. The man could eat almost as much as Wei, and most of it was meat. Xiong ate meat, but not in large quantities. Argus had to have some every day, and he was a skilled hunter. Only Ling was his equal with a bow.

Xiong was really missing his family. He also was missing Amal, especially his friend's ability to fly. Voices caught his attention. That was the thing about some parts of these mountains, voices carried. A whisper could sound like a shout and what sounded like it was right next to you could be quite a ways off.

"You hear that?" Argus asked.

"Yep."

"I'm gonna wake Kasan in case there is trouble."

Xiong nodded as he stood and drew his sword. He listened closer. The conversation seemed light, and one of the voices sounded strangely familiar. Then he heard his name. "Who is there?" He challenged. Argus drew his sword and picked up his shield. Kasan was on his feet and looked nervous. He struggled to pull his blade from its sheath.

"It's the boogie man come to call on you and your Spartan friend."

There was no way. *It can't be.* "Amal?" Xiong asked.

"And friends. Or I guess, relatives."

"How did you find us?"

Amal emerged from between two rocks, another man and two women, neither of them Meagan, right behind him. "Oh my god. I was just thinking about you."

"Well, you can thank our niece, Sona, for finding me, and then finding you."

"Niece?" Xiong looked at the girls. "My god, they are the spitting image of their mother." He could barely believe the resemblance they shared with Naina. And the man was undeniably Ling's son.

"Xiong, meet Marco, Shehani, and Sona."

Xiong smiled, sheathing his sword.

"Where is Meagan?" Argus asked.

"Good to see you to, ol' buddy." Amal frowned. "What do you think I just dumped her and left to come see you two?"

"Is she safe?"

"Yes, Argus. She took a side trip to speak with some old friends. Acquaintances of both of yours."

"Who?"

"She didn't say. She said she would be along in a couple of days."

Xiong walked over and reached out to Amal. The two shook hands, then Xiong pulled the tall man in for a hug. "So good to see you my friend." He then turned to Marcos. "It is as if I am staring at my brother once again. How is he?"

"He is fine, uncle."

"And who is Sona and who is Shehani? Goodness you two are as gorgeous as your mother." The twins smiled, both blushing a bit.

"I am Sona, and this is Shehani." Sona had her hair pulled up, while Shehani's was loose. If they chose to do their hair the same way at the same time, he wouldn't be able to tell them apart.

"So my brother and sister-in-law have three beautiful children. Amazing." Xiong grinned from ear to ear.

"Actually there are eight of us," Marco chimed in, "four sets of twins."

"What?"

"Yeah. Your brother and my sister have obviously been busy." Amal laughed.

"That is awesome! Where are the others? And what brought you three to us?"

"They are back in India. Well except Biao and Jie, they are in China helping Uncle Zhan and Uncle Wei." Marco answered.

"Biao? Jie?"

"Yes. Biao was born after we learned of Uncle Biao's death. Jie, the youngest, was named for a dear friend of yours. He also is passed."

"Is there one named Xiong?"

"No. My sister Mahika and I are the oldest, followed by these two, Biao and his twin brother, and Jie and his twin sister Chanda."

"Well good, that means I must not be dead yet." Xiong half laughed, trying to fight the pain of losing Biao.

"Biao's twin is Te, and as far as we know his namesake uncle is still alive. We have been searching for him for many, many years."

"Te. I know his heart is broken." Xiong teared up. "I just hope he is okay."

"We were tracking him to a place, where was that Sona?"

"Carthage."

"Yes, Carthage. We were headed that way when Sona felt Amal's presence and heard your pleas for help."

"My pleas for help?"

"Yes, Uncle Xiong. I could feel how much you were wanting Uncle Amal's help, so I brought him to you." Sona answered.

"Incredible. You all have powers then?"

"Yes," Shehani answered, "I have the power of magic. Marco, like our parents, is a speed freak."

"Gee, thanks, sis."

"You're welcome."

"Like dad, these two are real smartasses," Marco said, bringing a laugh from Xiong.

"I remember your father's sense of humor very well. Man do I miss him."

"Sona, over here . . ." Shehani started.

"I can speak for myself," Sona scorned. "I am like Uncle Amal with his telekinesis. Yes, I can levitate myself, thanks for asking."

"But I didn't."

"You thought it," Marco said, "she can read minds as well."

"Show-off." Shehani stuck her tongue out at her sister.

"Can I hug you first?" Xiong asked as he moved toward Sona, scooping her up in a huge embrace. "Wow, I just had such a strong urge to do this." He said as he held her off the ground while she giggled.

"She also has the power of suggestion," Marco added.

"But only over the weak minded," Shehani said, drawing a laugh from Argus. Kasan was standing there confused.

"Wow, you really are my brother's children," Xiong replied as he set Sona back down on the ground.

"So, how does the hunt for Ju-Long and Lalita go?" Amal asked.

"Almost had them in Sicily," Argus answered.

"Not sure where they are now, but they've left their calling card here in the mountains," Xiong added.

"More Raksasha?" Amal took a sip from his flask.

"That wine?" Kasan asked.

"Just water."

"Damn!"

"You wouldn't be getting any anyways." Argus shot Kasan a look.   "It's actually worse than that. There are two blood drinking Minotaur and a blood sucking cyclops running around here."

"Shit. That is worse." Amal shook his head. "Uh, what the fuck is a cyclops?"

"A one-eyed giant," Xiong answered.

"Hell, I got one of those." Amal laughed.

"Knew that was going to come up at some point." Xiong shook his head.

"Well, it's not technically up at the moment."

"Really? In front of the children, Amal?"

"I'm sixty, Uncle Xiong," Marco said.

"We are fifty-two."

"Seriously?" Xiong looked at the girls who didn't look a day over seventeen.

"Hell, the youngest twins are thirty-six," Amal said.

"Wow, time flies when you are in the middle of nowhere for close to a century." Xiong laughed.

"So," Shehani interrupted, "we are here to help. Where would you like us to start?"

***

"The chosen one named Xiong is close. And as a special surprise, it would appear our good friend Amal has rejoined him after all these years. I can't penetrate their minds, but I can see through their human companion Kasan what they are up to. They hunt our pets. They have the one you call Argus with them, as well as two nieces and a nephew, the spawn of Ling and your girl Naina. Apparently their disease is spreading as well," Ju-Long said sarcastically.

"So, what do we do?"

"We end this. There is a reason I have been procreating on our trip, and taken our time getting to Brontes, Agnes, and Ander.

We have twenty newborns, and a total of ten human servants. It was all in preparation for battle."

"I assumed it was for the cross man and his giant, in case they were pursuing us."

"It was, but it was also for them. They nearly got to us in Sicily. I do not want them, or that cross carrying freak on our backs when we get to Carthage." He stood up, waiting impatiently for his small army to rise. He wasn't going to wait for the enemy to come to him. Ju-Long would launch an attack as soon as night fell. His pets and his people would feed on chosen ones' blood this evening.

***

Amal, Sona, and Shehani (who could use magic to levitate) had scoured the area by air. They had found a couple of caverns, but no demons. They would have to fly at night, hoping to spot the giant and the Minotaur as they hunted. They had returned to camp, where Xiong and Argus had a meal prepared. It was maybe an hour until dark, when the threesome would return to the skies and search once more.

"I'm telling you they are here," Xiong said.

"Who is here?" Amal asked, moving over to where Marco, Argus and Xiong sat by the fire.

"Xiong thinks he can sense Ju-Long in the area," Argus answered.

"I know it is him. He is shielding hard, but he is here. And I believe he knows where we are."

"How? You have taught me how to shield, Amal already knew, and the kids were taught by your brother Zhan years ago in their training in China," Argus scoffed, "how could he possibly track us?"

"Hey guys, what's up?" Kasan walked toward them. "That smells delicious."

"Oh shit." Xiong shook his head.

"Oh shit?"

`'"Yes, Kasan. Ladies and gentleman, let me introduce you to the vessel Ju-Long is using to spy on us." Xiong waved a hand in Kasan's direction. "I am so stupid! Why didn't I realize it before?"

"What did I do?" Kasan looked puzzled.

"Nothing. Do me a favor and look me in the eye." Xiong stood. "Hello, Ju-Long. I can feel your presence in my friend here. I hope you are enjoying your last night on earth. I don't know what your plan is, but know that we are ready. See you soon."

Amal leaned down into Kasan's face. "Say hi to Lalita for me."

"Lalita. Yeah, tell her Argus says hello as well." The Spartan smiled.

Kasan's face changed, and a booming voice that was not his own came from his mouth. "You are all dead! I am coming!" Then their human friend screamed in agony, fell to the ground and seized right in front of them, his body convulsing, foam dripping from his mouth. Kasan's eyes rolled into the back of his head, his normal voice back pleading for help. Then he went still.

Xiong knelt beside him. "He still breaths." He placed two fingers on Kasan's neck. "His pulse is feint." Xiong looked up at Argus. "Kasan is ice cold."

"Let's move him closer to the fire. Marco, can you grab some blankets?"

"On it, Uncle Amal."

"Sona, can you lay hands on him and see if you can help?" Xiong asked as he and Argus carefully moved Kasan's body."

"I will try." She knelt down next to where they laid Kasan.

"Uh, we have another problem," Marco said. They all turned in his direction. A giant stood there, next to a smaller man, a little shorter than Xiong, holding two crosses. He wore a long black robe with a high collar, a small white square over where his Adam's apple set.

Argus and Xiong drew swords. Shehani readied herself, and Marco stepped back, his blade flashing in his hand almost instantly. Sona never took her hands off the sides of Kasan's face as she watched them.

"Who are you?" Argus challenged.

"Your friend is hurt. I can help."

Argus took a more aggressive stance. "Not what I asked. Who are you?" he growled.

"I am John of Judea. I was not sure if I was going to be friend or foe when we met, but sensing your auras I am a friend, if thou allows it."

Xiong got a puzzled look on his face. *John of Judea? Where do I know that name from?* His mind was churning.

"And who is your companion? Is he friend or foe?"

"He is a friend as well, Argus. He goes by Goliath."

"How do you know my name? Are you some sort of wizard or warlock?"

"Neither. I heard you say your name when you were asking someone to say hi to Lalita for you."

Goliath? So familiar as well. Xiong thought. "How long have you been here listening to us?"

"Long enough to know you are Xiong, the tall man is Amal, and this little man is Marco." Marco shot the one calling himself John a look. "I know the women are Shehani and Sona, though I know not which is which."

Then it hit Xiong. "Are you John the Baptist? From the Vulgate?"

"Ah, thou has read the Vulgate? The Word of the Lord my God, both before and after the coming of his Son, my Savior."

"Yes. But how do you live now? You were beheaded."

"There is that. By Herod Antipas. Well, it was his wife that ordered my death, actually. She was never a fan."

"There is only one way a man walks the earth after death, and that is in the form of a demon. A Vrykolakas!" Argus snarled.

"I am neither. When Christ rose from the dead, then ascended to heaven, I was resurrected. He left me and His Holy Spirit to watch over His flock and continue His work here on earth."

"I do not believe in such things."

John went to answer, but Xiong cut him off. "Did the demons not scatter, many being forced back to Hell when the Light came? Did you not witness that yourself my old friend?" He looked at Argus.

"The Light. Yes my Savior Jesus Christ. Through him all things are possible." John smiled. He was starting to like this Xiong. "His life and death were for all of us, as we may someday inherit the Kingdom of Heaven."

Argus lowered his sword, but kept in his hand. "Okay, maybe there is a shade of truth to his story."

"A shade of truth?" John laughed. "He is the Way, the Truth, and the Light, my Jesus."

Another thought struck Xiong. "Is he the Goliath that was slain by David in the Books of the Hebrews?"

"Well now, you are a student of the Word. But no, he is not. I found him beaten and broken years ago and used the power of my God to heal him. He has been by my side for over three centuries."

"Something beat that into submission?" Shehani asked.

"Yes. Another giant. A cyclops named Brontes." Goliath grunted when John spoke the cyclops's name.

Xiong gave a surprised look. "We hunt a cyclops in these mountains, turned blood sucker by Ju-Long."

"Ju-Long? He is one of many demons I hunt. He escaped me, running like a coward from the power of my God when I first found him in Rome. He, his woman, and two others flew in this direction."

"He is here. We hunt him as well. I have hunted him from China, where he was created by the devils in Hell."

"There is only one devil in Hell. The others just serve him. Just as there is only one true God. All others bow to Him."

"What does he keep grunting for?"

"It is how he communicates, Argus."

"He cannot speak?"

"He has no tongue. Brontes cut it out. Conflict over a giantess. Brontes wanted her, but she was in love with Goliath."

"What happened to her?"

"When she saw Goliath was losing, she tried to intervene. That's when Brontes left my big friend here crumpled on the ground, his tongue already removed, and turned on her." Goliath let out a huge huff and pounded his forehead with his fist. "Brontes killed her." The giant turned his back on the group and let out a roar.

"Damn. Sorry big guy." Amal said honestly.

"There is not much I can do for him," Sona said, referring to Kasan. "His pulse and breathing are better, but his mind has been shattered. Other than keeping his heart beating and his breath flowing, his brain isn't really functioning."

"May I?" John asked.

"How do we know you are who you say you are? How do we know you aren't actually working for Ju-Long?" Argus remained skeptical.

"I promise you we share the same goals, if not the same ideals. But maybe this will help prove to you I am who I say I am." He tapped Goliath on the back. When the Giant turned he handed him the two crosses. "There is a reason I wear my collar so high." John took both hands and pulled it down to expose his neck. There was a scar running across the front and back the sides. "I assure everyone here that it runs full circle around my neck."

"Help him if you can." Argus relented. "But big boy there keeps his distance." He pointed his blade at the giant.

John nodded and walked over to where Kasan lie. "If I may trade you places young lady," he asked Sona. She stood and moved back. John knelt where she once was, placing his hands on the man's cheeks just as she had. He bowed his head and closed his eyes.

Xiong was standing close and could feel something in the air, it wasn't like what he felt when Te did his thing, but it was peaceful and brought love to his heart. He wondered if anyone else felt it. A smile came across Kasan's face. Then Xiong noticed his chest was no longer rising and falling.

"What the Hell? You killed him!" Argus had noticed it too, the point of his sword nearly touching the collar on John's neck.

"I have merely released him, as he asked me to."

"Asked you? He never uttered a fucking word." Argus caught Goliath stepping toward them. "You might wanna back off monster, lest I shove this through his neck faster than you can blink."

"Be at ease my friend. I will be fine. Do as the man asks." John looked softly up into Argus' eyes. *"Yea, though I walk through the valley of the shadow of death, I shall fear no evil: for Thou art with me."*

"Yea, though I walk through the valley of the shadow of death, I shall fear no evil:" Argus mocked him, *"for I am the baddest motherfucker in the valley."* This drew an abbreviated giggle from Shehani.

"What do you mean you did what he asked?" Xiong tried to ease the tension.

"I asked your friend if he believed that Jesus died for his sins, and if he sought that forgiveness now."

"And?" Argus spat.

"He said yes. Then I asked him if he wanted to be with his wife and children in heaven, or if he wished to return to this life. He smiled and said *Arianna*. That was his wife's name?"

Xiong nodded.

"Thou sees the smile on his face, the peace that has come over him. Do thou not?"

"I felt something, and it was positive," Sona said.

"As did I." Xiong wiped a tear from his eye. "Do you know if my brother Biao is in heaven? He never knew your God. We are Buddhists."

"My God is a loving God. He died for all. If you know and believe in Him, paradise is yours. However, he does not shun those who did right in life, but were never taught of His Glory. If you brother was a man like you, rest assured he has entered Heaven and is the loving arms of the Lord."

Another tear streamed down Xiong's face. "Thank you. Argus, please allow our friend to stand." Argus looked over at him and Xiong nodded. He pulled his sword back and lowered the tip to the ground.

"I will make a believer out of you yet." John smiled at Argus.

"Yeah, good luck with that." Argus frowned.

***

"Did you sleep with the fucking Spartan, too?" Ju-Long yelled.

"That was a long time ago, Ju-Long."

"I know. It just gives me another reason to kill him. Him and that smug Amal. That one I want to torture."

"And so we shall, my love." Lalita would like to bring Amal death as well. Fuck him to death.

"They know I am here, and they have backup, but they don't know about the little army I have collected, so surprise is still on our side." He grinned.

"You said earlier Naina's twin daughters are with them. What do they look like?"

"Just like their mother."

"Oh! Can we keep one?" She licked her lips.

"I wouldn't mind if we kept them both, but first we must destroy the rest. If the girls survive we will make them our play things."

Lalita smiled. "I want to take you right here, right now," she whispered as she wrapped her arms around her man.

***

"So, we have three high points around our camp, there, there and there." Argus pointed to the three peaks. "Amal, you take the one north, Shehani you cover east, and Sona gets the south. Xiong and I will be right here, using the rocks for cover until we see the enemy approaching. Marco, since you are our speed merchant and great with the bow, I want you to find a comfortable spot that doesn't leave you exposed, but puts you in the best position to use your skill set."

"What about us?" John asked, referring to Goliath and himself.

"You said Ju-Long saw your display when you deployed one of your crosses on a Vrykolakas right in front of him and he ran like a coward?"

"Technically, flew off like a coward."

"Either way, we want to end this here. Your presence might spook him, so I want you and the big fella out of sight until we have drawn them in."

"And where would thou like us to hide?"

"Down the trail heading east there is a cavern on the right. Conceal yourself there until the battle begins, then come out crosses blazing." John laughed at that statement.

"Will do, Argus."

"And if Goliath there wants a piece of the cyclops, tell him to go for it."

"He can hear and understand you, he just can't talk."

"Right." Argus looked at the giant. "I'll be your backup, or you can be mine. Either way, that is going to be one dead cyclops after tonight." Goliath nodded and let out a grunt.

"That grunt mean yes?" Argus looked back at John.

"The nod was a yes. The grunt was . . ."

"Good god, what is that smell?" Argus coughed. The others, save John, were gagging.

"A fart," John finished.

***

"Five of our newborns can fly. You and I will lead them, coming in from the south. The Minotaur will pair up with three of our non-flyers and come from the west, another two will attack from the east with Brontes. Then each of the remaining will be paired up with a human servant and come in from the north. I will send a mental signal to everyone so we are all converging on the enemy simultaneously from all directions. We will use arrows to take them out if we can, and swords when the fight gets in close," Ju-Long said, reviewing the plan with Lalita. "Your main job, besides staying alive, is to capture one of the twins. I will be killing Xiong, then capturing Amal. The Minotaur will be taking out Argus, and Brontes will be grabbing which ever twin you don't."

"You trust Brontes not to eat her?"

"He has been given implicit instruction not to consume the child."

"That's a relief." Lalita rolled her eyes.

"His penalty for doing so is death. Now, all have risen, all know their jobs, and we are set to go."

"What about the twins' brother? You haven't mentioned him."

"Well if one of the twenty newborns and ten servant's don't get him, I guess I'll have to add killing him to my list of things to do," Ju-Long huffed.

***

"Shit! I am sensing xiang shi on all sides. Ju-Long has brought reinforcements."

"How many?"

"At least a score. I need to let Amal and the twins know. At least five are coming by air!" Xiong closed his eyes and started with Amal, then Shehani, and by the time he reached Sona, his niece was in a fight with Lalita.

"Incoming!" Argus shouted. Ju-Long and the two Minotaur were flying right toward them. He sent and arrow flying, and the larger of the two Minotaur rolled out of the line of fire. *Damn! They are faster than before!* He thought, reloading just in time to have the other Minotaur slam into him.

Marco saw Argus' arrow miss its mark before firing his own. He caught the one he assumed was Ju-Long in the side. The Raksasha spiraled in the air, letting out a roar. He reloaded and took aim but could not fire safely on the second Minotaur as it tackled Argus to the ground. He located the other one and took aim as a huge hand came out of nowhere and grabbed him.

Xiong had instantly dropped his bow at Argus' warning and grabbed his sword. An arrow had caught Ju-Long before he reached him. Xiong looked over to see Argus fighting a female Minotaur and prepared to help him when an arrow struck him in the leg, and then another in his right arm. He fell to the ground and heard two more whiz by him.

Goliath saw his mortal enemy just as he grabbed the young man. *Brontes!* He leapt on the cyclops' back with all one thousand pounds of him and wrapped a heavily muscled arm around its neck, grabbing that arm with his other hand to sink the choke in deeper. Brontes let go of the boy as they both fell backwards.

Marco laid on the ground gasping for breath. There were broken ribs on both sides as the cyclops nearly squeezed the life out of him before something caused the behemoth to drop him.

He struggled to his hands and knees, wincing in pain. He looked around for his bow but it was nowhere in sight.

There were two vampiros with the cyclops. John jumped on the one's back sending them both to the ground. He brought the cross down on the demon's neck and it turned to dust under him. The other had disappeared on the other side of the fighting gargantuans.

Argus had kicked the Minotaur off and freed himself. Xiong had pulled the arrow out of his arm and was trying to get the one in his leg. Argus stood to help his friend and caught two arrows himself, one in his lower back and one in the back of his deltoid.

Amal watched his second friend go down from his northern perch. He had tracked and sent an arrow through the heart of one of the Raksasha that had fired on Xiong, and the eye of the human servant with him. He spotted the pair that had just taken down Argus and sent two their way.

Ju-Long had hit the ground hard, and was momentarily dazed. He had landed behind a boulder, out of the line of any fire, but this shit was getting old. With a roar he yanked the arrow from just below his rib cage and stood, peeking over the rock he was concealed behind. To his delight Xiong and Argus were wounded and on the ground. Agnes was heading toward them and she looked pissed. Ander was in the air flying at them from the other direction. *Time to die!* Ju-long flew over the rock and headed straight for Xiong.

Amal saw Ju-long emerge. He had taken down four and had no other visible target, so he grasped two arrows and readied to send them in Ju-Long's direction. Something hit him from the right and Amal tumbled, the arrows sailing in two different directions. A

Raksasha was on him. They landed on a ledge six feet down from the one he had been on, its fangs sinking into his left shoulder.

Sona was nowhere near strong enough to fight this bitch hand to hand, and the demon was too old to fall for her mind tricks. Luckily the woman was not trying to kill her, but seemed to be trying to take her prisoner. She felt the power she held, attempting to . . . *seduce me?* Sona was blocking with all she had but there was something stirring inside her. A need was growing and she wasn't sure she could stop it.

Shehani had let the flying Raksasha get closer before she unleashed her stun spell. When she hit them with it the two stalled and dropped out of the air. One plunged out of sight while the other fell twenty feet smacking head first into a rock. She heard its skull crack and saw the blood spatter everywhere. It looked dead, but she grabbed a stake from her belt and levitated down to be sure.

Marco looked up to see the vamp coming at him. He waited til the last minute then rolled left as it lunged for him. It sailed by, but as he laid there on his back he could see the demon spin around and come straight for him. The roll had aggravated his injuries and there was no way he was going to avoid it this time.

Just as it was about to pounce, a light flashed blinding him momentarily. When he could see again he was covered in ash and John was standing over him. "You alright, young one?" Marco tried to answer, but only managed to cough up blood. "I am going to take that as a no." The man said as he knelt down beside him.

Brontes was stronger and faster than the first time they fought, but then again so was he. The cyclops and its nearly two thousand pounds had knocked the wind out of him when they landed, but Goliath had managed to keep his grip. The beast stood, rammed him into a boulder, reached back and grabbed his hair trying to throw him, resulting in a clump of it being yanked out and blood trailing down the back of his neck, but he held on for dear life.

Xiong was lifted off his feet and tossed across the camp. When he landed and looked up, his shoulder on fire from taking the brunt of the impact, Ju-Long was bearing down on him again. He caught a glimpse of Argus being beaten by both Minotaur as he desperately worked to keep them from sinking fangs into him.

Ju-Long saw the arrow too late as it took him in the chest, just missing his heart. The pain was the worst he had ever felt, and he stumbled to the ground. He reached for the arrow and pulled it, but was weak from blood loss and the placement of the second bolt to find him tonight. He slumped to the ground still trying to free himself of the missile.

Xiong heard hoof beats approaching even before the arrow took Ju-Long in the chest. He glanced behind him to see Meagan on the back of a creature that was part horse and part man. Close behind was a female version of the man horse. Meagan had fired the shot that hit Ju-Long, while the other creatures sent two arrows into the male Minotaur, giving Argus a fighting chance.

Agnes ate a right from Argus as she watched the centaur and its female rider sink two more arrows into the fallen Ander. Her lover went still. The blow she received knocked her sideways, and into the back hooves of the rider less female centauride whose kick sent her flying twenty feet through the air.

Amal had found a large stone to his right and picked it up. He bashed the demon on the side of its head three times before it released its bite. He smacked it again as he rolled on top of it.

Amal dropped the rock and grabbed a stake plunging it into the heart of the unconscious blood sucker.

Brontes had finally broken free from Goliath's chokehold and the two behemoths were now trading blows. Bronte's punches were staggering, and hitting him was like hitting a stone wall. Goliath was holding his own, far better than their first fight, but both of them were bleeding and getting weary. Brontes had never tried to bite him in their original go round, but now all he seemed to want to do was sink fangs in him.

A vicious left sent Goliath to the ground. He countered with a leg sweep that put the cyclops on its back. The giant got to his feet first and planted a foot in the one eyed freak's face as it sat up. He reached down and hefted a boulder next to him and pressed it over his head.

Brontes had taken the moment to grab a handful of dirt and slung it into his opponent's eyes. Goliath let out a groan and slammed the rock down. He was wanting to crush the cyclops head with it, but blinded as he was, he only managed to smash its foot. Brontes howled in pain as bones crunched beneath the weight of the stone.

Goliath stumbled backwards as he rubbed his eyes. He tumbled over a bush and landed on his ass. He needed water to flush his eyes with, but that wasn't going to happen anytime soon. He grunted three times, hoping John was near enough to hear his call.

Xiong got to his feet about the same time as Ju-Long. He watched his nemesis finally pull the arrow from his chest. The demon was weak, but still dangerous, He drew two stakes, one in each hand, from his belt and strode toward the enemy.

Angry and injured, Ju-Long weighed his options. One of his Minotaur was down, Agnes was nowhere to be seen, and there were new players in the game. Some bitch had come to Xiong's rescue, bringing two human horse creatures with her. He glanced skyward and saw Lalita overhead carrying an unconscious woman, one of the twins.

He stared at Xiong for a moment as the chosen one advanced on him. He peeked over his shoulder and saw the woman had dismounted and was helping Argus up. They were both looking in his direction. The horse people were gone. He looked back at Xiong who was moving slow but getting closer. "Next time, you die. Right now I have a date with your niece. I bet she tastes sweet."

"Damn it!" Xiong yelled as Ju-Long flew off. "They have one of the twins!"

"Which one? Argus asked.

"They have my sister?" Shehani walked up behind her uncle.

Amal killed the one flying Raksasha just in time to have another one jump on his back and sink fangs into his opposite shoulder. This one was a female. He was weak from the previous blood loss, and this wasn't going to help. He knew how to play this one though. She was in for a surprise. He reached back and grabbed her hair. Not harshly, more like a lover would, and ran his fingers through it.

She let out a muffled coo, still drinking from him, but he could feel energy starting to trickle from her into his fingertips. He concentrated harder, using his telekinesis to work her womanhood. She released her bite and moaned. He let go of her hair and turned himself until he was looking into her eyes.

Amal put his mouth on hers and she accepted his tongue. She moaned as he continued to kiss her, lost in pleasure as he sucked the life force from her. He felt her mouth go dry and her breasts shrivel up. He broke the kiss and drew back. She looked to be two hundred years old. He grabbed a stake and jammed it through her chest.

"Thanks, honey," Amal said, feeling great. The ancient looking, now rotting corpse was disgusting, but his injuries were healed. "Next!"

Marco was healed. John had laid hands on him, and at first he worried the man might be 'freeing him from this existence', but he actually repaired the damage and let him live. The pair had went on to kill three more vampires and two human servants. Then John heard Goliath grunt for help, and the duo ran to him.

"It's his eyes. Get some water Marco, I need to rinse them out for him."

"Can't you just pray them clean?"

"It's not an injury, sort to speak. Quickly, get the water. Hang on Goliath. I got thee."

He turned back and saw Marco still behind him. "What are you waiting for?"

Marco handed him a flask. "Here it is."

"You had some on you?"

"Nope. Other side of camp."

"My God, you are fast."

John washed the giant's eyes out as Marco held his bow at the ready, scanning all around them. When Goliath could see, he made several grunts and threw his hands in the air.

"I don't know where Brontes went."

"You can understand him?"

"Three centuries together, you learn a lot of things."

Agnes was being pursued by the centaurs. She was moving through the trees as fast as she could, but they were gaining on her. She just needed an opening in the thick canopy the trees provided to take flight. She wanted to kill them for killing Ander, but that would be another time. Right now she had to protect what was growing inside her.

Amal landed to find a bloody Xiong hugging a crying Shehani. Argus was hurting and the only good thing about the whole scene was Meagan was there. "What is wrong? We are all still alive, aren't we?"

"They took Sona." Meagan answered.

"What? Who?"

"Ju-Long and Lalita."

"Which direction!"

"They are gone," Xiong said.

"I asked which fucking direction!"

"Southeast."

Amal wrapped a long arm around Meagan and flew into the air. "I'm coming too!" Shehani said, joining the couple in the air.

Amal looked back at her. "Stay here!"

"Fuck you!" Shehani said. "See, I can curse as well!"

The threesome turned southeast, flying as fast as they could.

Goliath, John and Marco went down the east trail, following the small puddles of blood and the awkward footsteps of an injured giant. They followed the step drag pattern right to the cavern where John and Goliath had hidden before the battle began. Brontes was inside, but only by a few feet. The cyclops was bleeding heavily, his breaths coming in gasps.

"John the Baptist," Brontes let out in a moan, "never thought I'd see you, or your lackey, again."

"I will show mercy and end this quickly for thou, demon." John twirled the crosses in his hand. Goliath shot his hand out, nudging his small friend back. He grunted twice, shaking his head and jabbing his thumb into his chest. "You Sure?" John asked.

Goliath nodded, picking up a big stone in his right hand. He straddled the cyclops chest and was ready to bash Brontes' skull into a million pieces. The enemy was playing possum. As Goliath lifted his right arm over his head, Brontes lifted his hips off the floor, simultaneously bringing his right arm hard behind Goliath's back, reaching all the way to his left. When both of their bodies landed, Bronte's head was between Goliath's legs, but he was on top.

Marco drew a dagger. "Where is the cyclops heart? Same place as a human?"

"Yes," John answered. "But that..." A flash went by him. Brontes and Goliath were engaged once again. The cyclops had popped up to where his torso was above the giant's waist, but Goliath had his legs around his opponent's hips and there was no way Brontes was going to mount him.

The cyclops made a critical error. He pinned Goliath's left hand down with his own right and proceeded to choke the giant with his left. Goliath still held the stone in his right hand and clobbered Brontes with it. Blood came from a new place on the behemoth's left temple. The cyclops roared. Goliath quickly blasted him again and again as Brontes fell right, becoming unconscious.

Then Marco was there, driving the pointed end of a small tree trunk into Brontes' thick chest. Almost instantly the smell in the cavern went from bad to worse as the demon cyclops began to rot. "Step aside, gentlemen," John said as he laid both crosses side by side on Brontes' huge abdomen. Light flashed from the crosses, however, this time it wasn't so bright that Marco was blinded. He watched as rivers of red-yellow-orange ran through the gargantuan's body just below the surface of the skin. It seemed to be following the network of veins and vessels that traveled through the cyclops. Then, as the glowing streaks running down from the lower cross hit the giant's feet, and the ones traveling up from the top cross reached the head John yelled "Close your eyes and your mouths."

The light flashed bright and ash flew everywhere. All three men choked and coughed as some of the flying particles ran up their noses. A few minutes later when the ashes began to settle they were able to open their eyes enough to exit the cave. The threesome were all covered in dust. Sucking in the cool night air was refreshing, but threw Marco and John into another brief coughing fit. They held their breath as they brushed themselves and each other off.

"Well, this has been a quite exciting night. Shall we see what's left?" John commented.

Petraios had gotten one shot off, hitting the Minotaur in the lower right leg, as the beast escaped through the forest canopy and into the night sky. His wife, Hylonome had only been a second behind, but that was long enough to keep her from having a clear shot. Disappointed, the centaur and his woman headed back toward the camp.

There was a momentary showdown as Marco and company met up with the centaurs. John and Goliath knew what they were, but had never met the pair. Marco had no clue as to what these creatures were. Thankfully, one from either side had a cooler head. Cooler heads always prevail. John and Hylonome, the female centauride, had started a dialogue that led to someone named Meagan that John had never met, Argus, who he was quite familiar with, and a mutual disdain for Minotaur.

"You two smaller ones want a ride?" Petraios asked, "It will be faster."

"You think so?" Marco asked, then shot off in a blur.

"Can you do that, too?" Hylonome asked.

"I'm fast, but not that fast. Probably not even as fast as either of you. I'll take a lift."

"Well, hop on John of Judea." She smiled at him.

Goliath looked at Petraios. "Don't even think about it, big fella. I'm a centaur, not a cent-ox." The centaur snorted before taking off behind Hylonome.

The bleeding had stopped for both Xiong and Argus, but the pain wasn't going to go anywhere soon. "What the hell were those things that rode in with Meagan to save us?"

"You mean the centaurs, Petraios and Hylonome?"

"Whatever those horse people were."

"They are centuries old my friend. Meagan and I have known them for a long time. They are good folk. Not all centaur can be trusted, but these two I'd walk through the gates of Hades with and never worry about my back." Argus had found two flasks and tossed one to Xiong. His was water, but he knew the flask Argus had held something stronger.

The two talked and drank until they saw the centaur, the giant, and John approach. "What took you so long?" A voice called from their right. Marco was perched on a boulder off to the side laughing. *How in the hell did we miss him coming back?* Xiong thought.

"We got the cyclops and a couple of the vampiros. I see the Minotaur there has had better days," John said. "How is everyone?" He looked around. "And where are the rest?"

"Ju-Long and Lalita took Sona. Amal, Meagan and Shehani went after them by air."

"Which way did they head?" Marco asked.

"Southwest," Xiong said. Before he could say anything else his nephew was gone.

"You are hurt," John asked, seeing the dried blood all over Xiong and Argus, "who would like me to heal them first?"

"I'll be just fine on my own. The last one I saw you *heal* is no longer with us," Argus spat. "Petraios, my old friend, can I get a lift? I'm going after the kid and the others."

"Climb aboard, Spartan." The pair headed down the trail.

"What sayeth thou? Whilst thou allow my Lord to heal thee through this vessel? I assure thee I will not be sending you to meet my God at this moment."

"Heal away," Xiong answered.

Soon enough John was riding on the back of Hylonome as Goliath and a renewed Xiong ran down the trail with them. They found two stray Vrykolakas along the way, taking them both prisoner. When they refused to talk, John touched the more defiant one's head with the cross in his left hand. Xiong had never seen it before. There was a blinding light and then a pile of ash.

John reached toward the second vampiro with the cross in his right hand. "And do you have anything to say, now?" The blood sucker coward, closing his eyes and turning his head away from John.

"I will take you to our lair, where we were last night and yesterday. Please just promise you will set me free!"

"I promise," John answered. Unfortunately, the vampire didn't know what John meant when he said that.

***

Ju-Long had found Capri and Renzo on his flight out of there and blood fed enough off both of them to heal himself. They, along with Lalita and the twin, had bypassed their cavern from last night and headed to the city of Volsinii, far enough northeast of Rome so they wouldn't be recognized, yet out of the mountains where the chosen ones would undoubtedly spend quite a bit of time looking for them.

They had taken over a good size esstate, killing and or consuming the residents, their servants, and three annoyingly protective dogs. He and Lalita had two good human servants watching the perimeter, and a beautiful plaything they could use for their pleasure until night fell once more. Lalita was even more excited to get to work on the young beauty than he was.

***

Agnes headed east out of the mountains, then north toward a cavern she was familiar with. It was a safe distance from where the battle commenced, where she lost Ander, yet close to Ravenna, a good sized city on the Adriatic Sea. That would allow her to have ready access to food during the gestation period.

She removed the arrow from her calf and fed on three villagers she happened upon, consuming blood, bone and flesh. There were two more with them, a male and a female. Agnes knocked them both out, then continued to the cavern. She was contemplating a couple of different options. Agnes had not had to survive on her own since she met her first love on the island of Crete. She had been forced to leave there because of Argus' presence and dedication to Ju-Long, her new master at the time.

Agnes wasn't even sure he was still alive. What she did know was that Ander, the father of her offspring, was truly dead and never coming back. Those fucking centaurs would pay for that one day. For now she just needed to focus on her pregnancy.

Agnes had seen Ju-Long create more of his own kind, and turn regular humans into superhuman servants. She looked at the man and woman, still unconscious, wondering if she too could pull such things off.

***

It was nearly dawn when Xiong and company reached the lair where Ju-Long and his minion had stayed yesterday. Argus, Petraios, and Marco had joined them, while Amal and Meagan along with Shehani had checked in earlier, and only now flew in again as they all readied to enter the cave. They found two

Vrykolakas and three human servants held up there. The fight was brief and unproductive, as none of them had any clue where Ju-Long was. Xiong reached out but couldn't find any sign of them. Sona was either dead, or Ju-Long was shielding hard to keep him from finding her.

This was turning into a disaster, harder than any of them could have imagined. Marco and Shehani knew the peril their sister was in/ They had all walked in on their mother and father being raped by a coven of blood suckers. Marco was fuming, and Shehani was bawling her eyes out. Xiong went to comfort his niece, while John went to Marco.

"Peace be with you, my child," he said as he laid a hand on Marco's shoulder. Marco could feel the tension release from his body, even though he didn't want it to. "We will find her. She will make it through this. I have prayed. The Lord will lead us to her. We must remain strong and believe. Trust in my God. Through Him all things are possible."

"I hope you are right, John."

***

Sona awoke to the dark. They had blindfolded her and she could feel her wrists and ankles were chained. She was cold, shivering actually, and knew that except the dark cloth covering her eyes she was naked.

"Oh, you are awake? I knew I had drained you more than I had planned on, but you just taste so fucking good, I couldn't stop myself. I haven't tasted anything so sweet since your mother and I rolled in the sand on the west coast of India a long time ago," Lalita said, smacking her lips at the end. "Oh, and then there was your uncle, who gave me the same power of telekinesis you have. But you have a couple of tricks up your sleeve he doesn't, don't you?" She giggled. "So sorry that I am way too old and powerful for you to read my mind, or fall for your pathetic power of suggestion."

Sona remained silent. She could feel the bitch's eyes roaming over her body as she heard the light footsteps circle around her. She knew she was going to be molested. She knew it was going to be painful and violent, especially when the male demon came along. *I will not scream. I will not cry.*

Lalita looked over the young girl's incredible body. There was a lot packed on that five foot nothing frame. She was petite, but blossomed in all the right places, from her heavy breasts, to her curvy hips, bodacious ass, and smooth, toned, thick thighs. Lalita, who was in Sona's head, laughed a little when she heard the girl's thoughts.

"Oh you will scream, and moan, and coo, and beg for more! Just like your uncle Amal did. Wow, what an enormous unit he has. Do you know if your brother is endowed like your uncle?" Lalita took in the sight of the girl's unblemished creamy tan skin. She was covered in goose bumps. "Cold?" Lalita asked, "I will warm you up soon enough, darling."

***

They had all decided to take a couple hours break to regroup and rethink. Xiong had now seen John's crosses turn four xiang shi into ash with a mere touch. He was curious as to what made those crosses so powerful.

"I have heard that the cross, a symbol of your God, has the ability to ward off evil. The ones you carry not only ward it off, they annihilate it. Why is that? Is your faith that strong?"

"My faith is strong, but the power comes from God, not me. These crosses are special. Jesus Christ, my Lord and Savior was crucified, giving His life and blood so that man could be forgiven from sin and know eternal life with Him. These crosses were made from the wood my Lord was crucified from. His blood has become a part of the wood itself, having soaked in while He hung there. The blood from the many lashes about His body as they beat and whipped him, the blood from the crown of thorns they shoved on His head, and then the blood that flowed from the stakes they drove through His hands and feet to hold Him in place during His crucifixion."

John paused and pointed to an area that was stained darker than the others. "This spot is from the wound that occurred when a Roman soldier drove a spear into His side. They didn't just kill Him, they tortured Him, made Him suffer as if He were a common criminal."

"So the Blood of Jesus, the Blood that washes away our sins, according to your Bible, is ingrained in that wood?"

"Exactly."

"So how does it turn blood suckers to dust?"

"The Light turns back the dark. No evil can handle the touch of something so pure—lest they burn," John explained, "it is only younger or lesser demons who turn to ash in one big flash, older more powerful ones are more resilient, and rarely stick around long enough to be destroyed by it once they realize what it is."

"Just curiously, if something happened to you in battle, could someone else pick it up and get the same results?"

"I'm not sure. That's never came up. I've let Goliath hold them for me so I could tend to the injured or what not. He has never tried to deploy them on the enemy." John shook his head. "Good question. I imagine if we ever find out it means I'm having a really bad day. The worst day since Herod's wife had my head lopped off."

***

Lalita fed from the energy in Sona through touch, and bit into the girl's neck to sample the sweet nectar that ran through her veins. After, she helped her prisoner sit up and brought her fruit, bread, and water.

"You must eat and drink, dear. You have a long, long day ahead of you."

"You mean a 'Ju-Long' day ahead of her." The demon chuckled as he entered the room. Sona cringed at the sound of his voice and knew things were about to get worse.

"Well hello, lover. Where have you been?"

"Renzo found two more people hiding, a servant girl and a teenage boy. They were having sex in an oversized closet."

"Did you kill them?"

"Nope. But we have two more servants now."

***

Argus was still being too stubborn to let John lay hands on him. The wounds would take a couple of days to heal on their own. He sat in the saddle on Petraios' back, emptying his fifth flask of wine. If he was in pain, he sure didn't know it. To Xiong it looked like he was getting drunk enough to be a liability instead of an asset in battle.

Amal and Shehani were in the air, staying together as they scanned the mountains for any sign of the enemy. On the ground Xiong, Argus, and Petraios made up one group. Hylonome, Meagan, and Marco made up a second, while John of Judea and Goliath ventured together. They had not seen a single trace of the Vrykolakas since the cavern.

This was going to be another situation where you'd have as much luck if you were trying to find a maggot in a huge pile of rice. Frustration and desperation were setting in with everyone, save John, who seemed to be at peace no matter what situation he was in. Frustration and desperation led to impatience, which led to mistakes. *Why did I leave either of my nieces on their own?* Xiong thought.

243

From now on it was the buddy system for everyone. No one would go anywhere without a second. That would include Argus, who might not like it, but would have to learn to accept it.

***

Hours later Sona was exhausted. She could see and feel how drained her body was both physically and mentally. Tears rolled down her cheeks. That demon bitch had been right. Sona had moaned, screamed and begged for more. Now, the humiliation had the waterworks flowing steadily.

Sona remembered that uncle Amal had had sex that involved both the demons, and had been bitten at one time or another by Ju-Long and Lalita. He wasn't sure when their ability to feed off sex transferred to him, but he always felt the flow of energy between them. Typically the energy was flowing out of him.

She was doing her best to pay attention to the flow of energy and how it was occurring. If she could figure out how to harness and pull some of it into herself, she stood a chance of surviving this. Hopefully she could figure it out by the time they came calling on her next. Right now she couldn't even find the energy to keep her eyes open.

***

"I don't think they stayed in the mountains." It was late afternoon and they all had just met back up in a town called Perusia. Amal and Shehani had traveled as far south along the mountains as Beneventum and came up empty. The others had crisscrossed the mountains and found no trace.

"So, what now?" Meagan asked, responding to Xiong's statement.

"We scour this city and the surrounding area, then move onto the next," Argus spoke up. "We hit every place west of the mountains and south of our current location."

"And then?" Marco scoffed.

"Hopefully we catch a break, kid." Argus looked over at Xiong's nephew.

"Maybe Ju-Long will make a mistake, drop his shields for a moment and let me see where they are. Or maybe Sona will find a way to reach out to us." Xiong put a hand on Marco's shoulder.

"Or maybe John the Baptist over there will say some magical prayer and the Lord will guide us to her," Argus said, the sarcasm thick in his voice. He climbed on Petraios, "c'mon kid, let's do some looking." Marco looked at Hylonome.

"You want a lift youngster? I was going with them anyways." Marco nodded and hopped in the saddle. The foursome took off checking the outskirts of the town and any place the demons might be holed up.

***

Sona felt weak. While she could move quite a bit, they had her restraints fixed so there was no way to reach her blindfold and untie it. She was too exhausted to even worry about escaping. She had no idea how long she'd been out, but she was hungry and thirsty. Sona wasn't sure if she didn't solve the riddle soon she would ever wake up after the next sexual escapade.

There were voices inside the room with her, though they sounded so distant. Then a clearly female voice said, "I believe she is awake."

"I will sit her up if you grab her food and water, Capri."

"Do you remember what the master said her name was, Renzo?"

"Stona or Soma, something like that," Renzo answered as he scooted her back so she was propped against the wall.

"Wakey, wakey little girl. We need to get your energy back up. The master and his lady will want to play again soon."

Sona dreaded the thought of them coming for her. As much as she hated them, she knew once it started her desire would be so strong she'd have no choice but to be into it. She really needed to figure out how to steal energy back from them, working at it like there was no tomorrow, because there might not be.

***

Ju-Long finally let go of her, still roaring. Sona fell forward instantly, her head smacking hard on the floor. Lalita moved over to her. She was breathing but her pulse was weak. "She's got one hell of a knot on her head. It's only bleeding a little, but the smell is making me blood hungry."

"The sun is almost down. We will be on the hunt soon, and moving further south."

"Well, you need to be more careful with the merchandise. This one is too much fun to play with, I don't want to lose her by accident."

Ju-Long scowled at her, then softened at the sight of her face. "You are right, my love. I'll try to be more attentive and not kill the child. Now, let's go. My blood thirst calls as well."

"What do we do with her?"

"Have one of the servants tend to her, then tie her up and load her onto the cart outside and hook a horse to it. We head to Capua tonight."

As they left the room Sona refused to cry. They had drained her even worse than the last time. She had tried her best to pull energy from them, but the only amount she got was what they pushed into her to keep her going as the pair continued to violate her. At the end she even invited them to bite her. They both did, but there was little to take. She was sure Ju-Long was going to drain her completely.

Sona wished in some respect that he had. It seemed as if they planned to keep her around for a while longer. She dreaded that thought. The idea of just giving up floated through her mind. She pictured her twin sister, her family, and slapped that thought away. She wasn't dead yet. *I will keep hope alive til my last breath.*

***

"Any luck in the city?" Argus asked "There is no trace of them on the outskirts."

"Nothing," Amal and Xiong both answered at the same time.

"Well, some of us can head southeast toward Volsinii while the rest scour the area south of here and east of Volsinii," Argus said.

"Well, Shehani and I can cover more ground by air, so we'll take the wilderness route. The rest of you can head to the city, we will meet you there."

"Sorry, Uncle Amal. I trust you, but I have already lost one sister. I'm sticking with the other wherever she goes. Besides, a little ground support if you run into anything couldn't hurt."

"They'll have each other in the air. You will be solo on the ground. That's a deal breaker, Marco," Xiong chimed in.

"I'll go with him," John spoke up.

"Really?"

"Really. It is the way the Lord leads me." He glanced over at Hylonome. "Would thou also join us?"

"Want a ride?"

"I would appreciate it. Plus I love talking to you." He glanced over at Petraios. "No need to worry big fella. I know I'm not nearly big enough to replace you."

Amal and Shehani took to the air with Marco and company following behind. Goliath started to fall in the procession. "Yee may stay with them," John said. Goliath groaned. "I will be fine. Take care of them. I will meet you in Volsinii shortly."

"Did the preacher man make a dick joke between him and Petraios?" Argus asked.

"Come to think of it, I think he did." Xiong laughed.

"It was no joke. It is a fact, you puny peckered humans." Petraios snorted.

***

"Shall we double back and see if we can run into our pursuers after we feed? Mainly Sona's twin."

"Ah, my spoiled Queen is never satisfied. Always wanting more."

"And my King does not? Double the pleasure, double the fun."

"I do like the way you think, my love. Allow me to give instructions to the three that have risen. You may see that the servants have their orders."

"Head toward Capua?"

"Correct."

They met back up just fifteen minutes later. Ju-Long had the three newborns, two males and one female, in tow. None of them were particularly attractive. They would make good fodder though for the chosen ones. "They will follow us to feed, then they are to come back here and remain until we return." He winked at Lalita. "Shall we?"

"Lead the way, handsome."

"The Master wants us on the road as soon as possible, preferably before the newbies return."

"The two kiddos are watching the perimeter while we bathe and bag their newest toy?"

"Yep," Capri answered.

"Well let's get it done. We got a long road ahead of us. I was born in Capua, it's more than a hop, skip, and a jump from here."

Sona felt herself being touched. She could hear the sound of a cloth being swished in water, then wrung out. The cool rag floated over her skin and it felt so refreshing. It did not feel half as good as the bare hand that held her right wrist as her arm was being washed. Then a second bare hand grabbed her left ankle just above the restraint as that leg was being cleaned up.

Where there was skin on skin contact she could feel energy being transferred. It was flowing in, not out. *There is no way. I must be dreaming.* Sona faded out again.

***

Ju-Long and Lalita spotted Xiong, Argus, Meagan, the male centaur, and a giant walking with them. The giant looked familiar, but there was no sign of the man with the crosses back in Rome. *Could it be a different one?* Ju-Long looked at Lalita. "They are divided."

"Yes, and Shehani can fly so she is probably with Amal." Lalita commented.

"The question is where. And who else is with them."

"I don't see their brother or the female centauride. Who knows, maybe Brontes, Agnes, or some of the others took them out."

"Possible," Ju-Long replied, "that would be nice, especially if that giant with them is the one that was with the cross bearer in Rome, to find they took him out too."

"And if they didn't?"

"Then we need to be aware of his possible presence when we find the others."

"That would complicate things."

"Immensely." Ju-Long frowned.

***

"I'm getting something," Xiong said as he held a hand up for all to stop. "I think its Sona."

***

"Yes, we will be lucky to make it to Capua before dawn. Volsinii is where my parents moved to before eventually settling in Rome. That trip seemed to take us forever. I was eight years old and walked alongside the wagon most of the time. My mother was pregnant, my grandmother had bad knees, and my two younger sisters were only three and five. Dad drove the cart," Renzo told Capri as they rolled the girl on her side.

Sona woke up for a moment, bare hands touching her flesh. Warm trickles felt good on her cold body. She reached out with her mind hoping someone would hear her. *Help.*

"It's her. She is weak but alive. I'm losing her!"

"What do you mean by 'losing' her?" Meagan asked in a panicked voice.

"She is passing out. I couldn't see anything. They have her blindfolded. I did hear voices in the room with her. I heard a male voice say Volsinii. That is the city we head to?"

"Yes, let us pick up the pace," Argus said, running half speed down the trail.

"You all go ahead. I'm going to contact Amal and let him know."

Meagan climbed on Petraios and they bolted after Argus. Xiong looked up at a waiting Goliath. "Go ahead. I'll catch-up." Goliath stuck up one finger and shook his head. Then he put up two and nodded.

"Yes, the buddy system. Thank you my friend. Watch our backs, I'll only be a moment."

Amal had gotten the message loud and clear, Sona was alive and somewhere in Volsinii. They swooped low, informed the ground crew, and set a course for the city.

Sona woke to the sound of chains rattling. She felt the metal clasp around her left ankle fall open, followed closely by the right. Her legs were free, but she had no energy to move. Then her hands were unshackled and a female voice spoke.

"Did you bring the rope?"

"No, I thought you were getting it, Capri."

"Shit," she groaned, "I'll get the rope, you finish washing her."

"I can do that." Capri left the room and Renzo grabbed Sona's legs mid-calf and spread them out.

Energy sparked into her. She could feel the man holding her calves was getting aroused, and the more excited he got, the faster the energy flowed in. Her body was awakening. Her nipples began to stiffen and warmth filled her womanhood as the man slowly washed her inner thighs and what lie between.

***

It was like a game of flinch. Two people on one side, two on the other, flying at each other like bats out of Hell. Shehani cast a stun spell, but Ju-Long and Lalita rolled in opposite directions. The spell sailed harmlessly between them until it dissipated in the distance.

Amal readied four arrows, but when the blood sucking pair split to opposite sides he could only focus on one. That one was Ju-Long. Amal turned left and launched all four arrows at the Raksasha. He was directing them right toward the enemy. Ju-long looked back and went into an immediate dive for the tree line just ahead and below.

Lalita saw the arrows closing in on her lover. He might not make it to the trees in time, but he wouldn't have to. She used her power of telekinesis, stolen from the very man that had launched these four missiles, to knock them off course.

Something hit her from the side and knocked her silly. *That little bitch hit me with a spell!* Just as she righted herself, realizing it was a stun spell, an arrow came out of nowhere and pierced through her abdomen. As she clutched at it a second plunged through her neck. She fell from the sky like a rock.

Marco and Hylonome had both hit her with good shots and she fell into a treed area a ways ahead. Marco knew neither was fatal, so they had to get to her and finish her off before she recovered enough to escape. Marco was far faster than Hylonome or John. He bolted toward where she went down.

John hopped off Hylonome and worked his way toward Lalita via the wooded area. He didn't want the demons to know he was there. Not yet. If they could take out the two main players here, it would be a game changer in the fight against evil.

***

Sona felt the fatigue slowly being swept from her body. Then she felt someone in her head. *Shit!* She laid her head back and just stared at the ceiling.

Sorry, Uncle Xiong. This isn't as bad as it looks.

My apologies for the inconveniently timed intrusion.

You're fine. Believe it or not, this is all part of my brilliant plan to survive and escape.

Do you know where you are?

I think we are still in Volsinii.

Do you remember anything about the outside of the place you are being kept?

I was pretty out of it. It was by itself, surrounded by land, some of it being farmed. It's a big place, with a couple of big outbuildings. That's it. She let out a moan as Renzo worked his way up washing her abdomen. *Wait. There is another servant here. A female. I think her name is Capri. Maybe you can use her to recon the outside.*

Good thinking. Hang in there kid. We're on our way.

He had a good idea of what the house and surrounding area looked like thanks to Capri and a few little mind tricks. Xiong reached out to Amal. They were in a fight, and looking through Amal's eyes he could see Ju-Long was there. He had been riding on Petraios since he first started to hear Sona's call. It allowed him to close his eyes and concentrate without having to stop.

"Okay, here is what I got." He sent a mental image to Argus and Petraios of the house and its surroundings, including the position of the moon to give a sense of direction. "This is where they have her. She's getting stronger. I saw four human servants, no xiang shi. Ju-Long and Lalita are not with them."

"You sure?" Argus asked.

"Yes. They are in a fight with Amal and company east of us. I need you, Petraios and the big guy over here to get to Sona. Meagan and I are heading to help the others." Xiong nodded at Meagan.

"But . . ." Argus started. The two had already taken off toward Amal.

"Get my niece, Argus!" He heard Xiong yell as the pair disappeared.

Argus hopped on Petraios' back. He looked over at the giant. "You ready, Goliath?" The behemoth nodded.

Sona could hardly believe that it was working, but it was. *Time to close the deal.* She grabbed the man by his ears and practically dragged him up on top of her. He was so lust blind that he didn't even realize she had taken off her blindfold. "Kiss me," she growled.

***

Ju-Long saw his Queen go down, then saw the fastest thing he had ever witnessed bolting across the open field toward the tree line she had crashed in. The centauride was following, but quite a ways behind. She was probably the bigger threat, but he was the more immediate one.

Ju-Long shot through the sky, avoiding two more missiles fired by Amal and some energy blast the girl in the sky shot his direction. He would deal with them in a moment.

A fist came out of nowhere and slammed into his face. His head snapped back and with the force of the impact meeting the speed he was traveling, Marco was lifted off the ground and somersaulted head over heels several times. He was unconscious before he hit the ground.

Ju-Long's right fist, arm, and shoulder were on fire. The impact had spun him out of control and he landed hard on the ground. He looked up just in time to see two arrows bearing down on his prone body. He rolled left and the arrows hit his triceps and rear deltoid on his already injured arm. He wailed in pain, getting to his hands and knees. Ju-Long crawled like a wounded animal into the cover of the tree line.

Lalita got the one out of her neck, but with the pain and blood loss the arrow in her abdomen wasn't coming easy. Then she heard the hoof beats enter the forest. The centauride was coming.

Lalita hid behind a clump of trees, biting her bottom lip trying not to scream as she tugged at the arrow again. With a grinding sound followed by a sickening wet plop it came free. She could hear the hooves getting closer.

"I can smell you demon. Come out and play with me, Lalita."

"You still pissed about Petraios? You two weren't even together yet."

"Yeah, but you knew how I felt about him. I thought we were friends."

"Hey, how many hundreds of years ago was that? Ever heard of letting bygones be bygones? I was hungry. He was horny . . ."

"Yeah, after you made him that way! Succubus slut!"

Lalita heard her coming closer. With the arrows out she was feeling better, but nowhere near full strength. She ducked down and readied herself to pounce when Hylonome came close enough.

"Don't hide. It is just you and me. Your boyfriend took out Marco, and is giving Amal and the other twin a run for their money." Hylonome sniffed the air again, then nodded and looked over at a clump of trees. *There you are.*

Lalita sprang from her hiding spot, plunging the arrow she had taken out of her abdomen deep into Hylonome's chest. The centauride rose up on her back legs as she whinnied in pain. She punched with her front hooves as she used her hands to grasp the bolt stuck between her breasts.

Lalita ducked under her strikes pulling a dagger from her belt and climbing onto Hylonome's back as the mare came back down on all fours. She shoved the blade into her side, the tip meeting the bone of her human ribcage. The centauride fell to the right and rolled onto her back, crushing the unwanted rider into the earth.

Lalita cried out as Hylonome flipped back and forth from side to side with her trapped underneath. Her ribs were broken, her spine busted, and who knew what else as the snapping and crunching sounds continued.

Hylonome was hurting and losing a lot of blood. She rolled over one last time and got to her feet. She staggered to her left, hitting a large tree and sliding down its trunk to the ground. She had pulled the arrow out, and the dagger had fallen somewhere on the ground. Lalita was moaning and groaning, but not really moving. That was a good thing because she couldn't really move either.

John had heard the fighting that was happening ahead die down to some whimpers. Some or all were injured. Hopefully his friends were okay. He picked up his pace hoping he would arrive in time.

Ju-Long escaped into the trees. Amal ran after him on foot. "Shehani, I got this, check on your brother!" he yelled as he landed and moved into the woods.

***

Sona sucked energy in through her mouth, swallowing it down in huge gulps. She was bleeding his life force from him and he was letting her.

Renzo rolled off her, groaning as he did. "So tired." Sona got to her feet feeling like two satchels full of diamonds and gold. She looked down upon Renzo, who was a thin, under nourished, sickly version of himself.

"What the hell have you done?" Capri yelled, dropping the rope on the floor.

***

Ju-Long pulled the arrows out, but his right arm felt pretty useless. He heard the tall man enter the woods. Lalita was hurt badly. He needed to get to her, but so wanted to kill the big dicked freak. Then he heard her wail. It was a wicked, pained sound that echoed through the trees. He raced to the sound of her voice, fearing the worst.

"You are hurt," John said as he knelt by Hylonome.

"I'll be okay," she whispered. Her eyes were already becoming glassy, her breathing labored.

John could feel the succubus reaching out trying to steal energy from him and the centauride. That wasn't going to work on him, but it might be the final straw for Hylonome. "No you don't demon. He was over Lalita, both crosses pressed against her. She let out an unreal scream as her broken body began to turn yellow, orange and red. She was burning from the inside out. A dark, black shadow reached for John.

Demonic sounds rolled through the night air. "Back to the Hell from whence you came!" John growled.

***

Sona used her power to quickly wrap Capri up with the rope, catching her while she was still shocked and surprised. "You cunt! The Master will kill you for this." Then Capri convulsed, coughing blood. Her eyes rolled into the back of her head and she collapsed to the floor.

"Well, that's a first." Sona turned her attention to Renzo, who lay on the ground gasping for air. *I wonder if there is something decent to wear in this house.* She exited the room and began searching for clothes.

***

A huge flash of light lit up the forest. Ju-Long felt pain shoot through his heart as he could no longer feel Lalita's presence. *She is gone. She can't be gone! Not her. She was like me, indestructible!* The light died but left him blinded for the moment.

He fell to his knees. It was like a hole was blown through him, leaving an unhealable wound. His heart ached, his stomach was in knots, and true death felt like it would be sweet release.

But he was Ju-Long. He would not go out without a fight. He was sure the cross bearer was responsible. The man would die or Ju-Long would die trying to kill him. He looked around. He didn't see the tall one anywhere near. He crept toward the direction the light had come from.

"You are going to be okay, Nome." Laying his hands on the centauride. She was alive, but barely. He prayed and channeled the power of his God into her, feeling the wound on her side close, the muscles, bone, and flesh repairing themselves. John knew the more serious injury was the chest wound. *Lord, I call on thee though I am not worthy, to heal my friend from all injury and illness and make her body, mind and soul whole once again. In Jesus name I pray, Amen.*

Ju-Long saw the man knelt down praying over the centauride, his back to the crosses that lay on the ground several feet behind him. Ju-Long drew his sword silently as he moved in.

"You will need to eat and rest, but you will be just. . ." John saw Hylonome's eyes widen, but before she uttered a word he looked down to see the business end of a sword protruding though his chest.

Ju-Long twisted and turned the blade violently as his rage continued to grow. A storm was brewing, and he was the cause. "I have killed you, Christian man. Where is your God now?" He grabbed John by the hair and exposed his neck. The centauride struggled to get to her feet. Ju-long looked down upon her as he leaned in to feed. "You're next, bitch."

Ju-Long bit into John and sucked hard. He immediately withdrew his fangs and began hacking and coughing, spitting the blood out. His mouth was on fire, his cheeks burning. He touched his face and the flesh felt like it was melting. He tried to roar but his voice was gone, his mouth filled with blood as he choked and spit more of it out.

Suddenly Ju-Long was sailing through the air, propelled by some unseen force. *Amal!* He thought as he slammed into a tree.

Amal knelt by John. He was gone. *How?* Hylonome looked at him. "Are you okay?"

"Still weak. Help me up Amal."

"Just stay there and keep quiet." He glanced around in the direction he had thrown Ju-Long. "I'll be right back."

***

Sona heard a struggle going on outside. She had found nothing to put on, and just as she headed up some steps to where she knew some bedrooms must be, she felt someone near. Sona reached out with her mind and immediately found Argus.

"You will answer me or I will kill you as dead as your boyfriend over there."

"Argus."

"What!"

"Her face is turning blue. If she can't breathe, she can't speak," Petraios remarked.

"Oh." Argus released the girl's throat and she fell to the ground coughing and learning how to breathe again.

"Argus! I am here!" Sona ran toward him in a thin white dress. Even in the moonlight it was easy to see how breathtaking she was.

"Wow," Argus said.

"Oh, my!" Petraios added. Goliath let out two grunts that sounded like they were of the approving kind. She leapt into Argus' arms. She smelled heavenly. Sona kissed his cheek and began to slide down.

"Where are the others?" she asked.

"They are engaged in a battle with Ju-Long east of here."

"What are we waiting on? Let's go."

"You are okay then."

"Better than ever."

"I smell something foul," Petraios interjected, sniffing the air, "Vrykolakas!"

Three vampires appeared out of nowhere, looking just as surprised to see them as they were. Petraios wasted no time, firing an arrow into the heart of the tallest one who stood in the middle. The other two split, one taking off to the right, the other running left.

Sona lifted the one heading toward the house off the ground and sent him sailing toward Goliath. The giant caught him by the legs in its huge hand and smiled. He lifted him over his head then slammed him hard into the ground. Again. And again. And again.

Argus pulled a stake from his belt and took off after the woman. She was fast, but he had a good angle and intercepted her before she reached some trees off to the left. He tackled the demon to the ground driving the stake through her chest as they landed.

Argus trotted back to the others. "You smelling anything else?"

"No."

"And you are?" Sona looked at the horseman.

"Petraios, at your service." He bowed and reached for her hand. She offered it and he laid a kiss just above her wrist.

"I'm kinky, but I don't know that I am that kinky," she said, causing Argus to chuckle.

"It would matter not, for I am spoken for and faithful. However, I cannot help but admire beauty." Petraios released her hand. "May I offer you a ride? Or are you fast like your brother?"

"No, but I can do this like my Uncle Amal." She took off into the night sky. "East?"

"Yes," Argus answered. He turned to Petraios. "I'll take a lift."

"You would. Lazy human."

***

Ju-Long got to his feet, his right arm hurting worse than ever, his mouth and face deformed from whatever the man's blood had done to him. His throat was scorched and he was more than a little dazed from smacking into the tree. It didn't matter. She was gone. She was gone and they would die.

He spotted the tall man before he saw him and crouched behind some bushes. He dreamed of delivering a slow, torturous death to Amal, now he just wanted him dead. Him, his nieces, his nephew, Xiong, Argus, they would die . . . the centaurs, and that bitch that was riding the male, the giant. Dead. Amal was next.

Amal had an arrow in each hand. He was scanning for his target, but Ju-Long was nowhere in sight. He knew his enemy was hurt but still dangerous. The lightning that had lit up the sky moments ago was gone. It was a good sign. Maybe he was already dead.

Amal heard something rustle in the brush and looked down. Two hands reached out and grabbed him by the ankles, yanking his feet out from under him. His head smacked the ground hard, knocking him senseless. Before he knew it, his attacker was on him.

It was Ju-Long, but his face looked like it had been burned and melted. The stench was horrid. He had never seen anything so grotesque, and he had seen a lot. The mangled mouth of the demon opened wide just as something blasted into the right side of his head knocking him out.

Ju-Long looked down on the tall man and saw the terror in his eyes. He delivered a massive blow with his left rendering his opponent unconscious. He was in a lot of pain, but that would be over soon. Amal's blood would heal him.

Sona propelled herself at speeds she had never been able to achieve before. She scanned the woods for anything, any sign of the others. The canopy was thick, making it nearly impossible to see what was below.

Then she hit a clearing and could see one figure hunched over another. It was Shehani and Marco. Sona sped toward them. *Where is everyone else?*

Hylonome had managed to get herself to her feet, but was still woozy from the blood loss. A tear trailed down her face as she looked at the man who had given his own life to save hers. If she had just focused on killing the enemy, instead of letting her rage make her reckless, Lalita might not have bested her. She might have killed the succubus bitch herself, and John would still be with them.

She cautiously moved over to the pile of ash on the ground that the two crosses laid on. She bent down slowly, not quite steady yet and cautiously picked one up. It didn't light up, or start to burn her, so she grasped it fully and stood, looking for any sign of movement ahead.

"Amal is hurt somewhere in the woods. I can feel Ju-Long's presence with him, but your lover is knocked out. We need to get there fast, Meagan."

"How bad is he?" Sona asked as she landed beside her siblings.

"Bad." Shehani stood, tears in her eyes. She wrapped her arms around her sister and bawled.

Sona comforted her for a moment, but knew she had to lay hands on Marco as soon as possible to see if she could help. Time was of the essence.

Ju-Long felt his strength returning, the pain in his right arm gone. Even the searing he had in his mouth and throat had eased. He was so engulfed in the power of the blood he was consuming he didn't hear the hooves that were cautiously approaching.

Hylonome spotted the two on the ground, Ju-Long on top with a motionless Amal underneath him. She reached out, the cross in her right hand, attempting to press it into the back of Ju-Long's head. She leaned a little too far and felt her balance going. The centauride tried to regain her footing, but tumbled right. She let go of the cross as she fell over the pair, barely clearing their bodies. The cross landed in the middle of Ju-Longs back.

It felt like a thousand pound weight fell upon him. He looked over to his right to see the horse bitch land beside them. *If it isn't her, what the fuck is on me?* Then he felt the burn as light began to illuminate everything around him. *The cross!*

He felt it sear into his skin, the smell of burning flesh filling the night. With great effort he pushed himself up. Ju-Long reached for his sword and found his sheath empty. He had left it stuck in that damned Christian. He knew if he tried to grab it with his bare hands, the cross would just burn them as well. He twisted and turned trying to get it off of him. It wasn't working. The thing had melted his epidermis and was stuck to him.

He reached for the sword that was on Amal's belt. As he did he could see the orange-red fire that was spreading through him.

It was hallway to his elbow. He grabbed hold of the hilt and ripped it, sheath and all, from his downed enemy. Weak, he stumbled back and bumped against a tree. Ju-Long felt as if the cross were about to push through him.

Hylonome was trying desperately to get up. She watched as the demon struggled to get the cross off its back. It had grabbed a sword from somewhere and was sliding it between the cross and its own burning flesh. She needed to find a way to finish the Vrykolakas.

Ju-Long dug the metal into his own flesh, getting it between the top of the cross and his back. In agony he pushed it down as far as he could, feeling it slice through muscle and tissue along the way. He extended his arms behind him as far as he could. The cross tore from his upper back and he roared. He slid the blade down further until it reached the small of his back and the cross fell to the ground.

Ju-Long collapsed to his hands and knees. For the second time tonight, he found himself crawling for his life. The fire had died beneath his skin, but the pain that remained was unbearable. He longed to pass out. He was too weak to fight. The best he was going to be able to do was hopefully escape.

Xiong and Meagan were there. He was helping Hylonome up while Meagan went straight to Amal. "He's alive, but barely." She said, panic in her voice.

"Are you okay?" Xiong asked Hylonome.

"Weak, but yes."

"Where is Ju-Long?"

"He crawled off in that direction," she answered.

"Xiong, help me! What do I do? I don't have enough power to heal this much blood loss. He is almost completely drained," Meagan pleaded.

"Where is John?" He looked at the centauride. He could see the pain in her eyes. She just shook her head.

"Damn!" He looked back at Meagan. "Fuck him."

"What? I can't just give up and leave him to die! You're an asshole!"

"No, Meagan, fuck him. Literally. He can feed off sex."

"Oh. Yeah."

"Hylonome, knock an arrow in and watch their backs. I'm going after Ju-Long."

The Master had passed out just before he got there. The enemy was all around. If they were to live, he had to get them out of here now. He scooped Ju-Long up in his arms and shot into the air through an opening in the canopy. He only hoped he was in time to save Ju-Long, even though he hated him.

Argus and Petraios hit the clearing just in time to see a demon fly into the sky, holding an unconscious person in its arms. Argus slid off his friends back and the two raced ahead trying to figure out who the Vrykolakas had carried off. Then they saw Xiong coming running out of the woods firing his bow. It was too late, they were out of range.

Sona had hands on him, assessing the damage. This was way beyond her ability to heal. His jaw was shattered, his cheek bone crushed, nose broken, skull cracked, and spine snapped. He couldn't talk, didn't respond to any physical stimuli, and was breathing raggedly.

"Save him already, Sona!" Shehani pled.

"I can't!" She turned, tears in her eyes.

"You have to! Please!"

Sona turned back to her brother. "I am so sorry, Marco." Her tears dripped onto his face. She leaned down and kissed his forehead. "Please forgive me." She could feel his life force, his energy fading.

Argus, Petraios, and her Uncle Xiong were there. "Is he alive? Please tell me he is alive," Xiong asked.

"She can't save him, Uncle. He is too far gone," Shehani answered.

Sona felt her lips tingle and she sat up. She was accidentally stealing more life from him. *Shit!*

A thought popped into her head. *I wonder . . .* She pressed her lips to him once again and concentrated on pushing her energy into him. She was no longer draining him, but it was not going in. "Uncle Xiong, help me."

Xiong kneeled on the other side of Marco. "What would you have me do?"

"I am trying to push energy into him, but I think he is too weak to receive it. Maybe if we both use our ability to heal at the same time we can give him enough strength to take the energy in."

"You can push energy into another?"

"Yeah. I stole the ability to feed off and push sexual energy from the demons, same as Uncle Amal. I am not having sex with my brother, so let's try this."

***

Elena waited, crawling over and hiding under the wagon while they were distracted by the vampiros. Thankfully, they seemed in a hurry to get somewhere else now that they had the girl, so they forgot about her. When she was sure they were gone she bolted to the house to see if anyone else was alive.

Elena went room by room as she worked her way to the back of the house and the steps that led downstairs. She moved down a short hallway at the bottom and into the room where they had kept the girl prisoner. The site was horrific. Capri lay on the floor, rotting. And wrapped in rope. The scene made Elena want to vomit, and she did.

When she was down to just dry heaves, she wiped her mouth and nose with the back of her sleeve and headed back toward the hallway. "Help." She heard a whisper. *Oh God, don't let Capri still be alive in that condition.*

"Help." She heard again, followed by a feint cough. It was coming from the other side of the room. She spotted Renzo's body and went to him. He looked like he was half mummified, his once toned body shriveled up, his beyond handsome face riddled with lines and wrinkles. *Help? How in the hell am I going to be able to help?*

"Water," he mouthed, voice barely audible.

Water. That I can do. "Wait here." She realized as she said it Renzo wasn't going anywhere, anytime soon.

***

They had done what they could and Marco was better, but still in a lot of danger. His wounds were still bad enough to bring death, but Sona couldn't seem to push the energy into him. She implored her brother to fight, to feed from the energy she was trying to give him. "Damn it!' she yelled.

The energy was sexual energy, and there was nothing sexual about touching her brother. Then it hit her. Sona looked up at the only available option. "Argus,"

"Yes."

"I don't believe I am about to ask you this, but I need a favor."

***

Goliath sat holding his friend in his arms like a toddler. He was totally unresponsive and had been for several hours. He just

267

rocked back and forth holding the bloody remains of the only person he had on this earth.

The sun was rising in the east, and all else seemed to be well. John had killed Lalita and saved Hylonome, who was still in disbelief as she was being consoled by her husband, Petraios. Meagan had saved Amal, Sona had saved Marco with Argus' assistance, and Xiong and Shehani were none the worse for wear.

Ju-Long had managed to escape once more, carried away by a xiang shi none of them recognized. Where they were headed was a good question. The one who took him flew south. "So, what is our next move?" Argus asked.

"We head south to find him." He hesitated. "Well, those who wish to join us, that is."

"We are heading south to get to Carthage, looking for Uncle Te. We will join you for a while." Shehani said. Marco nodded in agreement.

"Sounds like a plan." Sona answered as she stole a glance at Argus. He put on a huge grin for her.

"We must head back. We have family that needs us, and we are so few now we have to have everyone on hand to defend against our enemies," Petraios said, wishing he could join them on their adventure.

"Your service has been appreciated, and your friendship and comradery are always enjoyed. Family first," Meagan said wrapping her arms around Hylonome, then Petraios.

"Meagan and I are going to check on things in Greece, then we are heading to my homeland to marry and see the family. You are welcome to join us if you would like, Xiong."

"First off, congratulations. I hope your future is as bright and beautiful as both of you," Xiong said, shaking Amal's hand, "My mission is not done so long as that demon exists. My place is here, this is my journey, and I am living my life now, instead of just existing."

"I don't know who your advisor is, but he is a genius." Amal chuckled.

"Please do give my regards to Ling, Naina, and the rest of their children. Tell them I love them," Xiong said, his eyes happy, but watering. He stuck his hand out to Meagan, who brushed it aside and pulled him in for a hug.

"Take care of yourself, Xiong."

"You too, Meagan. Watch after my friend."

"What do we do about him?" Argus said, nodding his head in Goliath's direction.

"I'll go talk to him," Xiong said, moving toward the giant as the others bid their farewells to each other.

"If I could speak to you for a moment, Sona."

"Sure, Uncle Amal. What's up?"

"You have stolen the same power as I did from the demons?"

"Yes."

"The succubus inside you will want to be fed. You must give it just enough to satisfy its hunger. Go too long and it will overwhelm you. Let it feed recklessly, and it will own you. You must find balance. If you do not, it will not discriminate between friend and foe. It only cares about itself."

"In time, with practice, you will be able to draw sexual energy from others without having sex. However, every once in a while it will desire a fuller feeding. Do not deny its call for too long. Be careful."

"I shall." She gave him a hug.

***

Elena brought him water several times. He was actually able to sit up and talk a little better, but Renzo still looked like death warmed over. He was asking for food, or milk, anything with sustenance. She had went out to the pen behind the barn and collected some goat milk, then picked some grapes from the vineyard and headed back to him.

She realized she was starving herself and ate several grapes to curb her appetite until she had him fed, wondering the entire time if the master and Lalita would ever be coming back. She wasn't sure why she was working so hard to nurse Renzo back to health. Maybe because she had no one left and nowhere else to go. Right now, he was all she had.

***

Goliath would not respond to any of his questions. It was as if he couldn't, or wouldn't hear him. Then Xiong decided to try a different approach.

Goliath, please hear me. I know your heart is heavy, and I share in your sorrow. If he had not stepped in, Lalita might still be alive, and surely Hylonome would be dead. I am sorry I drug you two into this.

Silence. Xiong was going to try again when he heard a voice inside his head. A deep, masculine, and surprisingly articulate voice.

John was a good man. He was dedicated to leading people to Christ, fighting the forces of darkness, and helping everyone he could. We were not drug into this, we became a part of this long ago.

Goliath? Xiong could hardly believe it was the giant that was in his head. *Why have you not responded until now?*

Yes, it is I. I have been deep in prayer, asking the Lord what He would have of me.

And did he answer?

Just now. I am to take John's body and the crosses to Golgotha, the site of Jesus' crucifixion and burial. I will be moving on, but pray the Lord will watch over and protect you. You are good people.

As are you Goliath. It is my hope that we will meet again in a world that we have all made a better place. That our friend John made a better place.

Goliath stood with John in his arms and looked over at Xiong making eye contact with him for the first time. He nodded and turned to walk away.

"Wait. Where is the big guy going?" Marco asked as he approached.

"He takes John to what I believe will be the Holy Man's final resting place."

"Alone? That's against the rules. No one goes anywhere by themselves." Marco caught up to Goliath and tapped on his huge leg. "Hey, you need some company?" Goliath looked down and shook his head.

"Well tough shit, I'm coming anyways," Marco said.

"And who will be with you when you have to return?" Shehani said from behind them. "You are not leaving my sight. I am going, too."

"That's going to leave Uncle Xiong way short." Marco stated.

"We will be fine," Xiong said, "getting John's body safely to where it needs to be is a mission as important as any other.

"Tell Sona to stay with you and Argus until we return. We will find you and then proceed on our journey to find Uncle Te," Marco said.

"It has been three days since I rescued him. His injuries would have been fatal to even one our kind, but he is Ju-Long. Our Master is apparently indestructible."

"But we have fed him two humans a night, and while the scars on his face, and the carnage that was his mouth have mostly healed, the damage from the cross on his back is still raw and seeping. Plus he sleeps all the time, and except yelling to be fed or crying out for Lalita, he says nothing. Maybe his mind is broken even more that his body."

"Yet he improves a little each day, Jia-Li. Not to mention that if he dies, you die. That's the whole reason I answered his cry for help."

"And I am thankful for it, but . . ."
"There are no buts. If he dies you die, and even if his death doesn't kill me as well, I would take my own life. I cannot live without you my love." Balavan said, a quiver in his voice.

Jia-Li sat crossways on his lap, wrapping her arm behind him as she nuzzled her head against his neck. "But what if when he finally recovers he has gone insane and he turns on us? He has already made it clear the night we faced him outside of Constantinople he would kill you the next time we met."

"And if that be the case, at the first sign that he may be headed in that direction we will flee. Until then we nurse him back to health until he is well enough to survive on his own."

"You are truly unlike any other xiang shi. You are merciful. You are kind. You put others before yourself."

"Yet I still murder to survive. Even if I prey upon evil humans, or the ones who are already dead but are just suffering as they wait for their infirmities to take them, I am a killer. My soul is gone, and my place in Hell is waiting for me. Let us never forget that."

Ju-Long had the same reoccurring dream. He had died and crossed over onto another plane. He was in the Hell for blood drinkers. He could see Yen-Lo, the devil that had created him through his emissary Niu T'ou, who was also present with a number of other demons. He recognized some of the souls he had sent here, and some of those whom he had created and wound up here after their true death.

Chang, one of his right hand men from the original army was there as well. He even saw his cousin Kong, the incompetent fool, being savagely beaten by the strongest warrior under his command, Piao. He scanned everywhere, looking at the seemingly endless number of faces, hoping to catch a glimpse of his beloved Lalita. She was nowhere to be found.

Every time he would begin to make his way toward Yen-Lo to demand to know the whereabouts of his Queen he would be stopped by some unseen force. The devil would look his way, shake his head, and point at Ju-Long. He would be thrown backwards, landing inside his own body, where he could see Balavan and Jie-Li in the home they had him secreted in.

Ju-Long would try to force himself awake, immediately feeling the fire in his back once his aura returned to his human shell. The pain would be so intense he would pass out in his dream and wake back up to the same scenario in Hell again. It was an unending nightmare that he only got relief from when he woke to feed, if that was actually happening. Then he would dream of Lalita, making love to her until a bright light blinded him and she disappeared, leaving his arms empty as he whimpered her name over and over. During those times the suffering in his heart and his head drowned out the pain in his back.

"What if we laid his body in the shallow bathing pool and filled it with fresh blood instead of water? Do you think his body might heal from the outside in?"

"I don't know, Balavan. Have you ever heard of such a thing?"

"No. Not with blood. But I have heard of healing springs, and certain things added to water that are used to cleanse and heal. The human body needs certain things to survive, and there are plants and roots that contain things that help the body recover. Xiang shi require human blood to survive. The blood provides things that allow us to heal when we drink it. The cross wound on Ju-Long's back is not healing like it should. I am wondering if direct application of blood would help. It couldn't hurt, right?"

"I don't know, but we won't know until we try."

"Then I will begin collecting some humans. We will feed him one, lie him in the pool, and drain the rest of them into it. Would you like to come with?"

"He is still vulnerable. I will stay and watch over him, Balavan. But I would caution you, my love."

"And that would be?"

"The sun isn't down just yet."

"Right."

Balavan had fed on an elderly man whose body was full of fever and infection. It made the blood taste bad, but it still did the trick. He had gotten used to such things, though the first infirm human he fed on had him wondering if the bad blood would not make ill him as well. It didn't, so whenever he could he would find a human already on their death bed and usher them along to their next existence. Balavan was always careful to remove the heart afterward and take it with him, discarding it a safe distance away from his victim's body.

Then he ran across a group of thieves. After knocking out, binding and gagging all five of them, he made three trips getting them back to the residence he and Jia-Li had taken over three years ago.

Because of the wound to his back they had kept Ju-Long shirtless, and rolled up on his side or laying on his stomach as much as possible. When he was on his back the seeping wound, constantly trying to heal itself, would stick to the floor tearing away anything that had healed and reopening the sore.

Jia-Li had also removed his pants in preparation for his 'blood' bath. Balavan took the first victim, who he had recently knocked out for the second time, used the nail on his index finger to open the vein on the man's neck, then pressed the cut to Ju-Long's mouth. He sucked slowly at first, then clasped his hands on the man's head and fed furiously. When the body was drained he released the head and seemed to go right back to sleep, his eyes never opening during the entire process.

Balavan carried him over to the pool and laid Ju-Long in it. Jia-Li drug the next body over and Balavan turned the man onto his stomach, pulled the head back by the hair, and used his dagger to slit the throat and let the blood drain over Ju-Long's chest and into the pool. He did the same with another, then pulled Ju-Long into a sitting position as Jia-Li opened the neck of a third and let the blood run over the Master's back.

Ju-Long's body seemed to react to that. His back soaked the blood in almost as quickly as it touched him. Jia-Li slit open the last man and let the liquid from him thicken the layer of blood under Ju-Long before Balavan laid him back down.

They left him lying in the pool until sunrise had come and gone and it was night once again. Amazingly he had absorbed every last drop of blood they had poured over and around him into his body during that time period. He was still out, but looked better, as Balavan took him out of the pool and checked his back. The wound was healed, its imprint a half inch deep. It was in the exact shape of the cross with the flesh inside appearing melted and then molded, looking just like flames. The scar was the same color as the rest of his skin, but pronounced enough that there was no way you could ever miss it.

"I will go and bring him back his evening meal. Maybe then he will wake and we can finally leave, or send him on his way."

"Or he will wake and kill us both."

"He told me long ago that he appreciated loyalty above all else. While we had our differences in the past, I believe he will do right by us for saving him from sure death."

"Merciful and full of hope. That is my Balavan." Jia-Li half smiled, half fretted as she let out a sigh.

Ju-long was turning his head back and forth, moaning Lalita's name. Jia-Li had gathered some water and rags and was cleaning him. She found suitable clothing and was going to dress him once he was bathed. There was no blood on him, but a fair amount of dirt on his feet, legs, and arms.

He began to become erect as she washed him, still whispering Lalita's name as a lover would. She washed up his thigh and found herself growing excited. It had been a long time since she had been with the Master. It had been a long time since she had been with anyone save Balavan. Jia-Li fought the urges she was feeling, even sitting back, taking her hands off him.

His hand reached up and ran gently through her hair. She felt the energy that flowed through both of them. Jia-Li had missed this about the Master. She wanted him to spill himself inside her and fill her with his power, like old times.

"Oh Lalita, my love, how I have missed you."

Jia-Li ignored being called by the wrong name, realizing the poor Master might be delusional still. She placed her hand on his length. "I just want to please the Master."

"And I you, my Queen." He opened his eyes and propped himself up on his elbows. "Li Na, you have come back to me, too.

Where is Lalita?" He had a smile on his face and a look of shock in his eyes.

"It is I, master. Jia-Li. Balavan and I have saved you!"

Instantly his mood turned, Ju-Long's smile turning to an evil grin. "Why, that is even better. I have been waiting for this moment for a long time."

Before she knew it he was on top of her, wrapping his hand around her neck, pinning her to the floor. "Where is your lover, you fucking whore!"

"Master," she coughed, "please, we came for you, we fed you, and we brought you back."

"Well, thank you. Now where is he?" He tightened his grip.

"Out," she whimpered, "getting you food."

"Then we will have to find a way to spend our time until he returns." Ju-long tore her dress from her in one violent motion. "Guess we will have to go with the only thing you are good for. Spread your legs!"

She looked up at him, tears streaming down her face. "Mercy, Master. Please."

He was brimming with power. He had taken her in every way possible, then drained every last drop of blood he could. That's when he felt them. The chosen ones were closing in. Ju-Long punched through Jia-Li's back and tore her heart out. He used the blood to write a message on the floor, licked his fingers clean, and quickly dressed in the clothes Jia-Li had gotten for him. As he snuck off into the night he thought how wonderful it would be if Balavan took out a couple of them before they killed him. Either way one of his enemies would be dead, and he would be on his way to wherever he was going. He just had to remember where that was.

"Ju-Long has to be in there. I am sure that was the Raksasha that saved him who just entered the place." Argus said.

"Looking at him, I know you are right, and I think I recognize him from long ago."

"So it is a demon with some age to him, meaning he is powerful in his own right."

"Yes, I believe he was a monk turned blood sucker back in the Caves of Ajunta."

"India?" Sona asked.

"Yes. He was the greatest warrior among the monks there, before he was turned. I can't remember his name at the moment, but I remember he was not there when we took the caves back from the blood suckers. Nor did we see him with Lalita or Ju-Long anytime thereafter," Xiong answered.

"That ups the ante then, especially now that there are only three of us. If Ju-Long is alive and well in there, we might need to rethink our strategy," Sona added, "should we wait until dawn?"

"I have never been good at waiting." Argus huffed.

"I know, my friend. But at least let me see if I can detect anyone else inside the place. Maybe there is a human servant I can tie my mind into and do a little recon before we go in blind."

"Alright, Xiong. Do your magic."

"Shall I try as well?"

"Couldn't hurt, Sona."

Balavan rushed to her side, seeing the hole in her back and her heart lying next to her. Her body was in shambles, her arm coming off as he tried to roll her. A century had caught up with her in one night. "NOOOOO!!!" he roared, shaking the house, "NOOOOO!!" He was gasping for air that he really didn't need. His roars went to a whimper as he cried, blood tears rolling down his cheeks. "Please, please, please come back," he sniffled. "Come back to me, Jia-Li."

He could not believe his eyes. *Maybe it is not her.* Balavan knew the truth though. It was his beloved. Ju-Long had killed her. They had saved the wretched demon just to have this be their thanks. "Why!" he yelled. Balavan balled his fists, punching himself in the head. *So stupid! Why did I leave her alone with that monster!* "I will find you and kill you Ju-Long!" his cry echoed through the night.

"I am sorry Jia-Li. I am so, so sorry my love." He fell forward, kissing the back of her head as he sobbed into her once silky hair that had turned brittle. "Please forgive me."

Balavan heard a door being kicked open. Instantly he was on his feet. "Ju-Long! You demon bastard! Bring it! I will tear you apart with my bare hands for this! You fucking coward! Face me!"

He heard another door opening softly somewhere from behind him. He put his back to the wall, his head on a swivel as he watched both directions. "Too afraid to fight me on your own you had to go get help? Bring one or bring a hundred, I don't care! You will all die tonight!"

Arrows came from his right. Balavan caught them in flight and tossed them aside. He could not see whomever had sent them. "Arrows? Really Ju-Long? I thought more of you than that!" From his left a strong male figure entered the room, firing a missile that was headed straight for his chest. Balavan caught it, snapped it in half, and dropped the pieces to the ground.

"Who are you?" he asked, then heard light footsteps on the other side of him. He turned to face a girl holding an arrow in each hand, and a Chinaman pointing a crossbow at him. He glanced back to see the one on his left had another arrow knocked and ready. His eyes turned back to the Chinaman. "You are a monk, just as I was in my former life."

"You are the one I saw fly away in Ajunta, right after you talked to one of Ju-Long's twin servants."

"Just kill me," he cried. "That was the night I fell in love with her. That was the night it all began. Jia-Li! I failed you!"

Xiong raised his hand signaling for Argus and Sona to wait as he watched the demon monk squat in place and bury his face in his hands. "I remember exactly. I was up on the high ground overlooking the cave you and her were talking in front of. Your friend, Devesh spotted you and said your name, *Balavan.* You heard him didn't you?"

Without looking up, Balavan said, "You are one of the chosen ones."

"Yes."

"I am not your enemy. I did hear him, and I knew you were with him. I saw the army of monks marching from Ellora. I could have warned the others. I did not. I came back to save the one I loved, the only one I cared about. Jia-Li."

"Is that her?"

"What remains." He shook his head. "You can kill me now, for I have nothing to live for. Well, nothing except killing Ju-Long. If you let me live, my sole purpose will be to avenge her death."

"We don't just let demons live," Argus growled.

"Who are you, I ask again. You look young, but you feel centuries old."

"My name is Argus. I am centuries old, and the last of the Spartans."

"A Spartan? A member of the greatest military force the world has ever known before or since. If I am to die tonight, it would be an honor if you did it."

"You know of my people."

"Yes," Balavan answered, "I trained a hundred monks in your style of warfare. We repelled every threat made against us with just that force. Until the Raksasha came and caught us by surprise."

"Truly a student of battle. I wish we had met under different circumstances. I believe you were once a man after my own heart."

"Thank you. I will not beg for you to spare me, but I can be a powerful ally if you could find the faith to trust me. Merciful. Kind. That is how my Jia-Li would describe me. While the demon took my soul and made me a blood drinker, he was unable to take my conscience." Balavan stood slowly, keeping his hands at his side.

"Ju-Long spoke of you on more than one occasion during our time in Ajunta." He looked at Xiong. "He wanted your brother Zhan to be one of the ones pursuing us, but it was you he found spying on him through his servants and newborns. You can read minds as well?"

"Yes, but in your case it would only be if you allowed me. You are too old and have learned how to block one from entering your mind," Xiong answered.

"Be my guest."

"It works better if I am touching you."

"I am at your disposal."

"Xiong, don't be a fool!" Argus yelled.

"I have already peeked into his mind enough to know he has no intention of hurting us."

"I don't like it."

"If it makes any difference, I also detect the same thing," Sona said.

Argus snarled as he watched Xiong reach out and grab Balavan's hands. The Spartan laid his bow aside, drew a stake from his belt, and moved in on the pair. If the Raksasha even twitched that stake was going right through his heart.

Xiong was amazed at the life Balavan had lived as a xiang shi. He had shown mercy on numerous occasions. The way he had fed over the past couple of decades, choosing only the dying or the corrupt, was something he had never seen from any demon. Then there was his love for Jia-Li. It was as pure as anything he had witnessed among the living.

Xiong saw him show mercy to a man who was as merciless as they come. "Really? You turned Attila the Hun just to save his life."

"He was good to Jia-Li and I. He was begging."

"Attila the Hun is not dead? He is a Vrykolakas?" Argus asked.

"Yes."

"As soon as we are done with this Ju-Long, I want to find Attila. Facing another legendary warrior in battle would be a dream come true. Especially since his new existence would put us on equal footing."

Balavan smiled. "Now that would be a battle for the ages, the last Spartan versus the King of the Huns."

"You are the most unique demon I have ever met. I don't know about trust just yet, but I have deep respect for how you have lived in this existence you were drug into."

"Thank you, Xiong."

"Well, I guess I could pick your brain for a while before I run a stake through your heart." Argus put the weapon back in his belt.

"And you Miss? Could you accept me?"

"I'm just a girl, what would I know?"

"If you are like my Jia-Li, you probably know more than all of us put together." Balavan gave her a slight bow. "Just so you know, Xiong, your niece ran through my entire mind in half the time you did, and she never laid a finger on me." He blushed. "Sorry about the adult stuff, Sona."

"Oh, don't worry yourself, she knows all about the adult stuff, and she is good at it." Argus chuckled.

"Since we are going to keep him, maybe we should focus on the message Ju-Long scrawled on the floor in blood. There is something for all of us."

"What does it say?" Xiong asked, stepping over to where Sona stood.

"This first part is hard to read."

"Want me to give it a try?"

"It's not hard to read like that, it's just really sick and offensive, Uncle." Her eyes were already wet. "I'll skip it until the end, okay?"

The three men nodded.

"Sona, my love, I can't wait to reunite with you. You taste so good, not to mention you are a top notch fuck, and suck dick like it

is your job. What an asshole," She sighed, *"Argus, it will be my honor to kill the last Spartan. I will make it quick."*

"Arrogant asshole." Argus added.

"Xiong . . . soon."

"I hope so you pompous asshole."

"Balavan, the message for you is the worst of them. Do you really want to hear it? With what you have been through already tonight?"

"The hole in me will never heal. I am destroyed, yet numb to all feelings at the moment. I would read it myself, but it might be better if you read it to me. Are you okay with that?"

"Of course."

"Do not sugar coat it. Give it to me raw and whole, exact word for exact word."

Sona cleared her throat. *"Your whore's last job was feeding me. I defiled her completely, filling and covering her with my seed as she begged for mercy and cried out your name. No one takes what is mine without consequence. I know, if you can stop your crying, you will hunt me and try to kill me. My goal is to evade you for as long as possible, letting you live every day in misery, longing for the slut lying on the floor in front of you. Oh, by the way, some of the chosen ones are lurking outside so I have to go. Good luck with that."*

Balavan didn't blink, didn't utter a word. *I am going after him. He heads southeast, with no particular destination in mind.* Xiong heard him whisper in his head. In a flash, Balavan was gone.

"What the hell?" Argus grumbled.

"He hunts Ju-Long."

"To the southeast."

"You heard him too, Sona?"

"Yes. And he has left his mind open to both of us."

Agnes stood on the shore overlooking the Adriatic Sea. Her enemy was on the other side in Greece. That is where she would head soon. The Minotaur had successfully turned two humans into Vrykolakas. The new creations looked like a cross between their kind and her kind. They were ugly as sin, annoying as hell, and extremely stupid. She cast them out on their own after two weeks. What happened to them afterward she did not care.

She had also created four human servants who kept their human form, and were quite adept at taking care of her as she came full term. They did an awesome job helping her deliver the twins. Unfortunately her children had no interest in mother's milk after the first month, and had grown at a tremendous rate. They were four feet tall and strong as oxen by that point, and when their craving for blood and flesh hit them, the poor servants became their first meal.

The three women and one man didn't even fight back or cry out to her for help. They simply accepted their fate as if they knew their sole purpose was to serve her and her young ones. She missed them at times, but knew she had two strong helpers that would only get bigger and better.

Agnes placed her left hand on her daughter Ambrosine's head. She wrapped her right arm around her son Ambroos' shoulder. "We are going on a journey little ones. Back to my homeland, Greece, then down to a beautiful Island named Crete. I will search for my long lost love there. He will make a wonderful father if he is still alive. He is not your father, for some horrible creatures and their human companions killed him well before I gave birth to you. Do you like the taste of humans?" She looked down at her twins in turn. They both nodded their heads. "Well, we will be making a special stop on our journey. If you like human flesh, just wait till you sink your teeth into a centaur."

Golgotha, 482 AD

The ground here felt different, as if there was magical energy to the place. Appearance wise there was nothing ornate or fancy about it, like some of the Buddhist and Hindu holy places she had visited. Yet there was something majestic about the simplicity of the lands on which the Christians' Jesus had been crucified. Shehani felt enamored with the place. Marco also felt something otherworldly, in a good way.

"I just feel love. It's incredible, sis. Even with all the turmoil in the world around us, this place seems peaceful and safe, as if nothing and no one could hurt you as long as you are here."

"Yet it is a site where He was beaten, tortured and agonizingly crucified," Shehani remarked.

"True, but John told me that his Savior was Love. Something about his God lovingly sacrificing His only begotten Son so that man should not die but have everlasting life. Or something like that, I don't remember the exact words he used."

The threesome wrapped John's body in a shroud early on in their long journey here. Now Goliath bent down, taking John's body into the tomb where Christ had been buried, and later rose from, before ascending to Heaven to sit at the right hand of His Father.

There had been soldiers in front of and around the tomb when they first approached—at least a dozen of them. Then, as if by some unseen force they were led away, giving Goliath the time to set John in his final resting place.

Not long after they slipped away from the tomb the soldiers returned to their post. The sun was creeping lower in the sky, and Goliath led the siblings to a place where they were out in the wilderness, but under cover that would protect them from the rain if it began to fall. Marco took first watch, then Goliath guarded them until dawn. Shehani had done her fair share along the way, including shifts the last three nights.

When the sun rose they ate what little food they had left, Marco and Shehani deciding to gather along the way.

"Ready to hit the road, sis?" Marco asked as he let out one last yawn, stretching at the same time.

"Toward Carthage?"

"Is that where the others are headed?"

"It appears so, though they are at least two days out."

"Any sign of Ju-Long?" Marco asked, digging in his pouch for any morsel he might have missed. He was still hungry.

"Not in a few weeks."

"That Buddhist blood sucker still with them?"

"Balavan? Yes, he is."

"I'll find Goliath." Marco began to scan the area. It took a moment but he finally found his giant friend. He was hidden, but within sight of the tomb.

"Saying your last goodbyes? I understand. I'll give you a few minutes." Marco turned to walk away. A huge hand grabbed him and pulled the little man in for a big hug. Goliath let out a happy grunt.

"I love you too, big guy." Then came a low whimper. "Of course I will miss you." Then it registered. "Miss you? Why would I miss you? You are coming with us?"

Goliath put a finger up to his own lips and looked back toward the tomb.

"You are not just going to stay here forever watching over his body, are you? It is sad, but he is gone. Come with us."

The giant shook his head as he put Marco down. Shehani approached. "What's going on?"

"The big lug thinks he is obligated to spend the rest of his life sitting here, guarding John's body."

Shehani looked up at Goliath. "Really?" He nodded, then pointed at her and Marco. He flapped his arms like a bird.

"You just want us to leave you? Just like that?"

The giant nodded, pointing at his chest, then to the ground.

"You sure you will be okay?" Shehani asked. He nodded again and snatched her up into a gentle embrace.

"What? We just go now?"

"Yes, brother. Goliath has his path and we have ours. The two crossed for a time, and may cross again in the future, but for now we must part ways," Shehani answered. "I will miss you my big bear. Nobody can keep a girl warm at night like you can." She leaned in and kissed his cheek. Goliath sighed, water threatening to edge over his eyelid.

"Well, that's that. Thanks for walking with me a million miles, Marco. Have a nice life."

Goliath lowered Shehani to the ground.

"Well, let's go, sis."

Goliath grunted, putting a single finger in the air, then jabbed his thumb pointing behind him.

"Really?" Marco questioned, a scowl on his face. Goliath nodded. "Oh, alright!" Marco climbed up on the giant's right shoulder and began scratching his huge back. "You could have this anytime if you came with us."

Goliath let out a pleasured moan.

Carthage, 482 AD

Ju-Long spent months trying to find his way again. Losing Lalita turned out to be the most devastating thing he had ever experienced. He traveled alone, no human servants, no newborns. Occasionally he would create a female member of his kind and make her a plaything for a day or two, before tossing her body out to meet the sunrise.

The chosen ones had gotten close a couple of times, and that fucking Balavan was with them. He tried to find an opportunity on those two occasions to steal Sona from them. The chance never materialized.

Now he found himself in a place called Carthage. That is when he remembered he had sent his human servants there with the treasures he and Lalita had accumulated over time. They were to build a new home.

He reached out and couldn't find a sign of any of them anywhere in or around the city. The whole cross fiasco that had nearly killed him, and the loss of Lalita really affected him, physically and mentally. The physical had recovered, except that cursed scar on his back. The mind still struggled at times.

Ju-Long stretched out further. He felt something that was his, but it was too far off to tell who or what it was. He flew low over the outskirts, searching for any sign of them. He circled around to the southeast side. That is where he found what he was looking for, but not in the condition he was hoping.

The outside walls were partway up. It was going to be the size of a castle. Unfortunately it would never be finished. The bodies of his servants littered the ground. Ju-Long landed to take a closer look at the damage. His people were in various states of decay and had been gnawed on here and there by the local wildlife.

Other than that there were no external wounds that would have caused their death. He did notice they all had dried blood around their eyes, ears, nose and throat. *Did some internal parasite kill them?*

That is when it hit him hard. His mind was being scrambled so he could not think. Ju-Long fell to the ground in a fetal position. His body was seizing and he felt his internal organs twisting and turning as they were ripped apart.

The ground shook, opened up and swallowed his victim. As quickly as it appeared, it disappeared, the dirt and sand filling back in leaving no trace the hole ever existed. The man, six feet eight inches tall with hair that hung to just past his waist and a beard that reached down to the middle of his chest, walked down to the scene.

The ground was as solid as ever, no sign that it has just been churned up then sucked back in. He looked around one more time at his handiwork from yesterday. Those poor fools, just like Ju-Long, had no idea what hit them.

He couldn't believe his luck when he found this place, with the demon's servants awaiting the arrival of their master. He had no idea after massacring the lot Ju-Long would be there so quickly. "Back to hell, demon."

Te flipped a coin he had been holding onto for a few decades. It was meant for this very moment. On one side there was a dragon, the other a tiger. If the tiger was up, he would head back home. If it was the dragon, he would keep traveling. His head and his heart could never decide, so he would leave it to chance.

***

Marco and Shehani had caught up with them just a few hours ago. Earlier, a surprise pair found them. Mahika, Marco's twin (though they looked and were built nothing alike) and their younger brother Biao showed up. They had just taken out a pack of wererats with Jing and Chanda in western India when they ran into Amal and Meagan.

Introductions were made, hugs were exchanged, and the news that Meagan was pregnant relayed. Chanda and Jie accompanied Amal and Meagan back to their parents' house. Amal mentioned that Xiong and company might be shorthanded and Ju-Long was still lurking about. That's when Mahika and Biao decided to head their way.

It was still an hour before nightfall when the group spotted someone headed toward their camp on the eastern outskirts of Carthage. "There is no way," Xiong said.

"Yes, there is," Sona answered.

"What is it? Who is it?" Argus asked, getting to his feet.

"My brother. Te! Is it you?" Xiong ran toward him, as the others prepared for the worst. They couldn't be sure which Te this was and what mental state he was in.

"Xiong? You have such long hair. But you still have that handsome clean shaven face."

"I have long hair? Look at yours! And that beard!" The two embraced.

"I am so sorry, youngest one."

"For what?"

"I killed our brother. I know how close you both were. I was surprised you ever separated."

"It wasn't you. You were being controlled by some very dark magic."

Te could feel the tension in the group awaiting them. He poured out his energy and soothed their anxiety. They all sat in a circle as Xiong, Shehani and Marco brought Te up to speed.

"So, you are named Biao? You are built much like my brother Wei, though you are far more handsome." Te smiled though his eyes were watering. "And your twin is Te. What does he look like?"

"He is tall and thinner like you, but he is much more handsome," Biao answered. The group laughed, including Te.

"You are truly your father's son." Te wiped his eyes, still chuckling.

"You should meet your namesake. He is extremely intelligent and totally smartass," Mahika stated.

"I hope to meet him. Where is he?"

"Back at home. Our home, in India."

"Then that is where I will head."

"And after that, brother Te."

"To our home. It has been too long."

"Well, we got one of two goals accomplished. We found Uncle Te. Now we get Ju-Long and we can all go home," Marco added.

"We have accomplished both. You found me, and I sent Ju-Long back to Hell."

"Seriously? He is dead." The voice was unfamiliar to her, but night had crept up on them and she could smell what the thing speaking was.

"Raksasha!" Mahika jumped to her feet drawing her sword in one smooth motion. Argus stepped between them.

"He is a friend, Mahika."

"Did you just call me friend?" Balavan asked.

"Yeah," Argus answered, "friend in that you're still a blood sucking demon sort of way."

"Uncle Xiong?"

"Yes, Mahika. He is a xiang shi, but unlike any I have ever met. He is a good friend."

She slowly sheathed her sword, keeping her eyes on him and refusing to sit until he did.

"Balavan, this is my brother Te. Shehani is Sona's twin sister."

Balavan nodded. "Yes, she is. Pleased to meet you both."

"This is Marco, my oldest nephew," Xiong continued "and next to him is Biao, my youngest nephew?" He made that last part a question.

"Third youngest or second eldest. I am five minutes older than your nephew Te, eight years older than Jie—but sixteen years younger than this old man." Biao laughed. Marco elbowed his younger brother, causing him to laugh even harder. "Weak."

"It is like watching Ling and our brother Biao in Wei's body all over again." Te smiled.

"Yep, sure is," Xiong laughed before turning back to Balavan, "and the beauty who gave you that warm greeting is Marco's twin sister Mahika." Balavan looked back and forth at the two several times.

"I know." Marco shook his head. "She got all the height and I got the good looks."

"You are quite handsome young man, but your sister is stunning . . . gorgeous" Balavan looked around. "Xiong, I'd like to buy an adjective."

"So dazzling she will steal your sight. So beautiful she will take your breath," Te said.

"Yes. Damn, you are good." Balavan smiled. "What he said." He looked over toward Mahika. She smiled, her face turning red.

"Thank you. Both of you." She looked down, more than a little embarrassed by the flattery, especially coming from a blood sucking demon.

Balavan was mesmerized by her. After he made sure Ju-Long was dead his plan was to have the Spartan kill him. Actually he was surprised Ju-Long's death hadn't killed him as well. He had no Jia-Li, no reason, no purpose to his existence. But he could not take his eyes off her. Even when she looked his way, he didn't try to avert his eyes to hide his gawking. Sometimes she gave him a dirty look, sometimes she smiled. Both looks blew him away. *What would she want with a demon like me?* It would be a discouraging thought if he weren't so instantly, passionately, madly in love with her.

***

They talked all night, reminiscing and telling tales of their various adventures. It was as close to 'home' as Xiong had felt in a long time. While some of them were heading back later, he knew he wasn't. There were still xiang shi, Minotaur, and other evil creatures to be dealt with, and they were not all back in China or India. Argus and him would continue the fight here and beyond. He wondered if any would join them on their journey as he drifted off to sleep.

Sona and Mahika took first watch as the others slept in an old, abandoned building nearby where Balavan had spent the day yesterday. "So how well do you know this Balavan? Shehani said you, Argus, and Uncle Xiong have been around him the longest. She, Biao and Marco didn't meet him until I did last night."

"He has been with us for months. He feeds on the dying or the wicked. He is intelligent, polite, and can fight like Uncle Wei."

"But he still kills to survive?" Mahika asked.

"Yes. But he can go a day or two without feeding and does, unless he is injured or needs to be at full strength for battle. He is truly the strangest of creatures."

"Sounds like it."

"He doesn't have to sleep during the day. I am sure if you have questions he would answer them."

"Nah," Mahika answered. "Just want to make sure he is safe to be around."

"He is a demon, yet he is less evil than many humans. He was a Buddhist monk in his previous existence, just like dad and our uncles. When we found him Ju-Long had just killed the woman he loved, one of Ju-Long's original human servants, Jia-Li."

"One of the twins? The ones who kicked Uncle Biao in the nuts, beat on Uncle Xiong, and punched dad in the face as they made their getaway back in China? Long before we were ever born? I love that story. Every time dad gets a little too cocky, mom reminds him of the twins, and how much more damage she would do to him if he didn't start acting right."

"Yeah, that one. That is one story dad should have never shared with mom." They both laughed.

"So why did Ju-Long kill her? Didn't I hear Argus talk about how Balavan had saved him just before they got a chance to finish Ju-Long off? And Balavan talked about how he and Jia-Li had nursed him back to health? How ungrateful!"

"That is where Balavan differs most from Ju-Long and other Raksasha. They are merciless, he has mercy."

"What about Argus? He seems a little cocky."

"Oh, he is 'cocky' alright. You can just back off that one. He's mine, for now, til I am bored with him," Sona said with a smirk.

"As if? Like I'm taking sloppy seconds from my kid sister. Get real."

"Oh my goddess! You like Balavan!"

"You're crazy!"

"You think he is hot! You're thinking about fu . . ."

"Get out of my head you little shit! I will crush you like a bug!" Mahika growled as she got up, snatching Sona to her feet by her hair.

"Ouch! What the hell you behemoth barbarian!"

"Take it back!"

"I can't take back what I just saw in your head!"

"What do you see in my head now?"

"Nothing! You told me to get out, I got the fuck out!"

Mahika let her go and walked a few feet away taking deep breaths.

Thank goddess she didn't punch me in the face like she was thinking. Sona began fixing her hair while considering launching her sister through the air and into a tree. *She is tough. She'll recover*

"Okay, so I like him a little. You can't tell anyone."

"I won't. Promise. He is pretty hot, tall, tan, muscles on muscles, retractable fangs."

"Did you have sex him?"

"No. He hasn't even looked my way like that."

"Do you think him staring at me like that last night is good or bad?"

"Good." The two heard a male voice say from the building.

"Balavan? How long have you been there?"

"The entire time. I couldn't rest, you were so heavy on my mind. I just wanted to gaze upon your beauty a little longer."

"Hiding in the shadows watching us, that's creepy," Mahika said looking toward the dark space his voice was coming from.

"I would have come out there and sat with you, but sunbathing is no longer my thing."

Mahika nodded. "I guess that makes sense, but why didn't you let us know you were there?"

"I was, but then the conversation turned to me. I wanted to hear what Sona really thought of me. Then when you had your mental images of us together that Sona was so kind to talk about out loud, my heart began to race and I felt alive once again. You stirred me from my fog last night. This morn you have awakened me."

"Well, you might want to go get some rest. I ain't easy and it ain't happening anytime soon, if ever."

"But there is a chance, so I once more have a reason to be."

"Don't hold your breath." Mahika turned away from his voice. "Well, I guess that wouldn't really matter anyways."

"I waited over two years before I laid a finger on my last love out of respect for her loyalty to the demon that killed her. That love lasted longer than you have been alive. As long as I have purpose, my patience is endless. As long as there is hope, I will always pursue love."

Oh, he's good. Sona whispered in Mahika's head.

Ya think? Mahika answered. "Well, good night mister demonic, patient, blood sucking, merciful, handsome, creepy guy."

***

Night fell once again and everyone was finally awake. They all talked about where they would head next. Te, Shehani, Marco and Biao were heading home. Xiong and Argus were headed back through Greece, then north from there. Balavan wanted to return to Ajunta, but realized all his friends were long dead by now. So he was headed south, deeper into this land that was unknown to him.

"Sona? Mahika? You girls ready?" Marco asked.

"Yeah, about that . . . I think I'm going to hang with Uncle Xiong and Argus for a while. They could use a third."

"We haven't been apart for more than a few nights our entire lives."

"I know, sis." Sona hugged Shehani. "I will miss you, but it is not a forever thing."

"You really do like that crusty, centuries old Spartan?"

"He's just the flavor of the month, one month at a time for now." Sona giggled. "But man does he taste good."

"You take care of yourself. You need anything you call out and I will be there."

"I know. I love you."

"I love you, too." Shehani looked around. "Where is Mahika?"

"Yeah, kinda going her own way for a while as well. Needs to explore an opportunity and sort some shit out."

"Well, she could at least say bye." Marco commented.

"She told me to tell all of you that she loved you and would see you in the future."

"She left on her own? Not cool." Marco grumbled. "Which way did she head?"

"I'm not telling, but she is not alone."

"Who is with…..the fucking Raksasha? She hasn't even known him for twenty four hours!"

"She will be fine."

"So says you!" Marco shouted. "Why are girls so dumb?" Marco suddenly felt a hand clasp him by the scruff of the neck. Mahika turned him in midair to face her. "You aren't going anywhere little girl!"

"Marco, I will be fine, I promise. Now go back home, find a girl, any girl, and get yourself laid."

"I have plenty of sex, thank you."

"With a partner?"

"What difference does that make?" he scoffed, "I don't have to cuddle afterwards, or listen to them talk, and talk, and talk afterward." He crossed his arms over his chest and gave her an indignant look. "Besides, like dad I am saving myself for the right one. Now put me down before this gets ugly."

"Dad was a monk, dipshit. That's why he waited. It was part of his vows." Mahika made a whistling noise and a horse that was several feet away come forward.

"What the hell is the horse for? You getting lazy in your old age?"

"It's not for me. It's for you, Marco."

"I don't need a . . . "

Mahika open hand slapped him up side his face just hard enough to knock him out. She threw him crossways over the horse's back. "When he wakes, tell him I love him. She pulled her two little sisters in for a big hug.

"Be careful," Shehani said.

"Have fun." Sona winked.

Epilogue

Carthage 483 AD

The voice that called to him for months and months was weak, and sometimes the signal totally disappeared. Finally, they reached the place the whispers were leading them to. It was stronger after dark, so Renzo and Elena bided their time waiting for the sun to go down. The two human servants saw the skeletons lying about the place. Someone or something had wiped them all out. The Master was still alive somewhere around here, but he wasn't in good shape.

The voice started again just before the sun disappeared in the western sky. Renzo concentrated. The whispers weren't just in his head, he could hear them aloud. The sound was coming from below the ground. He looked around for something to dig with and told Elena to do the same. The pair dug furiously, her using the hip bone of a dead animal and he a medium sized flat stone. They were making progress, but the hard ground was unforgiving, their split fingertips dripping blood.

They were maybe three feet down when the ground rumbled and exploded, throwing them both up and out of the hole.

Ju-Long could hear them digging. He wasn't sure which two, but two of his human servants were there. Then he smelled it. It was as if he could see it trickling through the ground toward him. He concentrated, calling the three thin streams to his mouth. When the blood hit his lips he felt life coming back

Ju-Long's body wanted more. The lure of the blood drew him upwards until he broke the earth wide open, sailing through the night air. He landed and looked left. The young girl he had made somewhere along the way was lying there. He fell upon her like a wild beast, sinking his fangs into her neck and draining her of her life giving blood. Ju-Long felt his muscles strengthen, his skin begin to reform. Her blood helped, but it wasn't enough.

He looked back to see Renzo slowly getting to his feet. Ju-Long was on him in an instant, pinning him back to the ground and tearing into his throat. *Better.* He thought. He wasn't there yet. He needed more blood. And sex. Carthage was about to experience Ju-Long's triumphant return.

I don't die. Ever, foolish beasts.

About the Author

Shawn Boyd was born and raised in Whitehall, Ohio, where he still resides.

Shawn served as a combat communications specialist in the U.S. Army Reserves. He has been a Deputy Sheriff for over twenty-four years, spending time working in the jail, court services, community relations, and as the Deputy assigned to the Children's Services Intake building.

He helped create and taught a program about gangs and gang awareness for almost ten years.

Shawn and his wife Kathy have been married for twenty-five years and have three children, Ashley, Andrew and Shawn Ryan.

They are also blessed with two granddaughters and four grandsons.

The publishing of Shawn's book The Evolution of the Vampire: Xiang Shi, culminates Shawn's life-long dream

Tell-Tale would like to thank you for your purchase. If you would like to read more by this or other fine TT authors, please visit our website: www.tell-talepublishing.com

***